The Lighthouse at the Cove

Other Books by Amy Clipston

CONTEMPORARY ROMANCE

The Heart of Splendid Lake

The View from Coral Cove

Something Old, Something New

Starstruck

Finding You

With This Ring

Second Chance at Sunshine Inn

THE AMISH LEGACY SERIES

Foundation of Love

Building a Future

Breaking New Ground

The Heart's Shelter

THE AMISH MARKETPLACE SERIES

The Bake Shop

The Farm Stand

The Coffee Corner

The Jam and Jelly Nook

THE AMISH HOMESTEAD SERIES

A Place at Our Table

Room on the Porch Swing

A Seat by the Hearth

A Welcome at Our Door

THE AMISH HEIRLOOM SERIES

The Forgotten Recipe

The Courtship Basket

The Cherished Quilt

The Beloved Hope Chest

THE HEARTS OF THE LANCASTER GRAND HOTEL SERIES

A Hopeful Heart

A Mother's Secret

A Dream of Home

A Simple Prayer

THE KAUFFMAN AMISH BAKERY SERIES

A Gift of Grace

A Promise of Hope

A Place of Peace

A Life of Joy

A Season of Love

YOUNG ADULT

Roadside Assistance

Reckless Heart

Destination Unknown

Miles from Nowhere

STORY COLLECTIONS

Amish Sweethearts

Seasons of an Amish Garden

An Amish Singing

STORIES

A Plain and Simple Christmas

Naomi's Gift included in *An Amish Christmas Gift*

A Spoonful of Love included in *An Amish Kitchen*

Love Birds included in *An Amish Market*

Love and Buggy Rides included in *An Amish Harvest*

Summer Storms included in *An Amish Summer*

The Christmas Cat included in *An Amish Christmas Love*

Home Sweet Home included in *An Amish Winter*

A Son for Always included in *An Amish Spring*

A Legacy of Love included in *An Amish Heirloom*

No Place Like Home included in *An Amish Homecoming*

Their True Home included in *An Amish Reunion*

Cookies and Cheer included in *An Amish Christmas Bakery*

Baskets of Sunshine included in *An Amish Picnic*

Evergreen Love included in *An Amish Christmas Wedding*

Bundles of Blessings included in *Amish Midwives*

Building a Dream included in *An Amish Barn Raising*

A Class for Laurel included in *An Amish Schoolroom*

Patchwork Promises included in *An Amish Quilting Bee*

A Perfectly Splendid Christmas included in *On the Way to Christmas*

NONFICTION

The Gift of Love

AMY CLIPSTON

Lighthouse at the Cove

Published in Nashville, Tennessee, by Thomas Nelson. Thomas Nelson is a registered trademark of HarperCollins Christian Publishing, Inc.

Thomas Nelson titles may be purchased in bulk for educational, business, fundraising, or sales promotional use. For information, please email SpecialMarkets@ThomasNelson.com.

Library of Congress Cataloging-in-Publication Data

Names: Clipston, Amy author
Title: The lighthouse at the cove / Amy Clipston.
Description: Nashville, Tennessee : Thomas Nelson, 2025. | Summary: "Sometimes the road home isn't on a map. The Lighthouse at the Cove is a tender, romantic escape to a coastal town where hearts heal, hope shines, and love finds a way—right when you least expect it"—Provided by publisher.
Identifiers: LCCN 2025023345 (print) | LCCN 2025023346 (ebook) | ISBN 9780840716453 paperback | ISBN 9780840716460 epub | ISBN 9780840716477
Subjects: LCGFT: Romance fiction | Christian fiction | Novels | Fiction
Classification: LCC PS3603.L58 L55 2025 (print) | LCC PS3603.L58 (ebook)
LC record available at https://lccn.loc.gov/2025023345
LC ebook record available at https://lccn.loc.gov/2025023346

Printed in the United States of America

25 26 27 28 29 LBC 5 4 3 2 1

In loving memory of Delia "Dee" Halpin.

Thank you for being a special friend to me and an honorary grandmother to my sons.

We love you and we miss you.

Chapter 1

A WARM SUN WAS shining as Kaiah Ross rolled down the windows of her Land Rover Discovery to breathe in the salty air that held a fresh hint of early spring. She curved her hands around the wheel of her SUV as she studied the open road hugging the coast that stretched ahead, a ribbon of possibilities that made her heart flutter with excitement. On the radio Taylor Swift began to softly sing about a Romeo and Juliet who were blessed with a much better ending than the original pair had, and Kaiah tapped the Volume Up button a few notches so the promise of the song could fill her ears and perhaps drown out her doubts that a love story could have such a happy ending, even for her.

Hey, Ky, knock it off. The vibes are immaculate right now. Just soak in this glorious day!

And glorious it was. As a native New Yorker, Kaiah had never visited coastal North Carolina, but she could tell from the sparkling blue water that matched the cerulean sky that perhaps this visit wouldn't be her last. She was on her way to Edisto Beach in South Carolina, the subject of an article in a series she'd been writing about hidden gems where people should spend time on the East Coast. From Maryland to Florida, she was documenting places off the beaten path for *The Traveler*, an online magazine. The assignment was one many travel journalists would snatch up in a heartbeat—a fun series of articles to write on someone else's dime, and . . .

Uh-oh.

Small, flashing lights dotted her peripheral vision. Her gaze locked on her SUV's dashboard where two red lights illuminated. She was sure they weren't there earlier. In fact, she couldn't remember the last time she'd seen a light glowing there—not since before her last tune-up.

But there they were, two red symbols glowing ominously in front of her. Wait, was one of them a thermometer? Kaiah shifted her attention to her temperature gauge and felt a jolt run through her chest. The needle had entered the red zone and was rising—quickly. She looked back at the dash and saw the dreaded Check Engine light shining like a big, scary warning beacon.

Oh no. No, no, no.

Her sister Kamryn had warned her about trusting the fifteen-year-old SUV on another long trip, and she'd tried to convince Kaiah to buy a newer vehicle. But Kaiah just shook her head at the warning. She had faith in Daisy, her trusty four-wheeled companion. Besides that, a new car wasn't in her budget.

Well, Kam, looks like you win. I should've listened earlier.

The muscles in Kaiah's shoulders felt like boulders as she guided the car to the shoulder and turned off the radio to assess her situation. She was alone on a road trip in an unfamiliar state, driving an overheating vehicle. What should she do? She could call Kam, but what did her sister know about fixing a car? And her brother-in-law was an accountant, not a mechanic, so he probably couldn't help much either.

"Okay, Ky," she whispered. "You've got this. You just have to find an auto shop. We'll take it easy until we get back into civilization."

She turned her key and shifted into Drive as she pulled back onto the road. Surely someone could fix her SUV in a jiffy, and then she'd be on her way. She still had five more hours to drive before reaching her destination in South Carolina.

But all she saw was an endless two-lane highway—blacktop and nothing else. She was somewhere in North Carolina, but where?

Before she could pull out her phone and check Google Maps, she spotted a sign up ahead, and hope surged through her.

"Come on, Daisy," she whispered to her car, gently patting the dashboard. "You can do this, girl. Just a little bit more, and then you get to rest."

The temperature gauge continued to rise.

Oh no. If the needle kept moving forward, the engine would burn up, right? Hadn't she read that somewhere? There was no way she could afford to replace the engine in this car. She'd opted for a used Land Rover, thinking the trusted name brand would yield a more reliable car. But the tune-ups on the foreign car were pricey enough, let alone replacing an engine. And as a freelance writer, her budget was *tight*.

The sign came into view: Coral Cove Next Exit.

Yes! A town! All was not lost!

"Coral Cove," she muttered. "Let's hope they have a mechanic close by."

She merged onto the off-ramp and held her breath, praying the sign for a repair shop would appear right in front of her, like a mirage in the desert.

Instead, an adorable Welcome to Coral Cove sign featuring a sandy beach and colorful umbrellas filled her vision.

"Nice," she whispered to herself. *So there's a gorgeous beach. What else do they have? Any mechanics?*

And then a postcard-perfect little town came into view. Kaiah slowly drove down Main Street and spied several small shops, a town hall, and an elementary school. Everything looked like it belonged in a coffee table book of Americana. In the distance near the shoreline, she spotted a tall column wrapped in black-and-white stripes. It took her a second to realize she was staring at a real-life lighthouse.

She'd found civilization! And not only that, a storybook beach town. Surely she'd end up okay in this place, right?

She felt the boulders begin to roll off her shoulders . . . until she noticed steam beginning to drift out from under Daisy's hood.

"Seriously?" she groaned. "This can't be good."

Although a new car wasn't an option, she should've at least taken Daisy into the shop before she'd left New York, just to be sure she was ready for another long trip. But she'd been in a rush to get on the road. And look what that got her.

"In a town this small, there's *got* to be a mechanic nearby," she muttered, trying to ignore the lights glowing on the dashboard and the steam pouring from the hood.

She gripped the wheel tight. Surely Daisy could make it a few more miles so that Kaiah wouldn't have to call a tow truck, which would be out of her price range, or ask someone to help her push the car.

And then the oasis she'd been hoping for appeared: a sign for Coral Cove Car Care. This time a surge of hope coursed through her body.

"Yes!" she exclaimed. "We've got this, Daisy. They're going to make you brand-new. Maybe we'll be out of here in a couple hours."

She steered the car into the right lane, and as soon as the parking lot came into view, she drove in and pulled into the very last spot.

Shouldering her backpack purse, Kaiah climbed out of the vehicle and hurried past the line of cars in the parking lot. Hopefully they weren't all waiting for service. If they were, she'd be stuck here until Christmas.

She jogged up to the one-story cinderblock building with six garage bays and a glass front boasting the business's name and logo. When she pulled open the front door, a bell rang as she inhaled the scent of rubber tires mixed with weak coffee wafting from the ancient coffee maker in the lobby. Several tire displays led to a long counter, where a middle-aged man with a name tag that read *Bill, Manager* stood talking on the phone. He nodded at her and then finished his conversation about air filters before hanging up.

"Can I help you?" he asked.

She pointed toward the door. "I'm on my way from New York to South Carolina, and my car is overheating. Could you possibly fix it today?" She folded her hands as if saying a prayer. *And do you take credit cards too?*

"Oh." He rubbed the gray scruff on his neck. "I can get the mechanic to try and diagnose the issue, but I'm not sure we can fix it today." He came around the counter. "Let's take a look."

They walked to the parking lot together, and Kaiah popped the hood.

"The temperature gauge and Check Engine light came on, and by the time I got here, steam was pouring out from under the hood," she explained.

"Hmm." His brow furrowed.

"Do you have Wi-Fi?" she asked.

He lifted a bushy eyebrow.

"So I can work while you figure out what's going on," she explained. "I noticed a little sitting area."

"We do, ma'am," he said. "But how about this? I doubt we'll be able to fix this problem today, so let's fill out some paperwork and you can leave the key with me. I'll be in touch after we take a look." He pointed toward the road. "If you want to find a place to work, there's a coffee shop a couple of blocks from here. I promise it has more comfortable chairs and much better coffee than we can offer."

Ten minutes later, Kaiah found herself strolling down the heart of Coral Cove's Main Street. She pushed her sunglasses farther up on her nose as she took in the quaint shops lining the street. Customers walked in the double doors of Beach Reads and came out of Crafty Creations carrying shopping bags full of yarn and knitting needles. The scent of freshly baked pizza dough drifted out of A Slice of Heaven as she hurried past, and a small smile played on her lips. Everything in this oceanside town reminded her of the summer trips to New England she'd taken with her family when she was a kid. Kaiah had loved perusing the stores with her parents and sisters, looking for something special to spend her allowance on. Warmth began to bloom in her chest as images of those sun-dappled days filled her mind.

The sign for a coffee shop called the Roast Shack came into view, and she crossed the street. The rich aroma of roasted coffee beans saturated her senses when she walked in. Her eyes roved around the shop as she saw tables of customers enjoying their brew, some chatting with a friend, some pecking away at their laptops. One wall featured a mural of the beach at sunrise, while the opposite wall featured the water at dusk. Her fingers itched to pull her camera from her bag and snap a photo. She could almost see the image sitting atop a story she'd write about this enchanting little town. But if her plans worked out, her car would be fixed soon and she wouldn't be here long enough to write a story about it.

At the counter, Kaiah spotted a woman with silver roots and bright hazel eyes serving a tall man with closely cropped dark hair and broad shoulders. There was a gap between the woman's two front teeth, but it didn't mar her beauty. The imperfection added to her charm and made her grin even more endearing. The man seemed to think so too, judging by the way he was laughing along with her. He rolled his head back slightly as he laughed, the sound casting a glow around him. Then he turned around.

And he was . . . drop-dead gorgeous.

Kaiah's cheeks flooded with warmth as she watched the man, probably in his late twenties or early thirties, make his way to the end of the counter to wait for his order. Only when he lifted his eyes to meet hers did Kaiah realize she'd rested her gaze on him a beat too long. She looked away quickly, chiding herself.

Good job, Ky. Creeping on a stranger in a coffee shop—classy. Oh well, at least he doesn't know your name. Even if you didn't just make a fool of yourself, it's not like you want to race back into a relationship anyway.

Pulling her attention away from the hot guy, Kaiah pulled her phone from the pocket of her jeans and scrolled through her social accounts until she moved to the front of the line.

"What can I get ya?" the woman with the silver roots asked.

"A vanilla latte, please."

"Sure thing, sugar." The woman grabbed an empty paper cup and pulled out a marker. "What's your name?"

"Kaiah."

The woman's eyes rounded, and Kaiah almost laughed. She was used to people not knowing how to spell her name.

"It's K-a-i-a-h."

"Uh . . ." The woman blinked. "Sure thing, honey."

The woman wrote on a cup, and Kaiah moved to the side of the counter and leaned against the wall. Her eyes darted back to the hot guy, who was now talking on his phone. Judging by his T-shirt and gym shorts, he'd just come from a workout. She noticed the way his dark blue shirt hugged his biceps, and clearly he didn't skip leg day at the gym. Good grief, were those things carved from granite?

Stop it, Ky!

She didn't have time to obsess over this guy. Instead, she had to worry about how much these car repairs were going to set her back and how on earth she was going to pay for them. She'd sublet her apartment to a former coworker for a couple of months while she was on the road, but this year her income as a freelancer hadn't been stellar. The assignments seemed to be drying up, thanks to a rise in social media travel accounts that people could access for free instead of paying for an online magazine. And now this reporting trip could end up *costing* Kaiah money? A dull ache began to throb behind her eyes.

She knew if she ever got a staff writer job at a world-renowned magazine like *Travel and Culture*, one of the most respected lifestyle and travel media companies, then she could finally count on a real salary and maybe even some benefits. But that seemed like a pipe dream.

"Reid," a young woman called from behind the counter, jolting Kaiah out of her low-grade misery. "Jamie, Laura, Mark, and . . . um, Cayenne?"

Kaiah resisted the urge to roll her eyes. It wasn't the first time she'd been referred to as the spice. If only her parents weren't obsessed with names beginning with *K*, then she could've been named something more normal, like Olivia or Madison. Those were names people could spell without an explanation.

Kaiah swiped the cup off the counter and started toward the

cluster of tables. She took a whiff of the brew the way she always did, so she could enjoy the rich scent of vanilla before devouring the drink. But she only smelled regular black coffee. The vanilla was missing.

"Excuse me, miss?"

She spun and found herself face-to-face with Mr. Tall, Dark, and Handsome.

Oh, hello!

"I think I took your coffee by mistake. And judging by your cup, I think you have my Americano." His voice was warm, deep, and smooth. "Did you order a vanilla latte?"

"Y-yeah," she managed to say.

"Here you go." He held out his cup, and they made the exchange. "Sorry about that." And when his very symmetrical face broke out in a sheepish grin, she thought she might melt right into the Roast Shack's floor. "I promise I didn't take a sip."

"I didn't either."

"Great." He nodded as she silently admired his chiseled jaw lined with a hint of dark scruff.

"Thanks," she said before he gave her another friendly nod and then sat at a table with a woman and a couple of men who seemed to be around his age.

She found an empty table and pulled out her laptop before connecting to the internet and checking her email. A message from her editor was waiting, asking how her trip was going and how soon she could expect the South Carolina story. Kaiah also read messages from both the Airbnb host and her tour guide in South Carolina, confirming her stay and her plans to check out Edisto Beach.

Kaiah took a sip of her vanilla latte and tried to allow the warm drink to calm her frayed nerves. The auto shop was busy, but maybe she could ask Bill if the mechanic could fix her car first thing on Monday. And since she was only five hours away from Edisto Beach, she could get there in the evening and not have to rearrange her schedule too much. But she couldn't modify her Airbnb reservation until she knew for sure . . .

Her phone began to ring, and she found her favorite sister's name on the display. "Hey, Kam," she began, "you'll never guess where I am."

"Hmm," Kamryn said. "Well, I hear voices, so not in the car."

"Nope. I'm in a coffee shop in Nowheresville."

"Well, that sounds cute. How'd you end up there?"

Kaiah told her sister how she limped Daisy to the mechanic's garage before retreating to the coffee shop.

"Coral Cove, huh? It sounds pretty."

"From what I've seen, it is. Reminds me of those trips we used to take to Maine when we were kids."

"Oh . . . oh wow." Kam sighed, her voice thick with emotion. "That feels like a million years ago, huh?"

A vision of their mother, young and healthy and beautiful, floated in Kaiah's mind. She felt a tug in her chest and was sure her sister was remembering her too.

Pushing the memories away, Kaiah pulled up her map app and looked at the route from Coral Cove to the Airbnb. Yup, almost five hours.

"You know, Ky," Kamryn began, "I'm not going to say I told you so, but . . . you have entirely too much faith in ol' Daisy. She's pretty, but she's also high maintenance. Devon said the same thing."

Kaiah sighed. "I know, I know. I hate to say it, but you and my brilliant brother-in-law may be right." Her gaze wandered from her laptop, and she paused when she found Mr. Tall, Dark, and Handsome watching *her*. He smiled, and she returned the greeting before his eyes shifted to the woman beside him.

Um, woooow, okay.

"Hey, sis, did you hear a word I just said?" Kam asked.

"Sorry," she whispered. "Just got distracted by some superhot guy looking at me!"

"Oooh," Kam sang. "Do tell!"

Kaiah tried her best to keep her voice down while she shared how she and Mr. Tall, Dark, and Handsome had wound up with each other's drinks.

"It's fate," Kam insisted. "You were meant to meet him. That's why Daisy chose to break down right outside of Nowheresville. It was all a grand plan for you to meet your future husband."

Kaiah laughed. "Yeah *right*."

"Did you introduce yourself to him?"

"No. Since 'Cayenne' was written on my coffee cup, he probably thinks Mom and Dad were hippies who named me after a spice."

Kam chuckled. "It wouldn't be the first time. But seriously, you should go introduce yourself! Tell him your real name and that you're a super successful journalist on her way to cover the next big story."

"Uh-huh. Which is why my car is broken down and I'm worried about how I'm going to pay for the repairs."

"Oh shoot," Kam said, her teasing tone evaporating. "Do you need money?"

Kaiah's smile faltered. "No, but thanks." She decided to shift the conversation back to the pressing topic at hand. "I'm not going to meet this guy. Besides, Mr. Tall, Dark, and Handsome is probably married."

"Is he wearing a ring?"

"I don't think so. But let's get real: I'm twenty-six. All of the good ones are taken by now." Though she was glad her younger sister had managed to find a good one. She and Devon had been married almost three years.

"C'mon, Kaiah. No, they aren't. It's time for you to get back out there. Once you do, you'll find someone too. And maybe Mr. TDH is one of the good ones."

"He might be, but I'm not going to be here long enough to find out. I'm putting this town in the rearview in the next couple of hours. So what's up with you? How's work?"

"Ugh, tax season," Kam said with a sigh. "It's been crazy. Talking to you is always a nice break, though."

Kaiah spent the next hour catching up with her sister and answering a few emails. Then she finished her drink and walked outside to Main Street, where people moved up and down the sidewalk and in and out of the shops. The afternoon air smelled like seawater mixed with coconut sunblock, and for a moment she considered wandering out to the boardwalk, if there was one.

She turned just as Mr. Tall, Dark, and Handsome exited the coffee shop. He held the door open for two young women who both eyed him appreciatively. A phone started to ring, and he yanked his cell from the pocket of his shorts before holding it to his ear and grinning. He sauntered over to a black SUV and opened the door. And when his dark eyes met Kaiah's, he grinned and nodded before climbing in.

A smile tugged the corners of her mouth as she let out a sigh. *Goodbye, Mr. TDH. It's a shame I never learned your name.*

She shook off the thought and turned her attention to the stores lining the street. She wandered over to a gift shop, and in the window she spied a suncatcher featuring a black-and-white lighthouse, similar to the one she'd seen as she rolled into town. Instantly she found herself gripped by a memory of her mother. Mom had purchased a similar suncatcher during their last visit to Maine, the summer before she died. Back in New York, Mom had hung the suncatcher in the dining room window. It had remained there, sparkling in the sunlight, until Dad sold the house and moved to Arizona with his new wife.

Kaiah tilted her head and wondered what could have happened to the trinket. Had one of her sisters snagged it when they were packing up the house? She rested her hand on the window as more memories of her mother flowed through her mind—her mother's bright smile, quirky sense of humor, contagious laugh, warm hugs.

I miss you, Mom.

She hugged her arms to her middle and turned toward the majestic lighthouse standing against the bright blue sky. As if it were a beacon drawing her in, Kaiah started to walk toward it, thankful she'd worn her comfortable sandals.

She traveled three blocks and finally arrived at the lighthouse. Disappointment swirled in her chest when she found a chain-link fence surrounding the structure, the ancient-looking lightkeeper's quarters off to the right. Standing there took her back a couple of decades, when she was surrounded by her family and gazing up at a similar lighthouse in Maine. That, too, was a beautiful old structure that filled her with awe. And it was the moment she'd realized she wanted to tell other people about amazing things she'd seen on her travels. She wanted to journey to all the corners of the world, sharing stories about people and their lives in exotic places. Kaiah was still sure this was what she'd been born to do.

She fished her camera from her backpack and began shooting photos of the lighthouse through the fence. The wind blew strands of blonde hair away from her face while she captured photos of the coastal blue water sparkling in the sunlight. Boats with colorful sails moved out in the cove while seagulls sang in the cool April air.

Glancing around, Kaiah searched for a plaque detailing the history of the structure but couldn't find one. She yearned to know the gorgeous lighthouse's history. Why was it locked behind a fence instead of open for locals and visitors to enjoy?

Her phone dinged with a text message from an unknown number, and she opened it and read the message:

> Ms. Ross, This is Bill at Coral Cove Car Care. Please come by the shop. We have an estimate for you.

Finally! Maybe she'd be out of this place soon.

She responded with: On my way.

Kaiah hurried up the four blocks to the shop, pushed open the door, and approached the counter, where Bill set a computer printout in front of her.

"My mechanic took a look at your SUV," Bill began, "and a few pieces in your coolant system cracked and need to be replaced."

"Okay," she said. Sounded simple enough.

"I've checked around, but I haven't found the parts to fix it."

She swallowed. "What does that mean?"

"Tomorrow's Sunday, and nothing is open, including our shop," he said. "My suggestion is to leave the car here, and I'll let you know how fast I can get the parts to fix it."

"Do you think you can get them by Monday?" she asked.

He shook his head.

So much for not rearranging her plans. "When do you think you can get them?"

"I'll make some calls and then give you an update sometime on Monday."

Her hope deflated like a balloon. She was stuck in Nowheresville until at least Tuesday. She gazed down at the estimate and her stomach bottomed out. It would cost thousands—*thousands!*—to fix her precious Daisy.

This day had quickly gone from bad to worse.

Now she had to find a place to stay—which meant a hotel bill, since the magazine didn't cover travel expenses anymore—as well as figure out how to pay this repair bill. Her head started to throb. Her entire travel piece, which she had pitched to her editor, was now in the toilet. And instead of making money, she was *losing* it, hand over fist!

Her sister's offer of money echoed in her mind, but she didn't want to have to lean on Kam. Kaiah would find a way out of this debacle herself.

She pulled in a deep breath through her nose. Kam would tell her to calm down and think this through, and that was exactly what she was going to do.

"Do you want to fix the car?" Bill's question pulled her from her worry.

"Yes," she said, meeting his curious gaze. "I don't have a choice."

He nodded. "I'll do my best to get the parts as quickly as possible."

"Could you recommend a place to stay?"

He rubbed his chin. "There's the Sunshine Inn and the Rosewood Inn. Would you like their numbers?"

"Yes, please."

He typed on his computer and wrote on a notepad, then handed her the piece of paper. "These places are a bit far to walk. Can I get you an Uber?" he asked.

"That's more than generous," she said.

"It's the least I could do for an out-of-towner." He typed on his phone. "A ride is on the way."

"Thank you so much." She spotted a sign for the restrooms beyond the counter and hurried toward it. She needed a moment alone to gather herself.

After using the facilities and washing her hands, she rested her hands on the sink and studied her reflection. She looked as messy as her life felt. She pushed her long, wavy blonde hair behind her ears, stood up straight, and lifted her chin. She was going to get through this, no matter what.

When she reentered the shop, she spotted Bill leaning on the counter talking to someone. She couldn't see the man, but his deep, smooth voice seemed so familiar. If only she could place it.

"I bet Piper's getting big, huh?" Bill asked.

"Yup. Growing like a weed." The man chuckled, and what a great laugh it was. "She's six going on eighteen."

Bill turned around and smiled at her. "Ms. Ross, your ride is here." He made a sweeping gesture toward the man. "Kaiah Ross, meet Reid Turner."

Kaiah crossed to the counter and found herself face-to-face with Mr. Tall, Dark, and Handsome once again.

Maybe this day wasn't so bad after all.

Chapter 2

"KAIAH," THE HANDSOME STRANGER said as he held out his hand. "I didn't *think* your name was Cayenne."

She shook his hand. "I may be a little spicy, but no, I'm just Kaiah," she joked, and he laughed again. "So you're Reid?"

"Reid Turner, at your service."

"Actually," Bill began, "Reid's real job is at Coral Cove's Fire Station Number 1. He's one of the lieutenants."

Impressive. That explained why his biceps were straining the sleeves of that blue T-shirt. Now she pictured Reid in his uniform, those biceps picking her up and cradling her against his brawny chest, and she was almost certain someone had turned up the thermostat in the shop.

Stop it, Kaiah!

Reid pointed to her laptop bag at her feet. "Can I carry that for you?"

Kaiah shook away the thought and painted on a smile. "Thanks, that's so nice."

After retrieving her suitcase from Daisy, Kaiah and Reid headed to his black Chevy Suburban, where he loaded her luggage into the back. Bill stepped out of the shop.

"Ms. Ross, I'll be in touch after I check in with a few parts dealers." He shook Reid's hand. "Good to see you."

"You too, Bill." Reid opened the rear passenger side door and held out his hand to Kaiah. "Climb on in."

She took his hand and stepped up on the running board before settling into her seat. Her phone dinged with a text, and she pulled it from her pocket.

Kam: Update on Daisy?

Kaiah: Car's dead. I'm stuck in Nowheresville.

Kam: What???

Kaiah: I'll call you when I get settled. And by the way . . . my Uber driver is Mr. TDH.

Kam: Get out! You HAVE to sneak a photo for me.

Kaiah snickered to herself while Reid buckled into the driver's seat.

His dark eyes focused on her in the rearview mirror. "You still headed to the Sunshine Inn?"

"I'm actually not sure. Bill recommended to stay there while I was in town, and I guess he plugged that into the address. I don't even know if they have room for me."

He swiped a hand over his five o'clock shadow, thinking. "I know the owners. Want me to call them for you?"

"Yes, please." She held out the piece of paper with the phone numbers on it. "Bill gave me their number."

"I got it." He pulled out his phone, and when he touched the screen, she spotted a photo of an adorable little girl with dark brown hair and a cheesy grin serving as his screensaver. Could she be his little girl? Or maybe his niece? Maybe he was married. And if he was, Kaiah imagined that his lucky wife cherished both him and that cute little girl.

Reid dialed and held the phone to his ear. "Hey, Cade," he said. "It's Reid Turner. How's it going? Is there any chance you've got a room for the weekend? I have a passenger who needs a place to stay until at least Monday." His handsome face clouded with disappointment while he listened, and Kaiah slumped back on the seat. "I understand. Thanks so much. Tell Everleigh I said hi. Bye."

Reid angled his body toward her. "They're full at the Sunshine Inn. Hosting a wedding. There's also the Rosewood Inn. I'll try them."

"Thanks," she said.

He dialed a number, listened for a moment, and then frowned. "I forgot. They're close for refurbishing." He rattled off the names of a few other hotels, along with their locations. Most of them were at the beach or the sound, which sounded way out of her price range. "I can call them if you'd like."

He must have read her hesitation on her face because he paused and appeared to be working through something in his mind. "I have another option for you."

She leaned toward him. "Okay."

"I know this might seem a little forward, so please feel free to say no. But I have a garage apartment you can stay in."

"Oh." She moved her hands over the thighs of her jeans, making a swishing sound. Sure, this guy was handsome and friendly, but she didn't really know him. Just because he was a firefighter and had a photo of a cute girl on his phone didn't mean he was trustworthy. "Um . . ."

"It's not extravagant," Reid continued, "but you'll have your own entrance. One of the guys from my station stayed there while he was having some work done at his house. He liked it. I was thinking about turning it into an Airbnb, but I haven't gotten around to it."

She bit her lower lip and debated what to do. Reid didn't seem like a total weirdo. But what if he was? And what would Kam say about staying with a stranger? Then again, Kam wasn't stuck in the middle of Nowheresville, nearly broke with nowhere to stay. It seemed like the choice was made for her. "How much?" she asked him.

"I don't know." He shrugged. "Free?"

She lifted an eyebrow. Nothing was free. Everything had a price.

"Okay, okay. How about you pay whatever you can afford?"

She hesitated. Reid *seemed* harmless. But was this a good idea? Would Kam tell her she was crazy for trusting this handsome stranger?

"I can take you by the motels if you'd like," Reid said quickly. "And if you'd rather find an Airbnb, I can look on my phone and then—"

"Your garage apartment sounds perfect," she said, shutting down the debate in her brain. For some crazy reason, she trusted Reid, and she decided to go with her intuition. She hoped that wasn't a grave mistake.

"Great," he said. "What are you comfortable paying?"

"Well, the repairs on my car are going to be a little over two thousand, so . . ."

"Yikes." He grimaced "Don't worry about it. We can work it out after you get your car back."

"Really?" This guy sounded too good to be true.

"Yeah, really." He started the big SUV, and it rumbled to life.

While Reid drove through town, Kaiah made a mental note of everyone she had to tell about her change of plans—her editor, her tour guide in South Carolina, and the owner of the Airbnb where she planned to stay.

And Kam. She needed to give her sister the address of where she was staying just in case . . .

"Where are you from?" he asked, looking at her in the mirror again while they were stopped at a red light.

"New York."

"Oh wow."

"You?"

"Here. A Coral Cove native."

"Seriously?" she asked. "It's really . . . nice here."

He laughed. "A bit smaller than New York, that's for sure. How'd you wind up here?"

"My car brought me here. I was on my way to South Carolina and eventually to Florida, but my car had other ideas." She explained how it overheated. "Now I'm stranded—at least until Monday. Hopefully Bill will find the parts and I'll be on my way."

"What are you planning in South Carolina and Florida—if you don't mind me asking?"

"I'm working on a series about hidden travel gems. I started in Maryland."

"Hidden travel gems?" he asked. "Like cool places no one knows about?"

"Exactly."

"So you're a journalist?" he asked. And he actually sounded impressed.

Score.

"Yup."

"That's pretty cool. I bet you've been to some interesting places."

She shrugged. "Yeah, I've traveled a bit and done some fun stories, but my dream is to write for a big magazine like *Travel and Culture*. I want to go to remote areas and write about interesting people and stories that matter. Not just fluff pieces, you know? I don't want to stick to beach towns. I want to update the world on the state of the rainforest and write about traditions in the Indigenous communities of Alaska. I want to change people's minds, not just tell them where to find the best corn dog on vacation."

Reid chuckled. "That sounds like a real adventure."

He steered into a residential area as she cracked the window and basked in the cool, salty air. She scanned the brightly colored beach homes sitting quietly along the street. Each home was a different shape and style—no two were alike—and each house sported a cute and creative name like *Rock 'n' Reel*, *Catch 'n' Relax*, or *Absolute Beach*. The neighborhood felt warm and welcoming, and for a moment she wondered what it would've been like to grow up here.

Reid motored slowly down the road before pulling into the driveway leading to a bright blue, one-story clapboard house with *Beachy Keen* written on a driftwood sign in a fun script font. A detached garage with an apartment above sat beside the home.

"What a cute place!" she exclaimed.

"Thanks," he said. "My wife picked it out. We got this place for a song after we were married. Our folks helped us with the offer, and the house needed a lot of work. We actually lived in the apartment above the garage while we fixed it up."

So he *was* married. She nodded slowly, trying to make her voice sound as normal as possible. "That's great."

He checked his watch. "My daughter should be home any minute now." He faced her and seemed almost apologetic. "I have to warn you—she's a chatterbox."

"No problem." Kaiah chuckled. "I love chatterboxes."

"Good." He pushed his door open. "Let's get you settled."

Reid carried her suitcase up the outside staircase leading to the apartment and punched in a code to the lock. He pushed the door open and made a sweeping gesture. "It's not much, but it's clean. I'll get you some linens."

Kaiah stood in the middle of the spacious den and turned, taking in the sofa, flat-screen television, and galley kitchen complete with a breakfast bar. Through an open door she spotted a large bedroom. "This place is actually bigger than my apartment back home."

He laughed and then stopped when he saw her expression. "Oh, you're serious?"

She nodded. "This is perfect."

He smiled. "Make yourself comfortable." He found a notepad and pen on the kitchen counter. "I'll write down the code for the door. Are you hungry? I can see if I have any food in the house."

"I can order something in. Just give me the address, and I'll be all set."

"Sure," he said before writing on the notepad again.

The rumble of an engine announced a vehicle pulling into the driveway, and Reid crossed to the window. "She's home."

Kaiah inclined her head to the side. He'd said, "She's home," not "They're home." So, where was his wife?

He pointed to the door. "You can come with me if you want, and I can get your linens. Or you can get unpacked, and I'll bring them up later."

"I don't have much to unpack," she said.

She followed him down the stairs to where a gray Toyota 4Runner sat in the driveway behind the Suburban. A tall brunette with long, thick hair and an athletic figure climbed out of the driver's seat while two little girls clambered out of the back. One resembled the girl in the photo on Reid's phone, and the other seemed to be about the same age and had light brown hair and hazel eyes.

"Dad! Dad! Dad!" The little girl with dark hair and chocolate-brown eyes bounced over to Reid.

He scooped her up into his arms. "How was the birthday party?"

"Sooo fun!" She wiggled. "Put me down. I need to show you our dance."

Reid grinned and set her on the ground.

"We're learning hip-hop!" She turned to the other girl. "Let's show 'em, Astrid." The two girls began dancing around the driveway, shaking their hips and waving their arms.

Reid and the woman exchanged a glance and shared a grin, but Kaiah didn't pick up any romantic vibes between them. Hmm.

"They're wound up," the woman said.

Reid waved a hand toward the two girls. "I see that."

Suddenly the first girl stopped dancing and made a beeline to Kaiah. "I'm Piper Elizabeth Turner. Who are you?"

Kaiah bent at her waist to make herself eye level with the girl and held out her hand. "I'm Kaiah Ross. Nice to meet you."

"Ky-ya?" Piper asked, and Kaiah nodded. Then the girl scrunched her nose. "How do you spell that?"

"K-a-i-a-h."

"Huh." Piper considered this, and then she pointed to the other little girl, who had also stopped dancing and was watching them. "This is my cousin, Astrid Griffin, and her mom, my auntie Becca. Auntie Becca and my dad are twins. Me and Astrid pretend we're twins too. Right, Astrid?"

The other little girl nodded. "Uh-huh!"

"Really?" Kaiah asked, and Reid grinned. Mr. TDH was a twin. Intriguing! And where was his wife? In the house already? Away on business? Working on a Saturday?

"Why are you at my house?" Piper asked. "Did you come to visit us?"

"Actually, my car broke down, and I'm staying in the apartment over the garage until my car is fixed. Is that okay?"

Piper nodded. "Sure." Then she took Kaiah's hand. "Want to meet my cat? Her name is Ariel, and she's a calico. And she's two." Then she dropped Kaiah's hand. "I'm six, and Astrid is six. How old are you?"

A chuckle escaped Kaiah's lips, but she couldn't help it. This kid *was* a chatterbox.

"Piper . . ." Reid's voice interjected, a hint of reprimand in his tone. "It's rude to ask someone how old she is."

"Really?" Piper's eyes widened with genuine surprise, turning her gaze toward Reid. "Is it because saying a huge number makes you sound really, really old?"

Kaiah bent over in a belly laugh. This child, with her unabashed curiosity and adorable bluntness, was super endearing.

"Piper, what am I going to do with you?" Reid shook his head. "I'm sorry, Kaiah."

"It's okay." She leaned down with a conspiratorial look and whispered, "How old do you think I am?"

Piper tapped her chin. "Well, my daddy is thirty-two, and my auntie is thirty-two, but my uncle Cash is thirty-five. Are you thirty-two?"

"Nope." Kaiah shook her head, and out of the corner of her eye, she spotted Reid cupping his hand to his forehead. "Guess again."

"Hmm . . . thirty-five?"

Astrid jumped up and down and announced, "Forty!"

"Not quite," Kaiah said with a laugh. "I'm twenty-six."

"Wooow," Piper and Astrid both exclaimed. Then Piper pointed at Kaiah. "You should stay for supper." She looked at Reid. "Can we order pizza?"

"Yeah!" Astrid clapped her hands and jumped up and down. "Pizza! Pizza!"

Piper joined in with the jumping and chanting. "Please, Daddy? Pretty please with sugar on top?"

Becca shook her head and then took Astrid by the hand. "Not tonight, honey. We need to get home. Your dad will be there soon." She smiled at Kaiah. "Enjoy your time in Coral Cove."

"Thanks."

Becca turned to her twin brother. "Can we come by for supper tomorrow?"

"You bet."

"Good, because we need to talk about the festival. The mayor's talking about pulling the plug on the whole thing, but I'm trying to figure out how to get her to keep it."

"Chad Morris mentioned something about that at the Roast Shack today. Glad you're on it, though. It'd be a shame to shut it down."

"My thoughts exactly. We'll talk more tomorrow. See you then." Becca waved to her niece and then loaded Astrid into the 4Runner and pulled out of the driveway.

Piper took Kaiah's hand and steered her toward the house. "Let's go see Ariel. She's a really nice cat. She sleeps with me every night. She likes my feet. Do you have a cat?"

Kaiah flicked her eyes over her shoulder at Reid, who gave her an apologetic look. "Not a cat, but I used to have a dog."

"Oh no." Piper stopped and frowned. "Did your dog go to heaven?"

"No. My friend took him."

"Like *stole* him?" she squeaked. "My friend Jasmine stole her friend Emma's favorite eraser at school, and she had to give it back and say she was sorry." Her expression became very somber. "It's not nice to steal."

"You're right," Kaiah said, trying her best not to smile. "It isn't nice to steal."

"Did you call the police?" Piper asked.

"No." Kaiah shook her head. "I just let my friend keep him." *Though I should've fought more for you, sweet friend.*

Piper patted her hand. "I bet you miss your dog."

Kaiah nodded. She did. In fact, she missed him so much that her heart hurt.

"What's your dog's name?"

"George."

Piper's wide smile was back. "That's a great name." Then she took Kaiah's hand and yanked her. "Come meet Ariel."

Piper led Kaiah around the house—through the foyer to the kitchen and breakfast nook, past a large den, and into the laundry room—in search of the cat.

"She has to be around her somewhere," Piper muttered, her hands on her little waist while they stood in the doorway leading to the laundry room.

"Piper." Reid rested on the doorway, and at that moment Kaiah realized just how tall he was. He had to be at least six inches taller than her own height of five-foot-eight. "I think Miss Kaiah is tired of searching for the cat."

Kaiah waved him off. "It's okay. Really."

He rubbed a spot on his neck. "You're very patient."

"Oh!" Piper took Kaiah's hand in hers again. "Maybe she's in my room." She started toward the doorway, which was blocked by her father. "Excuse us, Daddy."

Reid's lips twitched. "You're going to scare Miss Kaiah away on her first day."

"Nope. She'll stay if you get us pizza." Then Piper full-on grinned, and Kaiah spotted Reid's smile reflected in his daughter's.

Kaiah couldn't stop her laugh.

Reid's lips curled up in a smile. "You're encouraging my daughter's bad behavior."

"The kid's got a point." Kaiah shrugged. "Who doesn't like pizza?"

Reid laughed. "Fine. I'll order it."

"Yay!" Piper exclaimed, and when Reid stepped out of the doorway, Piper yanked Kaiah along.

"See ya!" Kaiah sang while they moved down the hallway.

"Do you like pepperoni?" Reid called down the hallway.

"Yes!" Piper and Kaiah responded at the same time.

Piper led Kaiah into a bright pink room decorated with copious pictures of mermaids, along with piles of dolls, books, stuffed animals, and other toys. It was the perfect girl's room with a cool beachy vibe.

"What a great room," Kaiah said, stepping over piles of toys. She pointed to a fluffy calico cat curled up in the middle of Piper's pink comforter. "And this must be the famous Ariel."

Piper flopped onto the bed bedside the cat and began petting her. "Ariel, this is my new friend, Kaiah."

"I'm pleased to make your acquaintance." Kaiah also stroked the cat. "I assume she's named after Ariel the mermaid?"

Piper seemed impressed. "How'd you know?"

"Lucky guess." Kaiah gestured around at the mermaid murals, posters, dolls, and bedding.

Piper picked up a photo beside her bed and handed it to Kaiah. "This is my mommy and me. She went to heaven when I was two. I'm six now."

Kaiah pushed against the anguish threading through her as she studied the photo of a beautiful young woman with golden-brown hair and sparkling brown eyes holding a baby in her arms. "Oh, Piper, I'm so sorry," she whispered as she took in the girl's sweet expression. She gave her small hand a gentle squeeze. "I'm sure you miss her."

"Her name is Brynn Elizabeth Turner," Piper said. "I'm named after her. My name is Piper Elizabeth Turner."

"That's so special, sweetheart." Kaiah studied the photo, and her throat felt thick. "I lost my mom when I was eleven." She met Piper's surprised expression.

Piper gasped. "You did?" she asked, and Kaiah nodded. "What happened to her?"

"She was sick."

"You miss your mom too," Piper said.

Kaiah nodded. "Every day." She set the framed photo down and took Piper's hand in hers as she sat on the edge of the bed. "But I keep her here." She touched her chest. "She's always in my heart." She gave Piper's hand a gentle squeeze. "Your mom is always in your heart too."

"Right," the little girl whispered while nodding.

Just then, the cat stood up, yawned, squeaked, stretched, shook her head, and then sat back down.

Kaiah and Piper's eyes met before they both started laughing at the silly feline. Shaking her head, Kaiah relaxed on the bed. Today had been an emotional ride, and she was grateful for the relief provided by her two new friends.

Chapter 3

REID HAD DEFINITELY LOST his mind. That was the only way to explain why he'd invited a stranger to stay in the garage apartment and why he was letting Piper drag her around the house to look for the cat.

Though, if he were being honest with himself, the *real* reason he was in this predicament was obvious. He'd found his gaze drifting toward Kaiah as she waited in line at the coffee shop. Her golden hair fell in waves past her shoulders, catching the morning light in a way that cast a glow around her. He liked the way the corners of her mouth curved up slightly as she pondered her order. He had even taken note of the way she'd walked around the shop, her vibrant blue eyes full of curiosity and warmth as she studied the art on the walls. It seemed he found everything about this woman captivating. His pulse quickened as he felt an unfamiliar spike of adrenaline. He'd been out of the dating game for too long to get back in now. Plus, as a single father with a demanding job, his life was already a careful balancing act.

But when his hand had closed around the wrong coffee cup—and he'd found himself standing before the beautiful stranger, stumbling over his own words as he tried to correct his mistake—he couldn't deny he'd felt like he'd won the lottery.

And when he got the call for a ride from his part-time Uber job, he'd never in a million years expected Kaiah to be his passenger. Then, when she shared she needed a temporary place to stay? Well, once again he felt like someone was handing him a gift—a reason to talk to this woman and maybe get to know her.

But what are you doing? a quiet voice whispered inside his head. *And what would Brynn say if she knew you'd invited a stranger to stay in your home? With your daughter here?* They'd always put their child's safety first, and he was committed to continue doing so. Piper was the center of Reid's life.

But Brynn did have a thing for helping those in need, the voice whispered.

He couldn't deny it. When Brynn was alive, she'd organized volunteer committees at their church to serve in the community. Each Thanksgiving she and Reid would hand out pieces of pumpkin pie at the Coral Cove soup kitchen. They'd helped out at shelters for the homeless and even built homes through Habitat for Humanity.

Reid smiled as he thought of his late wife. Then he sighed. His feelings were always so complicated when it came to starting a new chapter without Brynn. In many ways, she still felt so close to him, like she could walk through the front door at any moment. They'd never talked about what would happen if one of them lost the other so young. Imagining a life without each other seemed like a problem that was decades away. But Reid knew that Brynn wouldn't have wanted him to be alone forever. After all, he'd want the same for her if the roles were reversed.

And for the first time since his wife had passed away, Reid was interested in someone. It had to mean something, right?

What would Brynn think of all this? he wondered. *Honestly, she'd probably be happy you're finally getting back out there after four years.*

He could almost hear her say, *It's about time, Reid!*

He shook his head. Maybe he was making too much out of this attraction. After all, Kaiah would be back on the road working on her story, and he'd never see her again. And that would be that.

Just chill, man. She'll only be here for a few days. Just be kind and courteous to a stranger in need, and leave it at that.

After ordering a pepperoni pizza and garlic knots through A Slice of Heaven's app, Reid moved to the doorway of Piper's room and rested his shoulder on the doorframe. Kaiah sat on the corner of his daughter's bed with a mermaid doll on her lap while Piper talked on and on about mermaids and swimming in the waves. Kaiah's lovely face was fixated with a serious expression, her brows furrowed while she nodded along with Piper's story. She appeared completely fascinated with his daughter. He tried to ignore the warmth blooming in his chest.

Then Kaiah turned and grinned at him.

He returned the smile before focusing on his daughter, who had stopped talking about mermaids and started showing Kaiah her best dance moves.

"Piper?" he asked.

His daughter stopped flailing about and spun to face him. "Yeah, Daddy?"

"The pizza will be here in thirty minutes."

"Yay!" Piper whirled around again, her dark hair fanning around her.

"Need some help in the kitchen?" Kaiah offered. "I can set the table."

"No, thanks," he told her. "I got it handled. Paper plates are my friend."

She grinned at him again, a twinkle in those bright, intelligent blue eyes that seemed to keep drawing him in.

"Miss Kaiah!" Piper rushed over with a book. "Have you ever read *The Mermaid Sisters*?" She pushed the book into Kaiah's hands.

"No, I haven't." Kaiah beamed at his daughter. "Should we read it together?"

"Yes, please!" Piper snuggled up next to Kaiah while the cat beside her began to quietly give herself a bath.

Before the scene warmed his soul too much, Reid backed out of the doorway and moved to the linen closet. He retrieved a set of sheets and a stack of towels, then set the pile on the end of the kitchen counter before grabbing the paper plates and setting the table for three.

He stood by the counter and peered at the table. Memories of the last time the table was set for three brought a familiar stitch in his chest.

His phone dinged with a text, and he peered down and grinned at his twin's name on his screen.

Becca: Who's the pretty blonde? Do you have something to tell me?

Reid shook his head. He should've known his sister would want all the details.

Reid: Damsel in distress. Needed a place to stay.

Becca: Um, tell me everything. NOW.

Reid: Can't talk now. Piper invited her for supper, and pizza's coming soon.

Becca: A pizza date? Hmm! I'll let you off the hook for now, but I want details at supper tomorrow.

Reid swallowed a groan. He could already hear his mother and his sister ganging up on him, demanding to know about the mysterious blonde staying in the apartment.

He replied with: Will do. And we'll talk about the festival too.

Becca: Yep, that's priority number one. We've got to raise the rest of the money for those renovations. That wing HAS to be open again. The kids deserve better.

Reid: Trust me, I know. I can't imagine how cramped those classrooms are, now that half the elementary school is closed. We'll get it figured out. Night, Becks.

Becca: Night.

He busied himself with putting away the clean dishes waiting in the dishwasher since last night, and soon the doorbell rang, announcing their supper.

"Pizza!" he called toward Piper's room, and immediately Piper romped into the kitchen.

"Everyone, take a seat," he said while pouring three glasses of sweet tea.

Piper patted the seat beside hers. "Sit by me, Miss Kaiah."

Reid distributed the glasses and then sat across the table from the ladies.

Kaiah took a huge bite of pizza, the steam still rising from the slice as the melty mozzarella oozed down the side. "Okay, this is delicious," she declared. "And I'm a New Yorker. I *know* my pizza."

Piper nodded. "It's the best pizza ever. Me and Daddy eat pizza at least once a week. Auntie Becca and Nana like it too. What's your favorite food?"

"I like all kinds of food. It would be easier to tell you which kind of food I *don't* like."

Reid swallowed a bite of garlic knot. "Like what?"

"Hmm." Kaiah tapped her chin. "I'm not a big fan of brussels sprouts."

Piper scrunched up her face. "Me neither."

Reid held up his hand. "They're actually delicious if you prepare them correctly."

"Really?" Kaiah leaned forward. "And how do you prepare them 'correctly'?" she asked, making air quotes with her fingers.

"Roast them in kung pao sauce."

"Huh. I'd actually try them that way." She seemed impressed. "You like to cook?"

"I have to take a turn at the firehouse," he told her.

"So you've actually made brussels sprouts for your coworkers, and they didn't run you off?"

He shook his head. "Nope."

"Well, color me surprised. Roasted brussels sprouts in kung pao sauce sounds pretty fancy."

Piper made a face. "And yucky."

"I agree." Kaiah gave his daughter a high five, and he laughed.

Piper continued to pepper Kaiah with questions about her

favorite foods, movies, books, toys, cartoons, and colors while they ate pizza and garlic knots and then ice cream for dessert.

When Kaiah covered her mouth to shield a yawn, Reid stood and collected their empty bowls from their ice cream. "I think we need to let Miss Kaiah rest. She's had a long day."

"Awww," Piper moaned. "Will I see you tomorrow, Miss Kaiah?"

Kaiah froze like a deer in headlights, looking unsure of how to respond. "Maybe."

Reid touched his daughter's head. "Say good night to Miss Kaiah and then get ready for your bath."

Piper hugged her. "Good night." Then she scampered off toward her bedroom.

Reid turned to Kaiah. "She's a lot. Thanks for being so patient."

"She's great," Kaiah said, and she looked like she was telling the truth. "Talking to her made me realize how much I miss my nieces and nephew." Reid caught an emotion he couldn't quite detect flash across her face before she righted herself again.

"How many do you have?"

"Four. Two from each of my older sisters." Then she hesitated. "And a few more if I count my stepsiblings' children too."

He cocked his head. "How many siblings do you have?"

She held up four fingers. "I'm the middle of five girls. Can you imagine *five* girls?"

"Um, no." He shook his head, and she laughed.

"My poor dad, right?" She chuckled.

"And you have stepsiblings too?"

She nodded. "Four stepbrothers. My dad used to say we were like *The Brady Bunch*, where Carol brought three girls into the marriage and Mike brought three boys. But in our family, my dad brought five girls, and my stepmom had four boys. My older sisters and two of the older brothers were already gone from the house when Dad and Veronica married, but becoming a blended family was still . . . challenging."

She gave him a stiff smile, and he could almost feel the anxiety radiating off her in waves. But before he could ask her about the family, she picked up the stack of bowls, carried them to the dishwasher, and opened the door.

He came up behind her and touched her hand. "Don't worry about it, I got it."

"You fed me, and you're not even going to let me help clean up?" She reached into her pocket and pulled out a twenty. "At least let me help pay for supper."

"Put that away."

She made a face and stuffed the money back into her pocket. "You're too generous." Then she brightened. "I'll add it to the cost of the room after I get my car back."

"Deal." He patted the pile of linens. "Here are sheets and towels. There are blankets in the closet, along with some other supplies. Let me give you my number in case you need anything or want a ride somewhere." He rattled off his number while she programmed it into her phone. Then his phone dinged with a text. He glanced at the screen and found a message: Hi! This is Kaiah.

She pushed her phone into a back pocket on her jeans and then picked up the pile of linens. "Thanks for everything."

"You're welcome." He walked her to the door and opened it. "If you need anything, don't be shy."

"I won't. Good night."

He waited until she disappeared up the stairs toward the apartment, and then he headed into the bathroom, where Piper sat on the edge of the tub while it filled with water.

"Miss Kaiah is so nice," Piper announced as she climbed in. "I really like her."

Reid soaped up a facecloth and began washing her back. "You two seem to get along well."

"Uh-huh." Piper splashed her purple rubber duck in the water. "I hope she lives on top of the garage forever."

"She's only staying until her car is fixed, sweetie." He washed her arms and her neck.

"But I want her to stay forever and ever," Piper whined. "Why can't she?"

"Because she has a home and a job."

Piper's frown transformed into a bright smile. "I'll ask her to stay, and she will." She splashed her duck again. "I wonder what happened to her dog. Why would someone take George?"

"I don't know."

Piper continued to discuss Kaiah for the remainder of her bath. After Reid read his daughter a story and settled her in bed for the night, he returned to the den, found his laptop, and searched the internet for Kaiah Ross. He quickly found articles Kaiah had written detailing vacation destinations throughout the United States, along with a few articles about the best cruise lines and Caribbean resorts. He was swept away by her talent. The pictures she painted with her words were so vivid, he could see the destinations as if he were already there.

After reading her articles, he was even more curious about Kaiah. He found her Instagram profile and clicked on a few photos of Kaiah with a golden retriever wearing a happy expression. If dogs could smile, this one had the brightest smile Reid had ever seen. Surely that had to be George. A few other photos included a good-looking guy with light brown hair.

Could he be the guy who took George? But she didn't say the culprit was a dude.

The guy could be someone else—perhaps her boyfriend or her

husband. But Reid had noticed there weren't any rings on her left hand. So maybe she wasn't married. Maybe she was single.

Or maybe it was none of Reid's business.

Bro, seriously. She'll be gone in a few days, and you'll never see her again. Just let it go.

Kaiah drew in a long breath and then released it as she eased into the warm bubble bath. She was grateful she'd remembered to pack her favorite bubbles. For her, a bath was the best way to relax after a long and stressful day, whether the words refused to flow as she tried to write, or while grief surged through her veins as she thought of her golden retriever, George. She missed her best buddy so much. He'd been her constant companion, going out on stories with her, taking daily walks, watching television with her, and sleeping at her feet at night. In fact, she'd had to sleep with a pillow at the bottom of the bed ever since her ex had taken George. And that was on top of shattering her heart and her trust.

Now she was stuck in Nowheresville, but at least she had a warm bubble bath and some entertaining neighbors. She was still smiling after her supper with Reid and his precocious daughter. Piper had her in stitches with her nonstop questions and her funny anecdotes. It pained Kaiah to know that sweet little girl had lost her mother when she was only two. She knew what it was like to walk around with a permanent hole in her heart without her mother. Piper and Reid had been through so much. Yet she could see that Piper and Reid had persevered. She was struck by the love in Reid's eyes when he looked at his daughter. He seemed like a good man and a doting father.

She focused on the white ceiling and relaxed. She would somehow enjoy this unexpected detour until she hit the road again.

Once the bathwater cooled, Kaiah dried off and pulled on a pair of yoga pants and a T-shirt. She settled on the sofa and flipped through channels before settling on a Hallmark movie. Her phone rang, and she smiled at her sister's name on the screen.

"Hey, Kam," Kaiah sang.

"Last I heard, Mr. TDH was your Uber driver. Did you drive off into the sunset or what?"

Kaiah grinned. "Well, I'm staying in his apartment."

"*What?*" Kam exclaimed. "You're at his *place?* Kaiah, did you actually go home with him? What are you thinking? I mean, talk about dangerous—"

"Whoa, whoa, whoa!" Kaiah held her hand up while interrupting her. "Calm down, Kammie. I'm staying in an apartment on his property. I'm not staying *in* his house." Then she shared how he offered the empty apartment and planned to settle up after her car was ready. "For some reason I trust him. I met his six-year-old, and she's adorable. Kam, you'd love her."

"Oh!" Kam sounded relieved. "It's not exactly the hotel arrangement I would've expected, but I trust your judgment, Ky. So he's married."

"Actually, he's a widower."

Her sister clucked her tongue. "Oh no. I'm sorry to hear that. That little girl is younger than we were when we lost Mom."

"I know." Glancing around the apartment, Kaiah cleared her throat. She needed to change the subject. "Anyway, this apartment is perfect. It's bigger than my place back in New York."

"For real?"

"And guess what? Mr. TDH is a firefighter too."

"Woo! A man in a uniform?" Kam exclaimed. "Ky, you've got to send me photos of this guy."

Kaiah laughed and then cupped her hand to her mouth to cover a yawn. "It's been a long day, so I'll let you go."

"Okay, but I want photos of Reid in his firefighter uniform. Promise me you'll send some." A voice sounded in the background, and then Kam laughed. "Uh-oh, Devon's getting jealous. Honey, you have nothing to worry about. You're the handsomest accountant I know," she told him before laughing again. Then all Kaiah could hear were muffled voices that sounded as if Kamryn had covered the phone with her hand.

She shook her head. She could envision her sister and her husband joking around and pretending to bicker. Those two had the best relationship. There was a time she'd hoped to find a love like that. But she'd given up on those dreams six months ago when her last relationship fell apart. That was when she'd accepted that she was better off alone so she could concentrate on her career without any distractions.

"Okay, I'm back. I told him he has nothing to worry about." Kaiah could hear the smile in her sister's voice. "Since I'll never get to see my handsome husband in a uniform, you'll have to get me a photo of Mr. TDH."

Kaiah rolled her eyes. "I'll do my best, but I doubt I'll get to see him in his uniform before I get back on the road."

"Such a shame," Kam sang with a dramatic sigh. "Get some rest, Ky. And I want a full report on your fireman after you're back on the road."

"I'm sure there will be nothing to report, Kamryn," Kaiah told her. "Tell your husband good night for me."

"Will do. Bye!"

Kaiah disconnected the call and then chuckled to herself. She didn't know what she'd do without her favorite sister.

Chapter 4

REID PEEKED INTO PIPER'S room the next morning. "Hey, pumpkin, you awake?"

"Out here, Daddy!" her little voice called from the direction of the kitchen.

When he reached the kitchen doorway, he found her teetering on a chair, balancing on her tiptoes and reaching into a cabinet. Panic shot through him.

"Piper!" He scooped her into his arms and set her on the floor. "You know better than to climb up on chairs, especially when I'm not around. You could've fallen. What are you doing?"

"Making pancakes for Miss Kaiah."

Reid's eyes cut to the clock on the stove. "Honey, it's only eight. She might be sleeping or just enjoying some quiet time."

Piper pointed to the stove. "I bet she's really, really hungry after her trip. We need to make sure she has something to eat."

"Piper . . ."

"Pleeeease, Daddy," she whined. "Pleeease?" She bounced up and down on the balls of her feet.

He stroked the scruff around his mouth and released a long, weary breath. Surely Kaiah had enough of his loquacious daughter last night. If he invited her to breakfast, then she'd feel obligated to come. But on the other hand, Kaiah *seemed* to have enjoyed the company. And in all honesty, he certainly had enjoyed hers. What harm could it be to invite her for another meal? She was going in a few days anyway.

"All right," he said.

When Piper's whining morphed into cheers, he held up his hand, silencing her. "But you have to agree to a couple of things."

"Okay!"

"First," he began, pointing to her mermaid pajamas. "You need to get dressed, brush your teeth, and comb your hair."

She shuffled down the hallway, almost tripping over the cat lounging in the doorway.

"One more thing," Reid called after her. "We'll knock on the door once. If Miss Kaiah doesn't respond, then we'll leave."

"Deal!" Piper hollered.

"I'm hoping my car will be ready in the next couple of days," Kaiah said, holding her phone. She'd called Monica, the owner of the Airbnb in Edisto Beach, as soon as she deemed it an acceptable hour to ping her. "If it's okay, let's keep the reservation as is, and I'll call you when I'm on my way."

"I'll hold it for you, but please let me know if something changes," Monica said.

Kaiah released a shaky breath. Everything was going to be fine. She had woken up at seven and couldn't go back to sleep, so she'd started making phone calls to keep her plans on track despite the car issues.

"Thank you so much, Monica," she said while pulling a granola bar out of her suitcase. As soon as she got off the phone, she needed to order some actual food. She couldn't live on granola bars until tomorrow.

"Have a safe trip," Monica said before disconnecting the call.

Kaiah sat on the arm of the sofa and unwrapped the granola bar. What would go well with her minuscule meal? Coffee. Definitely coffee. A coffee maker sat on the counter, which meant there could be coffee grounds stored in a cabinet.

She hopped off the arm of the sofa and began searching but came up empty. She unlocked her phone and started to tap a breakfast order into a delivery app.

"I wonder if anyone in this town makes a better vanilla latte than the Roast Shack?" she muttered under her breath. She was on the hunt when a noise pulled her out of the zone—was that a knock?

Hushed voices murmured outside the door, and she peeked through the peephole. She smiled when she found Reid and Piper standing on the deck.

"Good morning," she said as she pulled open the front door.

"See, Daddy," Piper exclaimed. "I told you Miss Kaiah was awake."

Reid's smile was sheepish—and adorable. "Hope we didn't wake you."

"Nope. I've been up since seven." She leaned on the doorframe. "What's up?"

"Do you like pancakes?" Piper asked, her expression hopeful.

Kaiah bent and touched Piper's button nose. "I do. How about you?"

"Yeah." Piper clapped. "Did you have breakfast?"

Kaiah held up the empty wrapper. "Only if you count a smushed granola bar."

"Me and Daddy want to make you pancakes." Piper grabbed Kaiah's hand. "Let's go!"

Kaiah slipped the wrapper into the pocket of her jeans. "I'm ready." She allowed Piper to steer her down the steps and into the house, where Ariel lounged on the back of the sofa, snoring loudly.

"Hey, Piper," Kaiah whispered, tapping the little girl's shoulder. "Your cat snores."

Piper cackled. "Sometimes she wakes herself up because she snores so loud."

Kaiah shared a grin with Reid.

"Can I see a picture of George?" Piper asked when they reached the kitchen.

Kaiah unlocked her phone and scrolled to the last photo she'd taken of George, sitting on her deck smiling in a sunbeam. She felt a boulder drop into the pit of her stomach as she took in the photo of her best buddy.

"He's a beautiful golden retriever," Reid said, standing over her shoulder.

Piper pulled the phone closer to her. "He looks nice. I think he'd be best friends with Ariel."

"He likes cats," Kaiah said. "But most cats don't care for him." She set her phone on the counter. "How can I help with breakfast?"

Reid found the pancake mix while Kaiah started a pot of coffee. Her stomach was rumbling a few minutes later as the rich aroma of coffee mingled with the pancakes sizzling on the stove. Reid plated the pancakes, and the three of them sat at the table and smothered their breakfast in butter and syrup. Piper kept Kaiah and Reid in stitches while she shared stories about school.

After they finished eating, Piper jumped from the table. "I need to show you the story I wrote in school last week," she exclaimed before racing out of the kitchen.

"I wish I could bottle that energy," Reid said. "Want more coffee?"

Kaiah shook her head and then stacked their plates. "No, thanks. Everything was delicious." She carried the plates to the sink, where she began rinsing them off. "I feel bad that you're feeding me again. Maybe I can buy you lunch or something." When Reid remained silent, she craned her neck over her shoulder. He sat in his chair stone-faced, and his reticence sent heat surging to her cheeks. "Did I say something wrong?"

"No, no." He gathered up their coffee mugs. "I was just wondering . . ." He paused again. "Do you have plans today?"

"I don't have a car, so nope, no plans."

"Would you like a tour of Coral Cove?"

Piper slid through the doorway. "Are we taking Miss Kaiah out?"

Reid kept his focus on Kaiah. "Are we?"

Kaiah smiled. "Yep. I think I'd like that."

"What do you think of Coral Cove?" Reid asked Kaiah. He was holding his daughter's hand as the three of them meandered down the boardwalk that afternoon.

The sky above them stretched across in a soft blue, and seagulls called to one another while the waves crashed against the shore. Clusters of sunbathers scattered along the shore. Young families walked together along the water's edge, and teenagers played volleyball in the sand. In the distance, fishing boats bobbed in the water while sailboats glided along, their colorful sails flapping in the breeze.

Reid couldn't have asked for a better day to show Kaiah around town. Earlier that morning, they had jumped into his Suburban, and he gave her a windshield tour of the surrounding neighborhood before they parked on Main Street. They visited several stores before Kaiah insisted on buying lunch for them at Frank's Seafood Grill. He wasn't surprised to find that he was enjoying this day with Kaiah even more than the last. Their conversation effortlessly ebbed and flowed, and her genuine delight in his daughter's endless anecdotes warmed his heart.

Kaiah tented a hand over her eyes while she watched the waves. "As a travel reporter, I'm surprised I've never heard of this place. It's breathtaking here," she said. "I feel so at home, you know? It doesn't feel touristy. And the food was delicious—probably some of the best shrimp I've ever had." She turned toward him. "It reminds me of the beach towns we visited in New England when I was a kid. Those were some of my best memories of my mom. And you know what? Those trips inspired me to travel the world and write stories about the places I visited and people I met."

"Daddy! Daddy!" Piper appeared beside him and pulled on his hand. "My friend Megan's here." She pointed toward the sand. "Can I go say hi to her?"

Reid nodded. "Stay where I can see you. Miss Kaiah and I will sit on this bench."

Piper kicked off her sandals and took off running onto the sand. The other little girl saw her, and they both shrieked before hugging and dancing around.

Kaiah plopped on the bench and slipped on a pair of pink, mirrored sunglasses. "Your daughter is a ray of sunshine," she said.

Reid sat beside Kaiah. "I'm glad you're enjoying her, because she really likes you."

"She's a hoot." Kaiah crossed her long legs, and her eyes lingered on the beach. "That lighthouse is so beautiful. I saw it as soon as I drove into town, and after I met you at the coffee shop, I walked to see it. I felt like it was calling me." She grimaced. "I didn't realize how weird that would sound until I said it out loud."

He chuckled. "Not weird at all." He glanced at the lighthouse and then back at her. "It's beautiful, isn't it? Plus it has an interesting history."

"Is that right?" She angled her body toward him.

"It was built in 1805, and it saved a ship full of sailors from running up on the shoals during a storm right around this time of year, early April. One of the sailors was my great-great-so-many-greats-grandfather."

"Wow."

"The lighthouse is one of our historical sites. We have a museum just a few miles from here, and it details the history of Coral Cove, how it was a fishing village in the early 1800s and then grew from there. In fact, there was a port a few miles from here."

"You seem to know a lot about it."

"My twin sister is the president of the Coral Cove Historical Society. I help out with tours of the lighthouse sometimes, but the interior has been closed for a while because it needs some repairs. Plus the light hasn't worked for years."

"That's a shame. It's such a gorgeous lighthouse. I tried to get some photos of it, but the fence was in the way. Seems like such an integral part of this town." Kaiah nodded toward a banner. "I saw that sign for the Coral Cove Spring Festival. When is it?"

His mouth sagged downward. "In a couple of weeks, but Becks wants to talk to me about it. There are budget issues, and it might be canceled. But we really need the festival to help raise funds for the elementary school."

"Are you replacing the school?"

He shook his head. "There was a fire."

"Oh no," Kaiah exclaimed. "Was everyone okay?"

"Yeah. Thankfully, it was during Christmas break last year."

"Did you fight that fire?"

He nodded. "It was caused by faulty wiring and did a lot of damage in one wing of the school. The school board didn't budget for such a huge expense this year, and the town hasn't raised enough money to fix that wing, so the classes are doubled up right now. Plus the media center and the gym were also damaged, so we need to get those repaired too. We'd hoped that the festival would help raise the money, but last year the new mayor slashed the budget and gave the money to other projects. She just didn't know how much we'd need this festival."

"That's a shame."

A comfortable silence settled between them as they looked out toward the beach where Piper and Megan were digging in the sand. Taking in Kaiah's profile as she gazed at the water, Reid felt the urge to know more about her. "What was it like growing up as the middle of five girls?"

Kaiah chuckled. "Noisy. Do you and Becca have any other siblings?"

"Nope." He shook his head. "It's just Becks and me."

She leaned on the arm of the bench. "Our house was chaotic. Someone was always running to dance class, cheerleading, sports games, things like that. My sisters and I bickered a lot, but we had fun too." She paused, and her expression dimmed slightly. "At least, we had a lot of fun when we were younger . . ." Her voice trailed off, and she turned toward the lighthouse.

Silence stretched between them, punctuated by the sound of the waves crashing against the shore and children laughing and playing on the beach.

Reid longed to know what was on her mind. He cleared his throat and tilted his head. "Five girls . . . whew."

"Yeah." She angled her body toward his, and her warm expression sent relief filtering through him.

He shook his head. "I can't imagine. Are you close to your sisters?"

"Um . . . well, my older sisters moved away. One went to Ohio and the other is in California. My youngest sister is out in Arizona. She lives near our dad." She fiddled with the hem of her shirt. "I'm close to my one sister. She's only fourteen months younger than me. We talk just about every day."

"What's her name?"

"Kamryn."

Reid grinned. "Kaiah and Kamryn?"

"Oh, you haven't heard all of the names."

He shifted toward her. "I'm listening."

"My parents, Kristin and Kenneth, had . . . Are you ready for this?" she asked, and he nodded. Then she counted the names off on her fingers. "Kendra, Krystal, Kaiah, Kamryn, and Kimberly—all names beginning with *K*." She giggled, and a thousand butterflies fluttered in his stomach. He relished the sound of her laugh and wanted to hear it more often.

He rubbed his chin. "All *K*'s, huh?" he asked.

"Yup."

"Like that famous family that's always in the gossip magazines Mom and Becca read."

"Right, but without the money, California mansions, or drama."

They both laughed, and he enjoyed the easy banter between them.

As she tossed her hair, he caught the scent of her flowery shampoo and his heartbeat began ratcheting up. "You mentioned that you have nieces and a nephew. Do their names also begin with *K*?"

"No, thank goodness," she exclaimed with another giggle. "Kendra has Emilia and Jason, and then Krystal has Alyssa and Erin." She paused, and when her smile faded, he realized he'd been staring at her, lost in her ocean-blue eyes. She gave him a shy smile and tucked a lock of her thick blonde hair behind her ear. "I got the feeling you're close to Becca." She made a face. "Wait, should I call her Becca or Becks?"

"I call her Becks, but everyone else calls her Becca. I've been calling her Becks since we were kids." He rested his arm on the back of the bench. When his fingers accidentally brushed the back of her arm, he noticed she didn't pull away. "We're close. Always have been."

"That's cool."

He recalled how Kaiah's expression had darkened for a fraction of a second the night before when she talked about her stepsiblings, and curiosity nipped at him. "You mentioned that your father remarried." He hesitated, but her expression remained serene. "Are you close to your stepbrothers?"

"No."

She turned her body away, giving her attention to the waves again.

He immediately regretted the question, and a knot of guilt formed in his gut. "I'm sorry. I didn't mean to make you uncomfortable."

"It's okay." She turned to face him, and when her smile returned, it didn't quite reach her eyes. "My mom passed away when I was eleven, and my dad remarried two years later. Her death was completely unexpected. She'd been living with A-fib and none of us knew it—sometimes it goes undetected. She was fine one day and then . . . she was just gone. Sudden heart attack. I felt like I'd woken up in a nightmare where my world had been completely detonated."

She moved her fingers along the edge of the bench. "Then my dad met someone, and within a year, they were married. I was still grieving my mom, but I had no one to turn to. My older sisters were busy with high school and college. My stepbrothers were strangers. I mean, my stepmom was okay, but . . ." She shrugged and wrapped her arms around her middle before she continued. "She tried, but I was thirteen and I didn't want another mom. I pushed her away while my youngest sister clung to her. So Kam and I only had each other. We like to joke that we raised each other. I worked hard in school and managed to snag a journalism scholarship. I went away to college and never looked back. My dad moved out to Arizona, and I guess he never looked back either. I haven't visited him in a couple of years."

Reid swallowed back his frown. "I'm sorry. I didn't mean to dredge all of that up for you."

"It's okay." She turned toward him, and her expression softened as her hand brushed his, sending warmth racing up his arm. "Honestly, I don't talk about my family much, but it feels good to get that off my chest."

He was honored that she trusted him with something so personal.

"Are you close to your folks?"

"Yeah." He nodded. "They live in the house where I grew up, and I see them often."

"That's great."

They sat in comfortable silence and looked out toward the waves again.

After several moments, he examined his watch. "I didn't realize how late it was. If it's okay, I need to stop at the grocery store."

"Sure. I need to get some stuff too." She stood and shouldered her purse.

"I had so much fun today," Piper announced as her dad parked his SUV in the driveway later that afternoon.

Kaiah rotated to face her little friend in the back seat. "I did too. Thank you for taking me to see your fun town."

"You're welcome." Piper unbuckled her seat belt and pushed the door open.

Kaiah had not only enjoyed getting a tour of the town, but she cherished her talk with Reid on the boardwalk, where she'd somehow managed to unload her feelings about her family. Opening up to Reid had felt natural, even though she'd only known him for twenty-four hours. Was that because he was a stranger who didn't know her past? She was sure she hadn't felt that comfortable so quickly with her ex. There was something about Reid that she couldn't comprehend. It was as if she'd known him for years. They seemed never to run out of things to talk about. Goodness, she'd even enjoyed something as mundane as grocery shopping with him!

"Thanks for joining us." Reid climbed out of the car, and Kaiah met him at the back hatch.

She gathered up her grocery bags while he lifted his. "I guess I'll see you later." When she turned, something buzzed past her face, and she yelped while swatting it away.

"You okay?" Reid asked.

"Yeah." She tried to smile, hoping Reid didn't see her freaking out under the surface. "I think it was a bee or a wasp. I'm super allergic to bees."

"Oh." His lips twitched.

"Sorry. Kam always says I overreact when I hear something buzz, but I can't help it. I was stung by a bee when I was around Piper's age and had the worst reaction—lots of hives and I couldn't breathe well. Then I was stung by a wasp in high school, and it was *so* painful, plus my arm blew up like a balloon. So let's just say the buzzing things and I just don't mix." She started across the driveway toward the stairs leading to the apartment.

"Kaiah," Reid called after her, and she spun to face him. "Supper with my family is at six. Join us."

She was almost certain she saw hope in his eyes. "Thanks, but I don't want to impo—"

"You're not imposing." He finished her sentence, holding up his hand. "I have plenty of burgers."

"Yeah, Miss Kaiah. Have supper with us." Piper clung to three grocery bags in her hands.

Kaiah was tempted, but she didn't want to interfere with their family time. "I'm going to get started on my next article, but I'm sure I'll see you around tomorrow."

Reid appeared disappointed, which she found fascinating. Perhaps he also felt a warm friendship growing between them. Such a shame she would have to get back on the road as soon as Daisy was fixed. "If you change your mind, come on down and join us," he said.

"I will," she promised.

"Bye, Miss Kaiah." Piper flailed her arms around, jostling her grocery bags.

Kaiah waved and then scooted up the steps to her apartment. After putting her snacks in the cabinet and the six-pack of diet soda in the refrigerator, she settled on the sofa with her computer.

She opened her laptop and she couldn't stop herself from searching for information on Coral Cove. Soon she was reading about the history of the beautiful black-and-white lighthouse and surfing web pages displaying drawings of the ship that it saved.

As she settled back on the softa, she began to wonder if she should stop in Coral Cove on her way home and write a story about this fascinating little place. She'd have to run that idea by her editor . . .

Chapter 5

"I'LL GET IT!"

Later that evening, Piper rushed to the door. She threw it open and clapped when she found her aunt, uncle, and cousin standing on the porch. "Hi!" She grabbed her cousin's hand, and the girls ran down the hallway toward Piper's room, giggling the whole way.

Cash, Becca's husband, held the door open for his wife while balancing a covered dish in his other hand. "They act like they haven't seen each other in years every time they get together."

"How come you're never that happy to see me?" Reid teased his twin.

Becca rolled her eyes. "I see you enough." She held out a cake server. "We brought baked beans and a chocolate cake."

"My favorites." Reid took the cake server from her and opened the lid, the rich cocoa scent filling the room. "Yum."

His sister followed him to the kitchen and swiveled her head back and forth. "Where's the pretty blonde?" she demanded.

"Most likely in the apartment." He set the cake on the counter while his brother-in-law put the covered dish beside it.

Cash swiped a handful of chips from the bowl in the center of the table. "What pretty blonde?"

Becca quickly summarized how Kaiah came to stay in Reid's empty apartment. "Have you talked to her since yesterday?"

"Piper invited her for breakfast this morning. Then we gave her a tour of the town and stopped at the grocery store on our way home." Reid pulled a stack of plates from the cabinet. "I invited her to join us for supper, but she said she had to do some research for her next article."

Becca arched an eyebrow. "Well, that sounds like a full day. Did you have fun?"

Reid nodded. "Yeah. She and Piper seem to have clicked. Piper wouldn't stop chatting and sharing stories with her."

"Well, Piper is so shy," Cash joked, and they all laughed.

Becca grinned at her twin. "You should tell her to invite Kaiah for supper."

"Becks, the woman said no. She'll have her car back in a couple days and head to her next destination for her travel series."

His sister was quiet for a minute. The next time she spoke, her voice was soft. "Reid, it's been four years. You're allowed to open up to someone again."

He pinched the bridge of his nose and forced his eyes to keep from rolling upward. He'd heard this lecture so many times, he could almost recite it along with her. "Becks, come on. I know you mean well, but I have my daughter to think of. I don't need Piper to get attached and then have her heart broken when Kaiah leaves."

"So that's all this is about, huh? Just Piper?"

Reid shook his head and pulled cups out of the cabinet. He

wasn't in the mood for one of his sister's interrogations. Dating wasn't on his radar, and his twin knew better. But she still insisted on pushing him.

"Want me to warm up the grill?" Cash offered.

Reid was grateful for the change in subject. "How about you pull out the fixings, and I'll start the grill?"

While Reid concentrated on grilling the burgers, Becca and Cash readied the toppings and sides. As soon as his parents, Blake and Sue, arrived, the supper was on the table.

"Can we invite Miss Kaiah to join us?" Piper asked while she and Astrid sat in their usual spots across from Reid.

"Who's Kaiah?" his mom asked.

"She's busy, Piper. She told you that earlier." Reid glanced over at his mother and took in her intrigued expression. "Kaiah is an out-of-towner who had some car trouble. She's staying in the garage apartment while her car is repaired."

"I invited her for breakfast, and Daddy made us pancakes. Then we showed her the town," Piper explained to her grandmother. "Miss Kaiah and Daddy talked on the boardwalk while I played with Megan at the beach."

"Is that right?"

Reid could've sworn Mom had a twinkle in her eye.

"Miss Kaiah writes stories," Piper continued. "She used to have a dog named George, but her friend took her dog. She misses him—the dog, I mean. I don't know if she misses her friend. I have to ask her. I like her a lot, and I hope she stays a long time. I think Daddy likes her too." Piper took a bite from her cheeseburger and settled back on her chair.

His mother nodded slowly, a smirk on her face as she turned her attention toward Reid. "That's *very* interesting. Is Kaiah single?"

Here we go again . . .

Reid took a deep, cleansing breath. "I don't know, but she's leaving very soon."

"What a shame, son. She sounds lovely."

Reid glanced across the table at Cash, hoping his brother-in-law would rescue him with another subject change, but he was busy helping Astrid add copious amounts of ketchup and pickles to her cheeseburger. He decided to instigate his own subject change. "What were you saying about the festival?" he asked his twin.

"It's not good," Becca began, her expression turning grave. "Our marketing budget is slashed, and the newspaper doesn't have a huge online footprint. Somehow we need to get the word out about the festival, or it will just be a waste of money."

Cash rubbed his wife's shoulder. "It'll be okay. It always is."

"As much as I appreciate your enthusiasm, if nobody comes to the festival, we won't be able to raise any funds. Then who knows how long the school will be overcrowded." Becca picked up her glass of sweet tea. "We've done all of the fundraising we can with the PTO. Now we have to rely on the festival. But the attendance the last few years has been tiny compared to what it used to be. At this rate, we're going to spend more money putting on the festival than we stand to make from it. That's why the committee wants to cancel it."

Reid shook his head. "Don't cancel it. We can make it happen."

"I'm not so sure about that. We need to come up with a plan, and *fast*. We have an emergency committee meeting tomorrow," Becca said. "I'll let you know what happens."

"That's too bad, kids," Dad said. "I remember going to the festival when I was little."

Mom smiled. "Me too. It would be a shame to let that tradition die."

"There has to be a way to make it happen," Reid said. "And if there is, my twin will figure it out."

Becca sighed. "Let's hope so."

After supper, his mother and sister helped Reid clean up the kitchen while his dad and Cash took care of the grill.

"Daddy," Piper exclaimed as she flounced into the kitchen, pulling a rolling mermaid-covered suitcase behind her. "Me and Astrid are having a sleepover tonight."

Reid studied his daughter's serious expression. "Oh you are, huh?"

Piper glanced at her cousin, who nodded and then faced Reid again. "Yep! We've been talking about which mermaids are the fastest swimmers, and we're not done yet. So can I stay at Astrid's tonight?"

"What do you think, Becks?" he asked his sister.

"Fine with me. Are you working tomorrow?"

"Nope."

"We love having Piper over. I'll take them to school in the morning."

The girls cheered in unison.

Reid walked his family out to driveway and waved goodbye while they drove away. When he turned back toward the house, his eyes wandered to the apartment over the garage. An idea took hold of him, and he headed toward the stairs.

"You had a romantic walk on the boardwalk with Mr. TDH and his adorable daughter," Kamryn said while she grinned over FaceTime. "He sounds like a thoughtful guy and a good dad."

Kaiah nodded. "Yeah, I agree. Too bad I won't be here long enough to find out."

After spending over an hour researching Coral Cove and the glorious lighthouse, Kaiah had made some microwave popcorn and searched for a movie to stream. Then her sister had called and demanded the latest on Mr. Tall, Dark, and Handsome.

A knock sounded on the door. "Who could that be?" Kaiah asked.

"I bet it's Mr. TDH coming to whisk you away," Kam teased.

"Very funny," Kaiah deadpanned. But her heart did a flip while she worked to keep her expression blank. She peered in the peephole, and her stomach did a somersault.

Her sister was right. Reid was here!

"Who is it?" Kam asked.

"It's Reid!" Kaiah said in a loud whisper. "I'm going to hang up now."

"Noooo," Kam whined. "I want to meet him."

"You can meet him another time. I'll talk to you later."

"You'd better call me," Kam said before hanging up.

Kaiah pushed her phone into her back pocket, then combed her fingers through her hair before she yanked open the door. "Well, hello there."

Reid grinned. "Have you eaten?"

"Only if you count microwave popcorn."

"How do feel about Italian food?"

"I love it." She tilted her head. "But didn't you just eat with your family?"

"I did, but I thought you might be hungry since you didn't join us." He paused and gestured behind her. "Unless you're too busy working."

"I was just talking to my sister and thinking about pitching another article to my editor."

"Can you take a break?"

"For Italian food?" she asked. "Absolutely."

"Great."

They smiled at each other, and she lost herself in his bottomless brown eyes for a moment. He pushed up the sleeves of his long-sleeved T-shirt before resting an arm on the deck railing beside him. Kaiah couldn't pull her eyes away from the thick, ropey muscles of his forearm.

Whoa! He's one fit dude. Must be all that firefighting.

She gave herself a mental shake and tried to ignore the flush climbing up her neck. "I'll, uh, grab my purse."

~

Reid held open the door to Baudo's Trattoria, and Kaiah strolled inside. The savory aromas that hit her caused her stomach to gurgle, and she hugged her arms to her middle, hoping Reid hadn't heard it.

"This place reminds me of the Italian joints back in New York," Kaiah said while they walked together toward the counter. The walls were lined with photos of mouthwatering pastas alongside beach landscapes. The black-and-white tile floor was worn, and the matching checked tablecloths with small vases of fresh red carnations at each table evoked a feeling of yesteryear. "Do you eat here often?"

Reid grinned. "Oh yeah. It's been a staple in my life since I was a kid."

"What do you recommend?"

"Everything." He chuckled, and she enjoyed the deep, rich sound.

Kaiah grinned before studying the menu. Her eyes moved to

the glass cases, and she smiled when she noticed there were calzones shaped like lighthouses.

Reid sidled up to her. "What'd you see?"

As he leaned in, she breathed in his scent and picked up hints of evergreen mixed with sandalwood. Her heartbeat quickened.

"Those calzones are shaped like lighthouses," she explained. "How cute is that?"

"Would you like to try one?" he offered.

She nodded and then ordered a cheese and pepperoni calzone before they sat in a booth. She cut off a piece of the calzone and pushed the plate toward him. "Would you like a bite?"

He rubbed his hand over his flat abdomen. "I already ate."

"So you're going to watch me eat?" she asked, and when he nodded, she giggled. "Talk about awkward."

"Fine. I'll force myself." He cut off a piece, forked it into his mouth, and shook his head. "Superb."

She popped a piece into her mouth, and her tastebuds danced with delight. The soft dough burst with the perfect balance of tangy tomato sauce and rich mozzarella. "I agree." While she ate another piece, she glanced out the restaurant's front window. Her eyes rested on the gift shop across the street where she'd spotted the lighthouse suncatcher, and her heart lurched yet again.

"What's on your mind?"

Her gaze snapped to Reid's, and his warm chocolate-brown eyes melted any hesitation she had about sharing what was on her mind.

"There's a gift shop across the street," she began, "and the lighthouse suncatcher in the window reminds me of one my mom bought on our last trip to Maine. It hung in the front window of our house for years." She ate another piece of calzone while contemplating the lighthouse. She'd researched it earlier, and she was anxious to see it in person. "You mentioned you give lighthouse tours."

"That's right." He settled back against the booth.

"How would you feel about giving a nosy reporter a private tour?"

The bow of his smile reached straight to his eyes. "When?"

"Right now." She wrapped up the calzone and laid some cash on the table. "I'll finish this in the car, if it's okay."

He held up his keys, and they jingled. "Let's go."

The sunset sent a band of oranges and purples across the sky, reflecting on the water below. Reid thought it was a glorious backdrop for Kaiah's visit to the black-and-white-striped lighthouse.

She took several photos through the fence before turning to Reid. "I read online that it's been out of commission for almost two decades. What happened?"

"Faulty wiring." He leaned on the chain-link fence. "It was built in the early 1800s and updated in the 1950s to electrical. But over the years, the folks responsible for maintaining the building changed hands several times. First it was the mayor's office, then it was the parks department, and I don't even know who had it after them. The place just sat empty for a while. Around the town's two hundredth anniversary, the Coral Cove Historical Society wanted to get the lamp up and running for the town celebration, but when they assessed what needed to be fixed, the cost was much greater than they anticipated, so they abandoned the project. No one wanted to shoulder the extra expense to fix it."

"And now it just sits?" She stuck out her lower lip, reminding him of an adorable puppy. "That's a shame."

"When Becca took over the historical society, she opened the grounds for tours, and her goal was to also get the lantern room fixed." He ran his finger over the stubble on his chin. "But they still haven't gotten the funds to do it. Money for historical preservation in small towns isn't easy to come by, you know?"

"Hmm." She rested her hands on her hips and scrunched her nose in concentration. "I saw photos online of the inside of the lighthouse, but I'd love to see it for myself. The view from the top looks incredible. Any chance I can take a look?"

"Listen, it's not open to the public. But since this may be your only chance to see inside . . ." He trailed off as he cocked his head to the side, scrutinizing her. "Can I ask you to walk only where I say is safe?"

"Scout's honor." She held up three fingers. "And by the way, I *was* a Brownie and a Girl Scout, so that promise has some weight."

He chuckled. "All right, then. Follow me, ma'am." He unlocked the gate and held it for her before locking it behind them. They walked up the cobblestone path to the lighthouse.

"You could put this lighthouse on any shoreline in Maine, and I swear it'd fit in. It looks so much like the lighthouses I'd see when I was a kid. It's uncanny." She pointed to the small white building at the base of the lighthouse. "What's that?"

He unlocked the door and pushed it open, and a musty scent filled his nostrils. "The lighthouse keeper lived here. I don't think it's been opened since last summer during one of my last tours. I just let folks peek their heads inside."

"Let me get this straight. You're a tour guide, an Uber driver, a firefighter, *and* a dad." Her eyes studied him. "Do you ever take a day off?"

"What's a day off?" He flipped on the lights and made a sweeping gesture. "Go in but be careful."

"Yes, Lieutenant Turner." She saluted him and then proceeded into the building.

"These are the living quarters." He directed her around the small house. "There's a bedroom, a galley kitchen, a bathroom, and a small living area."

She pulled out her camera and took photos. Then she pointed the lens toward him and smiled, and her camera flashed and clicked a few times.

Reid smirked. "I promise the lighthouse is a lot more interesting than I am."

She shook her head, a coy grin on her lips. "I'm not so sure about that," she quipped, and her teasing tone sent his heartbeat racing. She headed through a doorway that led to the lantern room. "Can we go upstairs?"

He rushed ahead of her and held out his hand. "Let me go first."

Kaiah looped the camera strap around her neck before threading her fingers with his. He enjoyed the warmth of her soft skin on his as he guided her up the spiral staircase.

When they got to the top, she gasped. "*Wow*," she said, her mouth a small O shape.

Reid watched as she peered out over the 360-degree view that captured the cove and the edge of town. Darkness had begun to descend, and the streetlights created a warm glow, dotting the sidewalks. "This view is better than I could've imagined."

With the light from the sunset highlighting her golden waterfall of hair and kissing her sun-warmed skin, he couldn't have agreed more. "It sure is."

She turned her attention from the outside view back to the lantern room. Panels of glass surrounded a lamp the shape of a beehive. But instead of dripping with honey, ridged glass panels overlapped to create the lamp of the lighthouse. Kaiah had never seen anything like it. "So, Mr. Tour Guide, how does the lamp work? Or, at least, how did it used to?"

Reid cleared his throat and put on his most professional tour guide voice. "The lamp is housed in a glass enclosure called a lens. Lenses were specially designed to concentrate the power of the light so that sailors could see it from several nautical miles out. Originally they rotated with a mechanism powered by weights before they were upgraded to electricity. But obviously, now this guy doesn't work at all."

Kaiah nodded and took a few photos, then rested her hand on the doorknob to the gallery, the walkway outside the lantern room. "Can we go out there?"

"If you promise to be careful."

She saluted him. "Always." She pushed the door open, and the wind blew strands of her hair away from her face while she captured photos of the water. She rested on the railing and took a deep inhale of the fresh air. "It must be wonderful to breathe this fresh air all year round."

"I guess so. I've never thought about it." He touched her shoulder. "Please take a step back."

She gave him a cheeky smile. "Yes, Lieutenant." She moved away from the railing and pushed a few flyaway strands of hair behind her ears, but they immediately escaped and fluttered around her face once again. "Hmm, a fireman . . . It must be a great feeling to know you help people in your job."

"Except when you can't," he muttered, but immediately he regretted it. He wasn't ready to talk about the dark days, so he pushed them away in favor of a new topic. "So what's your favorite story you ever worked on?"

She paused for a moment, considering his question. "One of my first stories was for a small local paper in upstate New York, covering the upcoming holiday celebrations. It wasn't exciting, and I didn't get to travel, but I was finally writing for a paper. I wasn't a student or an intern. I was a real, paid journalist. Now granted, I wasn't making *any* money, but I had my own byline. That was enough for me."

"That's fantastic."

Her eyes shot to the water again, and a comfortable silence settled between them. Soon the sky was cloaked in darkness, and the only sound Reid could hear was the water lapping against the shore. He wondered what this beautiful stranger was thinking about.

"Lighthouses remind me of my mom," Kaiah suddenly said, her voice soft and almost reverent. "I've always been drawn to them because of her."

Suddenly he longed to take her into his arms, to soothe any pain this woman might've felt. When his hand brushed hers, she threaded her fingers with his as if on instinct. The intimate gesture sent a happy glow radiating through him.

"That's a nice way to remember her," he said, and then he internally rolled his eyes. *C'mon, man, don't be so lame!*

Reid frantically searched his mind for any subject to make up for his consummate lameness. His mind wandered toward Kaiah's "friend" taking her dog. Should he ask her if that "friend" was an ex? Before he could stop himself, the words came pouring from his mouth.

"You said your friend took your dog," he began. "Why?"

"My ex." Her voice vibrated with sadness.

"He sounds sweet." He hesitated. "I know this might sound weird coming from a guy you don't know, so feel free to say no. But . . . losing your dog is hard. Do you want to talk about it?"

A sigh seemed to bubble up from deep within her. "I know, I'm still reeling from it. It's my ex's fault. His name is Hayes Walker, and basically he changed his mind about me." She pushed her phone into her back pocket. "We met through work, which was probably my first mistake. We were both freelancing at the same online magazine. I thought he was arrogant, and I should have stuck with that assessment. But we worked on a story together, and I stupidly found his arrogance charming. Then we fell in love, or at least I thought we did, and then we started talking about a future together. And when we adopted George together, I thought that was like a real commitment." She scoffed. "Ridiculous, right?"

"No, not at all." Reid released her hand and rubbed her arm. "He would be so lucky to plan a future with someone like you."

He could feel her eyes watching him through the dark. "I thought I'd have it all like my older sisters—a career, a home, a family. But I was wrong."

"What happened?"

"Hayes decided he wanted a career more than he wanted me." She shifted to face the horizon, and a weight landed on his chest as he took in her sadness. "I didn't even know he was applying for jobs. I thought we were going to stay in New York together, but then one day he got a call, and the next day he was flying out to California for an interview."

"What job?"

"Staff writer at *Global Media*." Her posture wilted. "It was a position I thought about going after, but I stopped looking when we started talking about a future. I never considered putting my career before him." She barked out a bitter laugh.

He took her hand and cradled it in both of his. "I'm sorry, Kaiah."

Her eyes grew misty. "I was so naive. I thought I mattered to him. But obviously I didn't. We switched off which days George lived at his place and mine. On one of his George days, Hayes just took off. And he took George with him. My dog. *Our* dog." She blew out a breath. "I miss George so much. I've thought about getting a puppy, but it just doesn't feel right. Not yet."

"Hayes doesn't deserve you, Kaiah. You're way too good for him."

She waved her hand, as if to stave off the compliment. "That's why I'm done with love and all that." She nearly spat out the words. "It only leads to hurt. I'm just . . . I'm just better off alone."

An unexpected feeling wafted over him—disappointment?—but he nodded anyway.

Kaiah spun to face him, and he couldn't make out her features in the dark. "It's getting late. I guess we should go."

They flipped on their phone flashlights, and then Reid took her hand and led her down the spiral staircase.

Once they were back in his Suburban, she turned toward him and touched his arm. "Thank you for the private tour." The warmth was back in her voice.

"Anytime," he said, and his heart gave a happy kick while they drove to his house.

Chapter 6

KAIAH SPENT MONDAY MORNING multitasking. She googled everything she could about Coral Cove, wondering if she could convince her editor that this lovely town would charm readers the way it had her. But every few minutes, without fail, her thoughts would suddenly flit to Reid and the romantic lighthouse sunset they shared.

How could a man that thoughtful, that kind, that *gorgeous* still be single? By his own choice, probably. He and Piper had obviously been through a lot.

Too bad I have to leave them soon.

Wait. What?

Ky, you just met them. Of course you're going to leave them soon. You can't stay here. That's, like, something a stalker would do.

She'd known Reid and Piper for barely two days. But after spending forty-eight hours with them, she felt so comfortable, as if they'd spent a lifetime building an archive of memories and inside jokes. Kaiah was still surprised that she'd opened up to Reid about her mom and her weird family dynamic, not to mention Hayes.

She'd never shared such intimate details about herself with a man she barely knew.

She scrubbed her hands down her face. "Maybe I'm losing it," she whispered. "I for sure need a vacation when I finish my next article."

When she picked up her phone from the table, she found it was almost noon. Surely Bill knew by now when he'd have the parts to fix Daisy. The sooner Kaiah got back on the road, the better. She'd just head on over to the auto shop to get the latest news, then head out to savor the warm April sunshine. After all, it was cloudy back in New York. If she was stuck in Nowheresville, at least she could enjoy the great weather.

She lifted the window shade facing the driveway and saw that the Suburban wasn't there. Reid must've had some errands to run. She ignored the disappointment that bloomed inside her. *He doesn't exist just to give you rides, Ky.*

Instead, she requested a ride through her Uber app and, a short ride later, arrived at Coral Cove Car Care. She hurried to the counter, where Bill spoke on the phone. He nodded a greeting and finished his call before addressing her.

"Ms. Ross," he began, "I was going to call you."

"Oh?" Hope bloomed within her. "You were able to find parts for my car?"

"Well, I have good news and bad news."

She bit her lower lip.

"The good news is that I located the parts." He frowned. "The bad news is that they won't be here for a few weeks."

She blinked and then blinked again. "I'm sorry, did you say a few *weeks?*"

"Unfortunately, I did. The parts are coming from Great Britain, which means it'll take a while to get them."

Kaiah rubbed her forehead. This was not how she expected this conversation to go. "Any chance I can drive slowly to South Carolina and make it?"

"You want to take an overheating car on a five-hour ride?"

"Not a good idea, right?"

He shook his head. "Not unless you want to do even more damage and wind up stranded."

"Right." Her head started to spin as she ran through alternatives in her mind. She could rent a car, go to South Carolina, write her article, and then return to Coral Cove to pick up Daisy, but the cost of renting a car was astronomical these days. For sure it'd be more than her budget allowed. And if she had to come back to Coral Cove, that meant *another* detour and delay on her way to Florida, which would lead to spending more money she didn't have.

What if she took Kam up on her loan offer? Then she could rent the car and go down to South Carolina, but asking her sister for money was so humiliating. She was twenty-six years old and needed to get her life in order instead of—

"Ms. Ross?"

"Huh?" Kaiah's eyes snapped to his. "Sorry." She cringed. "I was just trying to figure out what to do now."

The older man pressed his thin lips together. "I tried to find parts that would be here sooner, but I came up empty." He paused. "Would you like me to go forward with putting the order in?"

"I would. Thank you."

After signing a few forms, Kaiah walked out to the parking lot and sat down on a bench. A warm, gentle breeze caressed her cheeks as she looked out toward the lighthouse. She longed for a beacon like that to show her where to go.

She pulled her phone from her backpack purse and considered calling Kamryn to give her an update. But at this hour, Kam was probably busy with clients at her accounting firm. No matter what she was up to, Kam had much better things to do than listen to her sister whine about her predicament.

Unlocking her phone, Kaiah pulled up Reid's number. She could text him and ask for his advice, but he most likely was ready for her to leave so that his life could get back to normal. He, too, had better things to worry about.

The weight of anxiety pressed down on her shoulders as she let her head fall into her hands.

She was stuck in the middle of nowhere for the next few weeks. *Weeks!*

All her plans were ruined. What was she going to do now?

After taking a few minutes to sit quietly on the bench, Kaiah sat up straight and shook her head. That was enough time spent feeling sorry for herself. *Chin up*, her mom used to say whenever her daughters were despondent. Kaiah had to keep her chin up and act like the adult she was.

Now she just had to figure out how to solve this predicament.

Reid crossed the parking lot toward his Suburban.

"We're not giving up," Becca insisted. "This town needs that festival, and we're going to make it happen, no matter what the committee said."

Reid blew out a deep sigh. At his twin's request, he'd met her at the Coral Cove Historical Society that morning to discuss the town's spring festival, and the meeting had not gone the way he'd hoped. Despite Reid and Becca making a case for how important the festival was, the board still insisted that years of low attendance were forcing them to cancel it.

"And how do you think we do it, Becks? Do you have a few thousand dollars lying around that we can use for the marketing budget?"

"No," she snapped. "But there has a be a way. We just haven't found the solution yet, so we'll just keep trying stuff until we do." She looked out toward Main Street and then back at him. "I'm going to talk to the mayor, and then I'll call the president of the PTO. I'll call you later."

"Sounds good."

Becca pulled her phone out of her pocket and began punching buttons. "Hi, Claire. Is Mayor Whittington available? Yes, I'll hold. Thanks."

As he climbed into his car, Reid heard his phone ding and was surprised it was a text from Kaiah. He thought maybe she would've asked for a ride today, but he was disappointed he hadn't heard from her all morning.

Kaiah: Any chance you can pick me up from CC Car Care?

Reid: I'd be happy to! I'll be there in a few.

He motored to the other side of town and spotted her sitting outside the shop. The deep crease in her brow told him something was wrong, and his stomach tightened. Hopping out of the SUV, he met her at the bench.

"Thanks for coming," she said while her fingers moved over the straps on her backpack purse.

"No problem." He sat beside her and angled his body toward hers. "Everything okay?"

She released a sigh that seemed to have filled her whole body, and she slumped back against the bench. Her defeated expression reminded him of when Piper had missed a dance step at her recital last year after practicing for weeks leading up to the performance.

"The parts for my car are coming from Europe, which means they'll take a few *weeks* to get here. I don't know what to do now. I could rent a car, but that doesn't seem too smart considering how much the repairs are going to cost me."

Reid picked at a loose piece of wood on the bench as a plan clicked into place. He glanced at his phone. It was almost twelve. "Are you hungry?"

"Uh." Her pretty blue eyes widened for a moment. "I guess so."

"Let's go to lunch." He stood.

She studied him. "Okay . . ."

"I think I might have a solution that'll help us both out."

~

"I have a proposal for you."

Reid and Kaiah sat at a table overlooking Coral Cove Bay in Frank's Seafood Grill. She folded her hands on the table, her gorgeous blue eyes focused on him. "I'm listening," she said.

He licked his lips as he gathered his thoughts. "I've mentioned how much the spring festival means to our community. It's been a tradition here for more than a hundred years, and for the most part, it's always been a revenue generator for our little town. This year we were counting on the festival to raise money for renovations on Coral Cove Elementary School after the fire."

She took a sip from her glass of water. "You mentioned that."

"The festival is only weeks away, and now the committee wants to cancel it. Attendance has been pretty low for the past few years, and we don't have the marketing budget to promote it the way we need to." He rested his fingers on the table. "Here's my proposal: You can stay in the apartment above my garage for free for as long as you need to. And in return, I was hoping you'd help us promote the festival. Maybe write a few articles to generate some interest."

She was silent for a moment, and Reid held his breath.

"Let me get this straight," she began. "You want me to write a few articles about Coral Cove and the festival. And you're not going to charge me a *dime* for staying in your house? For as long as I need to be there?"

"Exactly," he said. "It's a win-win, Kaiah. You can save a few bucks on lodging while helping us breathe some life into Coral Cove—not to mention help some schoolkids. Who can say no to helping the kids?"

She nodded slowly.

He gestured around the restaurant "Think of it this way: This is just the next installment in the Hidden Gems series, right? I think our coastal town fits with the theme."

That earned him a lopsided grin. "It sure does."

"So what do you say, Kaiah?"

She took another drink of water, and then the corners of her mouth tugged up. "All right then. Let's get started."

"Hi, Libby!"

Later that afternoon, Kaiah's voice rang through Reid's garage apartment as she sat on the sofa with her phone, folding her legs and tucking them under a throw blanket. After lunch, she and Reid had returned to his house so she could pitch the new articles to Libby, her editor.

"Are you on your way to Edisto Beach?" Libby asked.

"Not exactly, but I have exciting news." Kaiah took a deep breath. "I'm still in Coral Cove, and I'm going to be here a bit." She explained how the parts for her car were delayed. "But you know what's crazy about all this? I think my car led me to my next hidden gem. Seriously! This little town is in the middle of nowhere, and it's so charming, Libby. It has an adorable Main Street, local inns, tons of cute shops and mom-and-pop restaurants, even a lighthouse! There are practically zero chains here. I mean, it's like the town is on the set of a Hallmark movie."

"Uh-huh," Libby said, her tone distracted.

Kaiah knew her editor might be scrolling on her phone and decided to take a new tactic. "Plus, every spring they have a festival that celebrates the lighthouse and town founding, and it's coming up in a couple weeks. I'd like to write a couple features about the town and help promote the festival. I know our readers will go *crazy* for it. We could feature Coral Cove in all kinds of content—new road trip destinations, listicles about perfect long weekends, spots for a girls' trip. People need to know about this place *and* this festival."

At the end of her pitch, Kaiah swore she could've heard a pin drop on the other end of the line. *Oh no. She's not going to go for it.*

"Huh. Well, tell me this: Is Coral Cove going to be as interesting as Edisto Beach?"

"Oh, it definitely is," she promised. "Trust me, the photos of the lighthouse alone will sell the place, not to mention the history that goes along with it." She explained how the structure helped sailors lost in a storm. "I'll make sure to highlight it all in my stories."

Libby paused. "Well, get me your first article, and then we'll see if you can write some more."

Kaiah beamed. "Thanks, Libby! I'll have it to you in the next couple of days," she said before disconnecting the call.

She sank back on the sofa and peered around the apartment. This place was going to be her home for the next few weeks, and the realization settled a warm feeling over her. She could get comfortable here—and also get to know Reid and Piper a bit more. A ripple of happiness fluttered in her stomach just as her phone chimed with a text.

Kam: How's Daisy?

Kaiah knew the answer was loaded enough to warrant a call. She dialed her sister's number, and Kam answered immediately.

"Not good, huh?" Kam said when she answered.

Kaiah hugged one of the sofa pillows against her chest. "Um, I might be stuck here for three more weeks."

"Stuck?" Laughter erupted over the phone line. "Did you sabotage your own car so that you have more time with Mr. TDH?"

"Believe it or not, that plan never entered my mind," Kaiah said. "But Daisy took care of it for me. Actually, I have a new story to follow while I'm here. I can continue working on my Hidden Gems series before I get to South Carolina. I'm going to do some write-ups on Coral Cove first."

"That sounds super fun," Kamryn said. "Wish I could come down there to help you, but you know how it is during tax time. We're swamped. Actually, we're *so* swamped that I'd better get back at it. Call me soon, sis."

"I will," Kaiah promised before ending the call. After grabbing a pen and notepad, she rushed out the door, almost running into Reid.

He took a couple of steps back. "Hey! I was coming to see you."

"And I was coming to see you," she said.

They both laughed.

"You go first," he said.

"I convinced Libby to let me write about Coral Cove," she explained. "She wants to see the first article in a couple of days."

"That's great! Becks is coming over tonight to talk about a marketing plan."

"Awesome."

He rubbed the back of his head and almost seemed sheepish for a moment. "I'm going to pick up Piper from school. Any chance you'd like to ride with me?"

"Oh," she said, surprised by the offer. "You know what? I'd love to. I need to see more of Coral Cove for my first article, anyway."

"Great."

They drove out to the elementary school and took their place in the long pickup line. Kaiah looked toward the far end of the one-level brick building where nearly all of the windows were boarded up. "That's the section that burned?"

"Yeah." Reid shifted the Suburban into Park before leaning toward her. The scent of sandalwood, mixed with soap and something . . . uniquely Reid drifted over her, and her pulse picked up speed. "The fire started in the heating system, and if you can believe it, the fire alarm system was on the fritz too. So by the time we found out the school was on fire, the entire wing had been damaged."

She shook her head. "That's a shame."

"I know. But you're going to help us to raise the money to renovate it."

"Right," she said. "No pressure."

He looked into her eyes, his face brightening. "I've read some of your articles, and you're a talented writer." The warmth in his chocolate-brown eyes caught her off guard.

"You've read my articles?"

"Of course I have," he quipped, resting his arms on the steering wheel. "I googled your name after you mentioned you're a journalist. Your series on the beaches in Maine were brilliant. I mean, your words swept me away as soon as I started reading them."

A lump began to form in her throat.

Then a loud bell rang and movement in the corner of her eye drew her attention to the front of the school, where students began filing out and a line of adults ushered them to the waiting cars.

Reid pushed the button to roll down Kaiah's window and slowly motored along with the line until they reached Piper waiting with a woman who seemed to be in her mid-sixties.

Piper grabbed the woman's arm. "Mrs. Thompson, this is my new friend, Miss Kaiah!"

The older woman waved to Kaiah and Reid before opening the back door of the Suburban. "See you tomorrow, Piper."

"Bye!" Piper buckled herself into the back seat as Reid slowly steered through the parking lot toward the road. "Miss Kaiah! I didn't know you were coming to get me today."

She turned back and beamed at her small friend, touched by her enthusiasm. "I didn't either, but it turns out I'm going to be at your house for a few more weeks."

"For real?" Piper squeaked. "We're going to have so much fun!"

Reid's eyes met Kaiah's as he gave her a sidelong smile.

Kaiah settled back in her seat, taking a deep breath full of fresh spring air and basking in the warm rays of the sun. For a moment she wondered what it would be like to live in a town like Coral Cove forever, to feel part of a community, part of a family.

But that would mean giving up dreams like writing for *Travel and Culture*. Right? Surely there was no way she could have both. That only happened to people in the movies. Never in real life.

Chapter 7

KAIAH TUCKED HER LONG legs under her body and rested her back against the corner of the sofa in Reid's den later that evening. Her long, thick, sunshine-colored hair was styled in a messy bun on top of her head with tendrils falling around her face, and her eyes were focused on her notepad while she tapped her pen against her chin.

She was adorable, and Reid couldn't take his eyes off her while he sat on an armchair across from her and drank from his large glass of water. He felt someone watching him, and when he rotated toward the opposite end of the sofa, his twin waggled her eyebrows.

Great. Becks had caught him staring at Kaiah. She'd give him a hard time about it later.

"I have an idea," Kaiah announced. "To get more people to come to the festival this year, you need to give them a new reason why they should attend. And the easiest way to do that is to give them a new experience. Honestly, that can be as easy as changing the branding around the event."

The twins nodded their heads quietly, taking in the information.

"Instead of focusing on the beach," Kaiah continued, "let's focus on the town's rich history and the significance of the lighthouse. We could rebrand the event and call it the Light the Dark Festival. Think about it: The festival marks the transition from winter, which is the dark, to spring, which is light. Plus the name is a nod to the lighthouse's role in saving that ship of sailors on a blustery spring day long ago."

Kaiah glanced down at her notebook to gather her next point, and Reid couldn't take his eyes off her.

"And instead of holding the festival for just one weekend, let's stretch it out over a week. That way we can expand the list of activities and give folks some new things to look forward to. Plus extending the festival gives more people with different schedules the opportunity to attend. And in theory, the longer schedule will give us more chances to raise money for the school." Kaiah bit her lower lip and divided her focus between Reid and his sister. "What do you think?"

Silence hung over the room while Reid and Becca shared a look. Then their faces broke out into grins.

Becca clapped her hands. "Yes!"

"I agree. This is genius, Kaiah," Reid said. "We can invite different vendors and charge a fee for their participation. All of the money we collect can go to the fundraiser."

"And what about the lighthouse?" Kaiah asked. "I mean, if we center the festival around it, then I think we probably need to fix it."

The twins exchanged a look.

"I see where you're coming from," Reid said. "But to be honest, I don't know if we have the time or funds to get the lamp replaced."

"I get that. But if that's the focus of the festival," Kaiah said, "think about how powerful it will be for the town to see their lighthouse glowing in the night. They'll literally see the transition from dark to light."

Reid nodded. "That's true."

"And if it's the first time in years, then it's even more special, right?" Kaiah asked.

The twins nodded.

"If we fix the lighthouse, I can only imagine how many tickets we could sell for lighthouse tours," said Reid.

"You can sell tickets for everything, and all of the proceeds go to the school," Kaiah said before studying his sister. "What are you thinking, Becca?"

Becca tapped her finger on the end table. "I need to get the mayor on board. Then we need to have a meeting with the town council. I bet they could locate some funds for the lighthouse, even if it's just a makeshift fix. Then we need to talk to the school board and the PTO. I think we need to get a long weekend break approved so the kids can attend."

"Let's make a list." Reid nodded toward Kaiah's notebook. "We'll need banners, tickets, signs, to start."

"Does Coral Cove have a local newspaper?" Kaiah asked.

"Yup," Reid said.

"I'll talk to the editor and see if they'll run my articles there too." Kaiah twiddled her pen above her notebook. "Now let's brainstorm a list of new activities for the festival."

For the next several minutes, they tossed around ideas for events at the festival: a craft show, a town parade, a talent show, booths for selling food, a dunk tank for teachers and school administrators. Kaiah jotted down their ideas.

"I think this is a great plan," Kaiah told Becca when they were done. "For my articles I'll start with an overview of the town. The town's history is fascinating, and mentioning the town museum would definitely appeal to history buffs who'd like to see this little slice of Americana." She sat up straight and set her notepad and pen on the coffee table. "I can't wait to get started."

Becca turned to Kaiah. "Tomorrow morning I'll pick you up after I drop the girls off at school. We can get started on promoting the festival and also do some research."

"I'll be ready." Kaiah grinned at Reid, and he was almost certain his pulse fluttered.

Becca examined her phone. "Oh, it's almost eight. I need to get home and get the girls in bed."

"Piper!" Reid called. "Honey, you need to get ready to go to Auntie Becca's house."

The little girl appeared in the doorway with Ariel at her heels. "Can Miss Kaiah help me pack?"

Kaiah lifted an eyebrow at Reid.

"Do you want to?" he asked Kaiah.

She smiled. "Sure."

Piper took Kaiah's hand and towed her toward the doorway before they disappeared down the hallway.

His twin focused her gaze on him. "She's great."

Reid took another long drink from his glass. He agreed with her, but he wasn't about to admit it. He knew exactly where the conversation would go. And he wasn't in the mood for a lecture on his nonexistent love life.

Becca didn't quit, though. "Piper adores her," she said.

Reid nodded. "She's a great writer too."

"And that's why you offered to let her stay here for free, right?" Becca grinned. "Because she's a good writer. Not at all because she's beautiful and sweet, and your daughter is already attached to her, an—"

"Becks." Reid groaned. "Don't start. Having Kaiah here is all about saving our town."

"Riiiiight . . ." His twin drew out the word. "Inviting a woman to stay in your garage apartment is about the town. Not that you might be interested in someone again." She hopped up from the sofa and started down the hallway.

Piper set two more stuffed cats by Ariel and then zipped up her suitcase. "I'm ready!"

Becca and Kaiah watched as the girl gave Ariel a kiss before setting the suitcase on the floor and then racing out of the bedroom, pulling the bag behind her.

"It'll be quiet here tonight," Becca said.

"But not at your house," Kaiah quipped, and they both laughed.

They walked back to the den, where Piper was hugging her dad.

"Be good tonight," Reid told her.

Piper lifted her chin. "I always am." She ran to the front door and pushed it open before turning around. "Are you coming, Auntie?"

Becca gave Reid and Kaiah a wave on her way out. "I'd better get going. See you tomorrow."

Reid closed and locked the door behind them and then pointed toward the deck. "Would you like to sit out back?"

With you alone on a starlit night? Sign me up.

Kaiah nodded, and she swore she could feel her heart skip a beat.

He padded to the kitchen. "I'll get us something to drink."

Kaiah made her way outside, and Reid carried two icy glasses of sweet tea to the deck. He gestured for Kaiah to take a seat on the comfortable, cushioned chairs.

The setting sun sent vivid streaks of color across the sky while the cicadas and frogs sang their nightly chorus. The air was warm, and Kaiah breathed in the scent of salt mixed with freshly cut grass. She decided to try to get to know her host a bit more.

"So what's a normal week look like for you? What's your schedule like?" she asked.

He relaxed on the chair, resting his left ankle on his right knee. "As a firefighter, I work ten days a month. My shifts are twenty-four hours at a time."

"Seriously? Twenty-four-hour shifts?"

He took a drink from his glass and then set it on the table between them. "Yeah. Seven to seven. I'll start tomorrow morning at seven and then get off Wednesday at seven. That's why I also do rideshare, to break up some of the downtime I have. That's also why I volunteer as a tour guide and at Piper's school and the animal shelter."

"You sure like staying busy."

He lifted his eyes toward the sky. "You could say that."

She studied his profile—his inviting dark eyes, his chiseled jawline, his high cheekbones and perfect nose, his thick, dark hair. She had the distinct impression this man had no idea how attractive he was.

His gaze snapped to hers, and his eyebrows sailed upward. "What's on your mind?"

Oh no. He'd caught her staring at him. Her mouth dried up as she tried to recover. "What, uh, what was it like growing up here?" she asked. "What makes Coral Cove so special to you?"

He took another drink and then scanned the backyard. "Honestly? That's hard to narrow down. Seems like everything about this place feels special." He shrugged. "As far as growing up, we spent a lot of time at the beach—swimming, surfing, fishing, things like that."

A vision of an eighteen-year-old Reid, lean and tan on a surfboard, riding the waves, filled her mind. A tremor rushed over her, and she tried to banish the daydream. "Did you ever considering leaving?"

"No." He shook his head. "My folks are locals and grew up here, and all of our family is here. It's home." He took another swig of tea.

Darkness began to fall, blotting out the backyard. Reid hopped up and flipped a switch, illuminating a string of white lights that dangled over the large deck. A comfortable silence settled over them as Kaiah tried to commit every detail of this evening to memory—the vision of Reid sitting under the lights with her, the smell of the salt water, the soothing sounds of the frogs and cicadas. And here she was, sitting with a man as humble and solid as they came. She couldn't remember a night more peaceful than this one.

"Becca went away to college." Reid's deep voice broke through her thoughts. "But she didn't go far. She studied at Wilmington and then came home."

"What did she major in?"

"Guess."

She moved her fingers over the condensation clouding her cool glass. "History."

"Ding, ding, ding!" he exclaimed. "We have a winner."

She laughed. "She's a history teacher, right?"

"Yup. She taught at the middle school until Astrid was born. She considered going back to work since my mom was already retired and could take care of Astrid and Piper too. But Becks wanted to stay home. Cash had been promoted to fire chief, so they were doing fine financially."

"Cash is the fire chief?"

Reid nodded and took another drink from his glass.

"Does that mean he's your boss?"

"Yes, but not directly. I report to the captain at my station, and the captain reports to him." He set the glass down on the coffee table with a *clink*. "So he's my boss's boss."

"Does that ever get awkward?"

Reid shrugged. "Not really. We rarely disagree on things." He smiled. "Plus, he owes me. I introduced him to my sister, and I like to remind him of that when it comes time for him to sign off on my performance evaluation."

"Good thinking," she said, and they shared a smile. She recalled the photo of Piper and her mother in Piper's room, and questions buzzed through her mind. How did she and Reid meet? How long were they married? What happened to her? Dare she even ask?

Before she could open her mouth, his voice snapped her out of her head.

"I bet you think I'm boring."

Her eyes widened. "Why would I think that?"

"You're so adventurous. You were driving down the East Coast alone. You're a travel writer, so I'm sure you've been to plenty of exotic places. But I've stayed here my entire life."

"Reid," she began, "you fight fires and rescue people for a living. *Boring* is not a word I'd ever use to describe you." *More like brave, generous, kind, thoughtful. And so very, very hot.*

"Did you always want to be a journalist?" he asked.

She considered the question. "I guess so. I started pretending to write books before I could even write."

"Really?" He seemed impressed.

"Yeah. I made little books out of paper when I was a kid, and then I started writing ridiculous stories when I was around Piper's age. I fell in love with reading and writing. And when I got to college, I was drawn to journalism because I love telling stories," she explained, and he appeared fascinated. "How about you? Why firefighting?"

"It's not a very interesting story."

She rested her elbows on her knees and tilted her head in his direction.

He chuckled. "Fine, fine. I was part of an after-school program that was like a camp, and we spent some time working at the firehouse. I was a junior firefighter, and I loved it. I've always loved helping people. Once I figured that out, I knew what I wanted to do."

"Wow. You're pretty amazing," she whispered. When she realized she'd said the words out loud, she longed to shove them back into her mouth. Embarrassment bloomed in her cheeks while she winced, waiting for his reaction.

He smiled. "So are you. And it's obvious my daughter agrees."

An amicable silence covered them once again, and she took a long drink from her glass.

"Do you think you'll ever settle down?" he asked, gazing up toward the sky. "Have a home and a family?"

"Um . . ." She cleared her throat, stretching the time to prepare her answer. "I used to think I would, but now I'm not so sure."

"Why not?"

"Sometimes," she began and then stopped to gather her thoughts. "Sometimes I'm not sure where I belong."

He considered this, and once again she wanted to yank back the words.

"I always believed that home is where the heart is." He gave her a sheepish smile. "Corny, I know, but it's true. I guess you need to figure out where your heart is."

She nodded. "I think you're right about that."

Kaiah decided she had enough soul-baring talk for the evening and switched topics, sharing her and Becca's plans for tomorrow.

Then Reid stood up. "I suppose I should get some sleep before my shift. Let me get that for you." He held out his hand, and when she gave him her empty glass, her fingers brushed his, and an electrical current danced up her arm. "Have a good day tomorrow."

"You too," she said. "Be safe at work."

"I will. Sleep well."

As Kaiah climbed the stairs leading to the apartment, she imagined what it would feel like for Reid to hold her in his muscular arms, and her heartbeat tripled.

Chapter 8

KAIAH AIMED HER CAMERA down the street and snapped a few photos of the lighthouse with the adorable stores in the forefront. "I just love this place," she said, turning to Becca. "Tell me more about the town. Something you wish visitors knew."

"Well," Becca began spreading out her arms, "all of the shops are family-owned, and most of them have been here for decades." She pointed to the Beachside Bakery down the street. "The Watson family has owned the bakery for as long as I can remember. My mom told me they inherited it from their parents."

"They?" Kaiah asked.

"The Watson twins, Jenni and Jessica. They're both married and have families, but they're still 'the Watson twins' to everyone in town."

"No kidding." Kaiah jotted down some notes in her notebook. "What's it like being a twin?"

Becca shrugged. "I've always been one, so I don't know anything else. But it's interesting. It's hard to explain, but we get a feeling. I know when he's upset or in pain or scared. He feels it for me too."

She paused, keeping her eyes trained on the bakery down the street. "Sometimes it seems like I can feel when Reid is in danger. Which is . . . a lot when your brother and your husband are both fighting dangerous fires."

"Yeah, I bet. That has to make you anxious."

"Sometimes I'm prone to worry, especially when they're on a dangerous call together, but I hold on to my faith."

Kaiah nodded. "How'd you feel when Reid told you he wanted to be a firefighter?"

"Proud." Becca gave her a sideways glance. "And not very surprised."

"How come?"

Becca's brow creased. "Are you interviewing me for your story?"

"I'm just curious about you guys."

Becca seemed to consider the statement before she kept going. "Reid has always stood up for people in trouble. He'd stand up to bullies who were picking on smaller kids at school, even if he didn't know them, just because it was the right thing. Being a firefighter seemed like the most natural fit in the world for him."

Becca started walking toward the bakery, and Kaiah strolled beside her. Questions about Reid's late wife floated through her mind, but she suppressed them. She hoped someday Becca or Reid would open up to her about what had happened to Brynn, but now wasn't the time to ask.

They approached the bakery, and Kaiah pulled open the door. A bell above it rang, announcing their arrival. "Let's go inside and meet the owners."

The aroma of chocolate and butter filled Kaiah's nose as she glanced around the bakery. She took in the sea of wooden tables and chairs where customers enjoyed their pastries. Photos of mouth-watering cakes and cookies adorned the baby-blue walls.

Behind the counter, middle-aged identical twins waited on customers. Kaiah made a beeline to the counter and took her place in line. "What's your favorite treat to get here?" she asked Becca.

"Oh, that's a tough one." Becca examined the case of goodies in front of her. "I'll never turn down a cupcake." She pointed to a row of small cakes adorned with thick domes of icing, all in different colors and patterns. "But the cookies are out of this world too."

"What can I get you?" one of the twins, wearing a name tag that said *Jenni*, asked.

"I'll have a vanilla cupcake," Kaiah said.

Becca pointed to the cookies. "I'll take a big chocolate chip cookie."

Jenni rang them up, and Kaiah paid.

"Thanks," Kaiah said. "If I could, I'd love to talk to you and your sister." She held up her notebook. "I'm a reporter with *The Traveler*, and I'm doing an article on Coral Cove."

Jenni's eyebrows arched in surprise. "Oh! Okay. Just give us a few minutes to help the other customers."

Kaiah and Becca took a seat, and Kaiah made a few notes before taking a bite of her cupcake. The cake was light and airy, and the rich vanilla icing was luscious and thick on her tongue. "This is spectacular."

"I told you," Becca sang.

Kaiah smiled, then decided to return to their previous conversation. "So Reid told me you went away to school. What brought you back here?"

Becca swallowed a bite of her cookie. "Fair question. When I went away to college, I thought for sure I'd break the Turner family legacy and move somewhere else after I graduated. But when I was in school, I saw so many people missing their families who were far away. I always wanted to be a wife and a mom. And I decided that when I raised my family, I couldn't imagine doing it without my people around me." She shrugged. "Wilmington was great, but this is my home, you know?"

Kaiah nodded. She was happy for Becca but couldn't help but feel a twinge of jealousy. The woman knew exactly where she belonged. Why couldn't Kaiah feel that way?

Becca picked up where she left off. "I taught eighth-grade history for a couple of years, and then I met Cash, and well, here we are."

"Reid told me he introduced you two."

Becca grinned. "That's right. And I was not nice to Cash when I first met him." She rested her chin on her palm. "To this day, I'm surprised he even gave me a second chance."

Kaiah set her pen on her notebook. "Now *this* is a story I want to hear."

Becca laughed. "Reid couldn't stand my high school boyfriend. We were on again, off again both in high school and college, and Reid always said he never treated me right. I had gone to Wilmington for college, but Dawson stayed here in Coral Cove. In my senior year I thought we'd finally start making wedding plans for after graduation." She let out a long sigh. "Instead, he said he was tired of waiting and wasn't going to do it anymore. He married someone else in town six months later."

"Ouch. I'm so sorry."

"Yeah. I should've known better. In the meantime Reid and Cash were working together. Reid kept telling me that I needed to meet Cash, and I kept saying, 'No, thanks.'" She ate another bite of the cookie. "Finally, Reid wore me down, and I agreed to a double date with him and Brynn—and Cash." Becca glanced out the window toward Main Street. "I was such a brat that night. We went to dinner and a movie, and I hardly said two words to Cash during the meal." She ran her finger over the tabletop. "When we got to the movie theater, Brynn took me aside and told me I needed to be nicer."

"And what happened?" Kaiah asked.

"Cash bought me popcorn and a drink, and we went and sat down in the theater before Brynn and Reid came in." Becca shook her head. "And Cash said something like, 'Reid told me you recently had your heart broken, and I know what that's like. If you're not ready, I understand. But I hope you'll keep me in mind when you are.'"

Kaiah clucked her tongue. "That is the sweetest thing ever."

"Right?" Becca's lips formed a dreamy smile. "I was speechless."

"And what happened next?"

"We skipped the movie, went out to his truck, and talked until nearly two a.m. Half a year later, he took me out to the lighthouse and proposed."

"That's so romantic!"

Becca sighed. "I know. We married a few months after that. And I had to tell my brother he was right all along."

Kaiah smiled. "That's amazing." She couldn't help but notice that Becca had brought up Brynn naturally. That would make asking about her feel a little less awkward. Kaiah gnawed on her lower lip. Becca seemed so open and eager to share, but something this personal . . .

Jenni suddenly appeared beside Kaiah and sat down at the table. "What did you want to ask us?" Her twin sister sat across from her and beside Becca.

Kaiah sat up straight. "Oh. Right!" She cleared her throat, putting on her journalist voice. "I'm Kaiah Ross, and this is my first time in Coral Cove. First of all, this cupcake is out of this world. Second of all, Becca told me you inherited this bakery from your folks. Tell me more about that."

"Well, we inherited our love of baking from our parents," Jessica began, "so it only made sense that we'd take over the bakery when they retired."

Jenni held up her hand. "We kept their menu, but we tweaked it a little bit."

Kaiah wrote in her notebook. "What do you like best about Coral Cove?"

The twins shared a smile and then responded in unison, "The people."

Kaiah spent the next thirty minutes interviewing the twins before she and Becca thanked them and then returned to Main Street. She rubbed her hands together as excitement filled her. She turned to Becca. "This town is almost too good to be true. The people are kind and hardworking. This place is beautiful beyond words." She paused, thinking. "So you guys have the festival every spring. What other traditions do you have?"

"Good question," Becca said. "The farmers market is one block over. It's open every weekend, even in the winter." Becca pointed down the street. "We also have a big celebration for July Fourth. The entire town comes together for a parade and a community-wide barbecue. It's a pretty big deal. Anybody can be in the parade, even the kids. They all decorate their bikes for it." She chuckled. "I remember how excited Reid and I were to put red, white, and blue streamers on our bikes and ride along the parade route. The parade is so fun—the marching band from the high school is always fabulous, and different clubs and town organizations have floats."

Kaiah wrote it all down. "I'd love to see that."

"That means you'll have to come back in July." Becca looped her arm in Kaiah's as they strolled down the street. "We also have more fun little shops. Let's go into the jewelry store. All of the jewelry is handmade by Ted and Betty Sue Walker, and they teach classes."

She steered Kaiah into the store, where a couple in their sixties stood behind the counter.

"Welcome to Waterside Gems," sang the woman, sporting a silver bobbed haircut. "How can we help you?"

"I'm Kaiah, and I'm a reporter for *The Traveler*. I'd like to interview you for an article about Coral Cove."

"Oh!" The older woman's green eyes sparkled. "How exciting! I'm Betty Sue, and this is Ted. What would you like to know?"

"Tell me about your shop and what you like about being here in Coral Cove," Kaiah said, adjusting her pen to take notes.

After the interview, Kaiah and Becca returned to the sidewalk, where a young woman walked a golden retriever. Kaiah's heart squeezed as she approached the woman and the dog. The sweet canine reminded her of George. "Would it be okay if I pet your dog?"

"Of course!" The woman stopped in front of her. "This is Maizy."

Kaiah bent and began to stroke the dog's head. "What an adorable name," she said, and Maizy responded by licking Kaiah's hand. The simple gesture nearly broke Kaiah's heart in two. She missed her Georgie so, so much.

Kaiah gave the dog a few more pats before the young woman and Maizy headed down the street. Kaiah's heart felt heavy as the pair disappeared from view. "Want to walk on the beach for a while?"

Becca consulted her watch. "Sure. We have some time before I need to pick up the girls from school."

They walked out onto the sand, and Kaiah peered over at the glorious lighthouse that seemed to watch over them.

"Okay, Kaiah," Becca began, "I want to know about you." She rested her gaze on Kaiah's face. "Are you single?"

"Yes."

Kaiah was almost certain Becca's eyes sparkled.

"By choice?"

"Not necessarily." Kaiah took a deep, steadying breath. "I recently got out of a relationship. It was his choice to end things, but looking back now, I suppose it was for the best."

Becca's symmetrical face filled with sympathy. "He hurt you."

"He did. But what hurt the most was that he took my dog."

"Wait. He took your *dog*? Seriously?"

"Yes. Actually, George was *our* dog. We adopted him together. Some days he lived at Hayes's house, and some days he lived at mine. Taking care of George together—I thought that meant we were making a commitment to each other, a *real* commitment." Kaiah shook her head and looked out toward the waves where a few couples walked at the water's edge. "Ridiculous, right? How could a dog we picked out together guarantee we were going to get married and raise a family together?"

Becca stood next to her quietly, taking in the information. "I'm so sorry he hurt you, but it sounds like you deserve better. And you should *totally* sue him for custody of the dog. And add in a few bucks for emotional damages."

Kaiah burst out laughing, and Becca joined in.

They walked in silence for a few moments, and the sound of the waves and the crying seagulls filled Kaiah's ears. She recalled her conversation with Becca when they were sitting in the bakery, and she wanted to know more about Reid and his late wife.

Courage surged through her veins, and she turned to Becca. "You mentioned you and Cash went on a double date with Reid and Brynn the first time you went out," she began. "How did Reid meet Brynn?"

Becca slipped her hands into the pockets of her jeans. "Brynn had been my best friend since first grade, when her folks moved their family here. She always had a crush on Reid, but he never gave her a second look until the homecoming dance freshman year. I had no idea that they were 'talking.'" She made quotes with her fingers. "I guess Brynn was afraid to tell me, and Reid didn't think it was important to inform me that he was flirting with my best friend. But they went to the homecoming dance together, and that was that. After we graduated, Brynn and I went to college in Wilmington, and Reid went through the fire academy. He was determined to make it work with Brynn, so he came to visit her every chance he could."

Kaiah smiled. "That's so romantic. When did he propose?"

"After we graduated. They were married about a year later. She was a math teacher at the middle school where I worked. And when they got married, everything seemed like it just fell into place. She'd always been my best friend, but then she became my sister."

Kaiah crossed her arms over her middle and found the courage to ask the question that she'd been so anxious to ask. "What happened to her?" she asked softly.

Becca sniffed and then rubbed her eyes. "Car accident." Her voice was rough. "It was horrible. Reid still blames himself to this day."

Kaiah's breath caught in her throat. She could feel a twinge in her heart for Reid, for Piper, for Becca. Brynn was loved by so many, and they all still grieved for her.

And poor Reid blamed himself for it all.

"I knew something was very wrong that day." She touched her chest. "Before I got the call, I could feel Reed's anguish. It nearly tore me apart." She wiped her eyes.

Kaiah was quiet for a long time. "I'm so sorry," she finally managed to say.

"Thank you." Becca cleared her throat. "My . . . my mom and I do our best to stay involved in Piper's life. And I'm grateful that she and Astrid are close too." She looked up at the sky, sighed, and then pointed her gaze back at Kaiah. "It's been a long four years. I keep hoping Reid will meet someone and settle down again. I know it might feel hard—of course it would. But it would be so good for him, and for Piper." She paused. "He hasn't dated since Brynn passed away."

Kaiah nodded.

They walked toward the sidewalk, and then Becca nodded toward the intersection. "Want to visit a few more businesses before we go?"

"Absolutely."

Chapter 9

BECCA STEERED HER SUV into Reid's driveway, and Kaiah unbuckled her seat belt. "Thanks for your help with the article and for supper."

"You're welcome," Becca said. "I'm sure I'll see you soon."

Kaiah whipped around to see Piper and Astrid in the back seat. "Good night, guys."

The two little girls waved and yawned in unison.

Kaiah gathered her backpack and purse before exiting the SUV and then jogging up the steps to the apartment. After setting her bags on the sofa, she flopped down and examined the photos she'd taken since her arrival in Coral Cove. She smiled as she scrolled past photos of colorful shops and the gorgeous beachfront.

When she came to the picture she'd taken of Reid at the lighthouse, her heart thumped hard in her chest. She sent it to Kam, along with a message: Here's Mr. TDH. Cute, right?

Then she hopped in the shower, tilting her face toward the

warm water, letting it wash over her in waves. She thought about the first draft of the article she'd write, what angle she'd take. Maybe a description of the town, then featuring some of the store owners, a history of the lighthouse. But something was missing. She just wasn't sure what it was yet.

After her shower, Kaiah pulled on yoga pants and a loose-fitting pink T-shirt before styling her hair in a messy bun and moving to the kitchen, where she brewed a cup of decaf lemon tea. Mug in hand, she made her way back to the living room and picked up her phone, finding two unread texts. One was from Kam, a reply to her photo of Reid that simply said: Uh, YUM! Next time get him in his uniform.

Kaiah laughed and typed: I'll try to get that for you—and for me too!

When she found that the second message was from Reid, her breath caught.

He'd been thinking of her too.

That thought sent a delicious tingle gliding down her spine as she opened his message and replied.

Reid: How did it go with Becks today?

Kaiah: Great! We visited lots of businesses, and I interviewed the owners. We also took a walk on the beach, and we brainstormed my first article.

Reid: Any chance I can get the insider's scoop?

Kaiah hesitated. She never shared an article before it was complete. Although she trusted Reid, she didn't want him to comment on her work when it was only half-baked.

Kaiah: Honestly, I don't quite have the framing yet. Something's missing, but I don't know what it is. I'm going to sleep on it first. Hopefully the answer will hit me in the middle of the night.

She groaned after she sent the message. Now he knew for sure she was crazy. She needed to sleep on the *framing* of an article? *Lame.* Before she could berate herself too much, her phone buzzed again.

Reid: How about I take you out tomorrow? Maybe explore the town a bit more? You might uncover some inspiration.

Kaiah smiled as her heart rate spiked. I'd love that.

Reid: Great. I'll be home around 7:30. What time do you want to go?

Kaiah: Don't you need to sleep?

Reid: Hopefully I'll get some here tonight.

Kaiah: But if you don't?

Reid: I'll be fine. What time would you like to go?

Kaiah: How about you come and get me when you're ready?

Reid: What time is too early?

Kaiah: Honestly, as long as it's not before 8:30, I'll be ready to go. But you need to get some rest.

Reid: I promise I won't knock on your door before 8:30.

Chuckling to herself, Kaiah replied: Good. I'll hold you to that.

Reid: See you tomorrow, Ky. Good night.

A shot of adrenaline sped through Kaiah's veins.

He called her by her nickname.

A goofy grin spread across her face as she texted: Good night, Reid.

A yawn overtook her, and she put down her phone. She couldn't wait to spend more time with Reid. Surely the trip would inspire her, and then she'd be ready to type up her article and send it to Libby.

Reid jogged up the stairs toward the apartment the following morning. He pushed his hands through his wet hair and then rubbed them down his athletic shorts before checking his phone. It was eight twenty. He promised he wouldn't knock before eight thirty, but he was only ten minutes early. Ten minutes wasn't so bad, right?

Truth was, he'd been looking for *any* excuse to hang out with Kaiah. That's why he'd reached out to her last night. He would've read the dictionary to her if she'd have asked him.

He hadn't felt this way about anybody, especially since Brynn. The past couple of years, his sister and mother had tried to set him up with women. They'd invite him over for supper, only for Reid to discover a blind date sitting by his side. Not surprisingly, nothing had come of the awkward meetings. The women they'd chosen for him were nice, even pretty sometimes. But he'd never felt a spark with any of them.

But Kaiah was different. He couldn't wait to spend time with her, to ask her questions, to get to know her better. Even though their friendship—relationship?—was destined to be short-lived, he planned to cherish every moment with her.

After raking his hands through his hair one more time, he knocked on the door and then rocked back on his heels.

"Coming!" she called from inside the apartment.

After a few moments, the door opened with a *whoosh*. The warm aroma of freshly brewed coffee washed over him, along with something flowery—perfume, perhaps?

"You're early." Kaiah touched her hair, which was pulled back in a thick braid. She was effortlessly beautiful, clad in a pair of jeans and a light blue top that complemented her eyes. "I need a few minutes."

"No rush," he said.

She pointed to the kitchen. "There's some coffee in the pot. Help yourself."

"Thanks."

He pulled a mug from the cabinet and poured a cup before leaning against the counter. Pulling his phone from his pocket, he scrolled through social media while he waited. He heard a *ding* and spotted a phone sitting on the end of the counter. He considered picking it up, but he didn't want to snoop.

"I'll be there in a minute," Kaiah called from the bedroom.

He grinned. "No worries."

Footsteps sounded before the door opened and closed.

"Ugh!" she exclaimed. "I can't find my phone. I'm positive I left it in here, but I can't see it."

The phone dinged again.

"It's out here," he called.

"Oh!"

He picked up the phone so he could hand it to her as the screen lit with a text.

Kam: How's Mr. TDH today?

Reid lifted an eyebrow, wondering what the message meant. Who was Mr. TDH? Surely it was some sister code. Curious, but definitely none of his business.

Kaiah appeared in front of him and reached for the phone. "Thanks. I thought I'd brought it with me to the bathroom, but when I couldn't find it, I was sure I was losing my mind." She looked down at the screen, and her eyes widened for a fraction of a second before she quickly locked the phone. A flush tinged her cheeks, and his heartbeat thumped as she shouldered her backpack and shoved her phone into her back pocket. "Um, I'm ready."

He grinned and rubbed his hands together. "All right then. Let's go."

"How was work yesterday?" she asked while they drove out of the neighborhood.

"Not too busy," he said. "We had a couple of medical calls and one minor car accident."

"That doesn't sound too bad. What kind of calls do you see most often?"

"Medical. We get calls for people having chest pains or things like that. We help stabilize them, and then they're transported to the hospital. I'd guess the second most common is car accidents."

She nodded and studied his profile as she remembered recalling the text Kam had sent earlier. She hoped Reid hadn't seen it, but she was pretty sure he had. Embarrassment swamped her once again. She'd had to tell Kam to cool it with those messages including "Mr. TDH."

Reid lifted a dark eyebrow. "Something on your mind?"

Oh no!

He'd caught her staring. She was certain her face was as red as a ripe tomato. She sat up straight. "Uh, I was just thinking about the festival. I have an idea for an event."

"Great," he said. "What is it?"

"Well, you already know I love photography, and I'm obsessed with the lighthouse. It hit me that we need to have a photo contest. We could charge an entry fee, and folks can submit their best photos of the lighthouse in different seasons or times of day. Then we'll use the winning photo in promotional materials for the festival. We can call it 'the Shining Light Photo Contest.' What do you think?"

His expression warmed her from the inside out. "I think you're brilliant."

She beamed at him. "Thank you."

"I talked to Becks, and she's going to arrange for a town meeting tonight to talk about the festival. She said she was going to call the mayor's office first thing. That's when we can talk about your idea for the photo contest and how people can submit photos for judging."

"Right. We'll have to set up a website for the event and take submissions. And maybe we can have people vote on the best photo online and then use it for the promotional materials. I should probably talk to the managing editor of the local paper too."

"How about we get some breakfast at Pancake Palace and make a list of everything we need to do and then go to the newspaper? Sound like a good plan?"

She grinned at him. "I can't wait to get started."

~

"Those were some of the best pancakes I've ever had," Kaiah said as she and Reid stepped out onto the sidewalk. Then her eyes widened, and she held up her hand. "But not as good as the ones you and Piper made for me."

Reid chuckled at her adorable expression. "This restaurant is known for its fabulous breakfast, so you can be honest."

"That reminds me." Kaiah snapped her fingers. "Those lighthouse-shaped calzones were so fun and delicious. I was thinking: We should have a themed food event where vendors sell lighthouse-themed décor and food. We can call it a Light Snack. We'll sell tickets, and the proceeds can go to the fundraising goal. What do you think?" She clasped her hands together, and her eager expression filled his stomach with butterflies.

"I love it."

"Awesome!" she exclaimed. But then something buzzed past her head, and her eyes rounded as fear etched her face. "Oh my goodness! Where did it go?" She whipped around, looking frantically up and down. "Is it gone?"

"Is what gone?" he asked, glancing around.

"Was it a bee or a wasp?" She gripped his bicep as if it were a lifeboat. "Is it in my hair?" she asked. "Reid. Where. Did. It. Go?"

Reid peeked around and shook his head. "I don't see anything—no bee and no wasp. Scout's honor."

She took a deep, cleansing breath, and her expression relaxed. "Gotcha. Thanks for not making fun of my winged-creature paranoia. You're nice." Then she opened her notebook, pulled a pen from her pocket, and wrote something down. She was back to all business. "I'll add the photo contest and lighthouse snack to the list of events. Now we need to get the newspaper on board so we can get the word out locally."

Without thinking, he rested his hand on her shoulder. And when she smiled up at him, he had the feeling she liked the closeness as much as he did. "*The Coral Cove Times* office is just a few blocks from here."

Reid held the door open for Kaiah as she walked into the newspaper office. She crossed to the front desk where a middle-aged woman spoke on the phone. A name plate on the counter read "Ingrid Miller."

Kaiah glanced around the office before giving Reid a warm smile that quickened his pulse. Then she turned to the woman after she hung up the phone. "Hi there. I'm Kaiah Ross. I was hoping to speak with the managing editor."

The woman looked down at the desk and then eyed Kaiah with skepticism. "I don't see you on the schedule, Ms. Ross."

"No, I don't have an appointment." Kaiah took a business card from her pocket and handed it to the receptionist. "I'm a journalist for *The Traveler* magazine, and I'm in town. I was hoping your managing editor might have a few moments to discuss a collaboration."

The receptionist's expression warmed slightly as she stood,

grabbed the business card, and started down the hallway. "I'll see if Mr. Murray has time to see you."

"Thank you." Kaiah flashed a winning smile. Once the woman was gone, she pivoted toward Reid. "Let's hope he's impressed with my credentials."

"I am, even if he's not."

She laughed.

But he wasn't kidding. He was blown away with her ideas for the festival. He just hoped they could pull them off. If they could, it would be a blessing for the town.

"Ms. Ross," the receptionist said, returning from the editor's office, "Mr. Murray can spare five minutes."

Kaiah adjusted her tote bag on her shoulder. "Perfect. Thank you." She clasped Reid's hand. "Let's go talk to him."

Reid was grateful she left her warm hand in his while they followed the receptionist past a row of small offices to a larger office at the end of the hallway. A man in his mid-sixties sat behind a large wooden desk that seemed like it had been hit by a tornado of paper. His small, dark eyes peered at them through horn-rimmed glasses with thick lenses.

The man stood and held out his hand. "Ms. Ross. I'm Clint Murray."

"Kaiah." She shook his hand. "And this is my associate, Reid Turner."

"Turner." Clint studied Reid. "You're a lieutenant with the fire department, and your sister is the president of the historical society."

Reid shook his hand. "That's right."

"Have a seat. What can I do for you?" He gestured toward two chairs across from his messy desk.

"I'm in town doing an article about Coral Cove and the festival," Kaiah began.

"Festival?" Clint's forehead pinched. "I heard that was canceled."

"We're working to change that," Reid said.

"Exactly," Kaiah said. "Reid and I are working with his sister, and we have a plan to make the festival bigger this year, but we need your help." She summarized her idea for Light the Dark—a weeklong festival designed not only to raise enough money for the elementary school renovations but also to put Coral Cove on the map for a tourism boost. "I was hoping to partner with you to write articles and publicize the event."

Reid's phone chimed with a text, and he pulled it from his pocket and read it:

Becca: All set for meeting at town hall tonight at 7:00. Mayor, town council, and school board will be there. The wheels are in motion!

He tapped Kaiah's arm and angled his phone's screen toward her, and she smiled. Then he addressed Clint. "We're going to discuss it with the school board and city council tonight at seven at the town hall."

"When are you planning to hold this festival?" Clint asked.

"It will start on the usual weekend, but like we said, hopefully it'll run for a week instead of just the weekend," Reid explained.

Clint seemed skeptical. "You're putting together an elaborate weeklong spring festival in ten days?" He scoffed. "Do you have a magic wand to pull this off?"

"If the town pulls together, we can make it happen," Kaiah said.

Reid was certain he found determination shining in Kaiah's eyes, and he couldn't have been prouder.

"Maybe so, but folks around here are used to doing things a certain way." The editor plopped back in his chair, and it creaked under his weight. "Where are you from?"

"New York."

Her pleasant expression never wobbled, despite his sneer.

He studied her business card. "And you write for *The Traveler*?" He tossed the card onto his desk. "Never heard of it. Why are you here?"

It took all of Reid's patience not to go off on this guy. How dare he talk to Kaiah like that?

"She's here to write about Coral Cove," Reid said. "Can you help us or not?"

Clint pointed to the hallway. "We're a staff of three here. I'm not sure how much help I can be."

Kaiah rested her hands on her lap. "I'll write the articles. I just need your help sharing them."

Clint shrugged. "I guess we'll see if you can pull off your festival plans. And *if* you can, and *if* you write the articles, then we'll make room for them in our print and digital editions."

"Perfect." Kaiah stood and hefted her giant bag onto her shoulder. "We'll be in touch."

Reid eyed Clint. "I hope you'll join us for the meeting tonight."

"I'll try," Clint said without much conviction.

Then Reid rested his hand on Kaiah's lower back and steered her out of that jerk's office.

"I'm sorry he spoke to you that way," Reid said while they drove down Main Street. "I wanted to tell him off." He actually wanted to pop the guy until he had a shiny black eye, but Reid managed to keep his temper in check.

Kaiah seemed unfazed while she studied the to-do list she'd made in her notepad. "Thanks, but it's fine. I'm used to having to prove myself over and over again."

"Really?" He cocked an eyebrow.

She laughed, as if charmed by his innocence. "Yes, really. It's the nature of being a woman in this business." She focused on their list. "So do you think the mayor, the city council, and the rest of the town can *really* come together and make this happen?"

"I sure do."

Kaiah dropped back on the seat. "Me too. I think it's going to be a lot of work. But it's also a lot of fun." She turned toward the window. "I love this little town. I've never experienced anything like it."

He smiled at her. "I just hope we can get it all together in time." He slowed to a stop at the light.

"I know I've never been to this festival before. But I'm sure it's going to be the best one ever."

And the conviction in her eyes made him believe she was right.

Chapter 10

THE TOWN HALL BUZZED with conversations later that evening. The large open area featured a dozen rows of folding chairs, and nearly every chair was occupied. A podium adorned with the seal of the City of Coral Cove stood at the front of the room. Kaiah followed Becca and Reid down the aisle to the front row, where they found four vacant chairs at the far end.

Kaiah touched Reid's arm. "This place is packed, and it's not even seven yet."

Reid rested his arm on the back of her chair. And when his arm brushed against her shoulders, heating the back of her neck, her body responded by sending a shower of sparks through her.

"Everyone here takes the festival seriously," Reid said. "I'm not surprised it's standing room only."

The man shifted closer to her, and a nearly delirious grin spread across her face as she basked in his comforting scent of sandalwood.

He nodded past her. "Here comes the mayor."

A woman who looked to be in her late fifties with a sleek silver bob cropped to her shoulders, wearing black glasses with thick, stylish frames and a blue pantsuit, marched toward them, her heels clacking on the linoleum. "Becca!" she called.

"Mayor Whittington." Becca jumped to her feet and shook her hand. "Thank you for helping me arrange this emergency meeting."

"I'm just thrilled that we're going to move forward with the festival. This town needs it." She took Becca's arm and led her to the podium, where the mayor tapped on the microphone and said, "Good evening. Thank you all for joining us for an emergency town hall assembly. Tonight we want to discuss the Coral Cove festival."

"I thought it was canceled," someone called out in the back.

A murmur of agreement swept through the crowd.

Mayor Whittington held up her hands. "Let's stay focused, please." She made a sweeping gesture toward Becca. "Rebecca Griffin is the president of the Coral Cove Historical Society, and she's also active in the Coral Cove Elementary PTO. I'll let her share the plan for the festival."

Becca thanked the mayor and moved to the podium, where she placed her iPad filled with notes. "Good evening. I have a proposal that will not only save the festival but also raise enough money to finish the renovations at the school." She looked down at her twin, who gave her a thumbs-up. "Instead of having a short festival the third weekend in April, I propose the festival would start Friday night and end the following Thursday night. We'll sell tickets and take donations and host lots of activities during those seven days. That way we have something for everyone to enjoy whenever their schedule allows. We'll give all the profits to the elementary school so we can fund renovations to restore the closed wing."

Becca studied her notes as the crowd murmured, taking in the new information. Then her eyes slid around the crowd. "With the help of a nationally acclaimed journalist, we'll begin promoting the festival immediately and hopefully gain attention not only in the region but possibly across the nation. We're hoping to attract lots of new folks to come. What we need now are volunteers who can help us plan and execute a festival those folks will come to year after year."

She paused as a new rumble of conversations swept over the crowd.

"How can we pull this off in nine days?" a man called.

"If we all pull togeth—" Becca started, but another voice interrupted her.

"And who can take off a *week* to work a festival?" a woman yelled.

"What about the kids?" someone called. "They have school!"

A burly man stood up in the back of the room. "What guarantees do we have that anyone will come at all?" he demanded. "What if we put our heart and soul into this—not to mention our dollars—and then no one bothers to come?"

"And who's going to pay for all of this?" a woman hollered. "I heard that the historical society blew through their budget and there's nothing left for the festival. How about you explain *that*?"

Becca cleared her throat. "The historical society's budget and the town's recreation budget were both cut after the poor turnout for the last few festivals. But this event will be different."

"How?" a man yelled.

"So now *we* have to pay for it?" a woman asked. "How's that even fair?"

A chorus of complaints sounded, and Becca's posture wilted.

Kaiah's stomach pitched as she turned to Reid. "We need to help her."

"My thoughts exactly." He stood and held his hand out to Kaiah. She linked her fingers with his, and he steered her toward the podium.

"Excuse me," the mayor called out from her seat, her voice straining to be heard without a microphone to amplify it. "Everyone needs to hold it down. We need to be respectful. All of your questions will be answered, but there's no need for yelling."

But the crowd continued talking, their voices becoming louder.

Reid approached her. "Mayor Whittington," he began, "could we please have a chance to speak?"

A stoic expression creased the mayor's face. "Good luck."

Reid took his place behind the podium and gave his twin's shoulder a squeeze as she stepped aside, then tapped the microphone. When the crowd continued their ranting, he tapped it louder and it whistled.

The conversations stopped immediately, and a hush rushed over the town hall.

"Thank you," he grumbled. "I'm Reid Turner, and I'm a lieutenant with the Coral Cove Fire Department." His dark eyes scrutinized the crowd. "How many of you have lived in Coral Cove your entire life?" he asked.

Nearly two-thirds of the audience members raised their hands.

"My sister and I have too." He rested his glorious arms on the podium. "I love this town, and when I was a kid, I knew I wanted to stay here the rest of my life. I wanted to get married here. Raise a family here. My daughter Piper is six, and she's a student at Coral Cove Elementary School, the same school my twin sister and I attended. You all know how a fire ravaged the east wing. I want the students to have the school they deserve, the one Becca and I had when we were growing up, and the one I suspect y'all had too. That's why we need to find a way to raise the funds for the school. We want to give our kids the best, the way our parents and grandparents did for us."

Reid paused and eyed the onlookers once again. "I'm proud of this town, but I also believe that sometimes traditions need to change. The festival we've had every year since before I was born is one of the traditions we can not only change but improve for the better. Right now, all I'm asking you is to keep an open mind. Sometimes change is necessary, and sometimes it isn't easy. We know it's not been the same festival the past few years. Can we agree on that?"

A murmur of agreement spread throughout the crowd.

"Good." He nodded toward Becca. "Rebecca is my sister, and I don't appreciate how she was treated while she was trying to talk to you." He jammed his finger on the podium. "She deserves your attention, and I ask you to remain respectful while we finish explaining our proposal. And when we're done, we'll answer all your questions." He held up his hand. "In an orderly fashion. Is that understood?" he asked.

A few people responded, "Yes, Lieutenant."

Kaiah placed her hand over her mouth to cover her grin. She didn't think Reid could be any more attractive. But the way he defended his sister and politely chastised the crowd was possibly the hottest thing she'd ever seen a guy do in person. *Mr. TDH? Maybe we need to start calling him Mr. Smooth.*

"Good." Reid licked his lips and held out his hand to Kaiah. "I'd like to introduce a new friend of mine. This is Kaiah Ross, and she's a journalist with *The Traveler*, a popular travel magazine. She's working on a story about Coral Cove. Kaiah proposed many new ideas for our festival this year. Trust me, having Kaiah write about Coral Cove is not only a great way to raise awareness about the festival and money for our school; it's also an excellent opportunity to highlight what a hidden gem our town is and invite folks from all over to come and experience it for themselves. I'm sure you all wouldn't say no to a few more tourist dollars flowing into your businesses, right? So I know you'll be respectful while Kaiah shares her ideas."

Reid stepped to the side and motioned for Kaiah to join him. "Everyone give it up for Kaiah Ross," he said, and a few people clapped.

Kaiah took a trembling breath, and her hands began to shake while she pulled her notepad from the bottom of her large bag. "Hi, everyone. I've been working on a series called Hidden Gems, highlighting charming small towns across the East Coast. I was visiting places between Maryland and Florida when I accidentally found Coral Cove and was captivated by your stunning lighthouse." She toggled her gaze toward Reid, who watched her with an intense expression that sent a tingling chill through her, despite the warm room. "Lieutenant Turner shared the story about the sailors who were saved by the lighthouse." Kaiah faced the crowd again. "Since I've been here, I've found that the lighthouse is the spirit of Coral Cove. I see it in the artwork that adorns your walls, in the treats lining your bakery cases. And I see the bright light in each of you. Every person I've met in this town has been so kind to me, a stranger who came to you all in need. It seems like kindness is the guiding light of this place." She paused, taking in a deep breath. "So I believe we should celebrate that light. I recommend renaming the festival 'Light the Dark.' The festival marks the transition from the dark of winter to the warm light of spring. It also reminds everyone that the lighthouse saved other strangers—the sailors—one early spring day long ago."

She scanned her list of events. "We'll begin Friday night by illuminating the lighthouse to symbolize the transition from winter to spring. Then we'll spend the next six days celebrating Coral Cove with live music, a market with vendors, tours of the lighthouse, and other events and activities for visitors of all ages." She summarized their ideas for events, including the Shining Light Photo Contest and Light Snack before she covered the mic with her hand and addressed Reid. "I think we can take questions now."

Reid joined her at the podium, and he rested his hand on her lower back. "Now we're ready for questions."

"But it's already spring," a woman exclaimed. "Why not just have a summer festival?"

"The lighthouse saved the sailors at the beginning of April. The festival should remain in April." Reid pressed his lips together. "Who's next?" He pointed to a man in the back with graying black hair. "Yes, sir."

"How are we going to fix the lighthouse in ten days when it hasn't been lit in decades?" he asked.

"We're hoping that someone knows an electrician who can fix it," Reid explained.

The man threw his arms up. "And who's going to pay for that if the historical society has no money?"

Kaiah leaned toward the microphone. "We're hoping someone will donate their time and supplies. Everyone who donates to the festival will be honored as a sponsor. We'll have a sponsor tent and include their names on banners."

Reid lifted his eyebrows and grinned at her. "That's right," he agreed.

More murmurs of conversations erupted in the audience.

Becca came to stand beside Kaiah. "This can work. We just need to pull together." She pointed to Kaiah. "Kaiah is a journalist with a popular online magazine. She can get the publicity, and Clint at *The Coral Cove Times* has agreed to run her stories locally."

"Hold on!" a woman called. "We only have nine days. Even if we all pull together, how on earth do we get everything together in *nine days*?"

The mayor touched Reid's back. "Excuse me," she said. "I'd like to speak again." Reid and Kaiah moved away from the podium. "We can do this if we organize and volunteer." She looked at Becca. "Would you like to be the chair of the festival committee?"

"Yes, I would." Becca beamed at Kaiah. "And Kaiah will help me."

Kaiah nodded.

Reid grinned at her again, and her heart began to beat in triple time.

"We got this, people," a woman announced, and people began to clap.

Goodness. Seems like all it takes is one person to sow a little hope around here.

"Let's turn this meeting around," the mayor said, "and we'll start organizing right here and now. We need some volunteers." She studied the sea of faces. "Who can fix the lighthouse? We need some electricians to pull together."

"I'm Duke Johnson," a man said as he stood. "I run Johnson Electric in town. I have some contacts, and I might be able to find a specialist who can work on it and donate his time."

Reid's expression filled with relief as he clapped.

"My sister and I will make lighthouse and nautical pastries to sell," one of the Watson twins announced. "We'll donate a portion of the profits to the school fund."

Becca held her hand up. "We'll have a market at the base of the lighthouse," she offered. "Vendors can pay a fee for a space, and the fees can go to the school."

A woman in the center of the crowd jumped up. "I'm Brenda Jones, president of the Coral Cove Business Committee," she said. "I'll handle the Light Snack event along with the website and social media for the festival."

Kaiah and Reid shared a smile. The festival was quickly coming together.

Becca tapped on her iPad. "Who else wants to volunteer?"

By the end of the meeting, Becca had an iPad full of volunteers and their contact information. Only a few naysayers continued to insist that there was no way the festival would be a success in such a short amount of time.

"Thank you for making this happen," the mayor told Reid, Becca, and Kaiah while they walked out to the parking lot after the meeting. "I think this festival is going to be a great success."

"We plan to do our best," Becca promised.

A woman dashed across the parking lot toward them. "Mayor Whittington!" she called. "I want to discuss something with you."

Becca set her hand on Kaiah's arm. "That's Joanna Edwards," she whispered. "She's the school superintendent."

"I wonder what she wants," Reid added.

Joanna came to stand with them, and she nodded a greeting before addressing the mayor. "I think the kids would benefit from being a part of the festival. I'm going to talk to the school board about making the festival part of the curriculum. They can volunteer their time or even help with fundraising. We can make it a field trip—or, come to think of it, we could schedule a long weekend to coincide with the festival. It would benefit the community and let the kids learn while having fun."

"I agree. That's a fantastic idea," the mayor said.

Joanna shook her hand. "Great. I'll talk to the school board." Then she started across the parking lot again.

"This has turned out even better than I thought it would," the mayor told Kaiah, Becca, and Reid. "I'll be in touch."

"I'll call Brenda Jones and talk to her about working on the website and social media tonight. We can incorporate the events and have sign-ups for volunteers." Becca hugged Kaiah. "I'm so glad you're here. We couldn't have made this happen without you."

Kaiah's heart swelled as she and Reid climbed into his Suburban.

"Tonight was amazing," Kaiah told Reid while they drove down Main Street. "You're my hero now."

Reid sneaked a glance her way. Although he was touched by the compliment, he couldn't understand how *he* could be *her* hero. "And why is that?"

"The way you told the audience to get their act together and to be respectful was just . . . it was amazing, Reid. You said all the right words and made them realize they were being immature and rude. I'm super proud of you."

Her words sent a ribbon of warmth through his chest.

"I'm going to stay up all night and finish my article," she continued. "I'm going to add the details about the festival to the one I already started and then send it off to my editor. Then I'll contact Clint and asked him to share it on the local paper's website."

She continued to talk about plans for the festival, but he was still playing back *I'm super proud of you* over and over in his head. He was sure he felt a connection growing between them. And for a moment he allowed himself to wonder what would happen if Kaiah decided to stay in Coral Cove. For the first time since he'd lost Brynn, he wondered what it would like to date again. To fall in love again.

No, no, no. He was being crazy. He didn't have room in his life for a relationship. And how would Piper feel about it when it all fell apart?

He already knew the answer to that question. Piper was growing attached to Kaiah too, and that was a slippery slope. They would both be heartbroken when Kaiah left. And okay, hypothetically, why would a sophisticated woman like her want to stay in a small town like Coral Cove? She told him she dreamed of going to exotic places and writing about them for a huge magazine. Staying in a small town like Coral Cove? That would be torture for her. Even if she *wanted* to stay, he couldn't imagine asking her to give up her dreams. And he never wanted to leave Coral Cove. His family was too important to him. So maybe they were just destined to live their lives apa—

A hand on his arm jolted him from his thoughts.

"Reid?" Kaiah asked, worry coloring her features. "You okay?"

He motored through an intersection and turned onto the road leading to his neighborhood. "Yeah."

"You seem preoccupied," she said. "Want to talk about it?"

He glanced over at the radiant woman in the seat beside him. How could he begin to express his confusing feelings for her? He hadn't even known her a week, and he was already feeling something deep and powerful for her.

"Sorry. I was thinking about the festival and everything we have to do."

"No worries. We'll work on it together tomorrow, right?"

"Right."

Reid parked in the driveway, and they climbed out. His eyes wandered to the clear, dark sky where stars sparkled above them and the moon sent bright beams cascading through the dark. He turned toward Kaiah, and for a moment he was struck by how beautiful she was standing haloed by the moonlight with her golden hair falling in waves past her shoulders.

"You said I'm your hero, but you were great tonight too," he said. "You made the audience understand how special the festival will be."

She wagged a finger at him. "But you convinced them to listen. I couldn't have done my part without you." She touched his hand. "I'll see you tomorrow."

She sauntered toward the stairs leading to the apartment, then turned around. The smile lighting up her face was nearly as warm as the midday sun. "Good night, Reid."

He couldn't help but beam back at her. "Thank you."

"For what?"

"Helping to save our town."

She did a mock curtsy. "My pleasure."

Kaiah turned and jogged up the stairs. He waited until the apartment lights illuminated before he walked inside the house.

Chapter 11

KAIAH RUBBED HER EYES and yawned as she pushed herself out of bed. It was after nine, but she'd only been asleep since five. She'd been up working on her article, researching Coral Cove, and thinking about Reid. Not necessarily in that order.

Even after she'd sent the article to Libby and crawled into bed, Kaiah stayed awake, replaying the events of the previous evening—how Reid had handled the raucous crowd, how he had encouraged her to talk to them, how he had rested his hand on the small of her back, how they'd held hands like it was the most natural thing in the world. He was kind, thoughtful, caring. And clearly he was becoming important to her. Which had never been part of her travel plans.

Great. Just great.

She groaned and covered her face with her hands.

After taking a hot shower, she dressed and ate a quick breakfast of cold cereal. Just as she sat down in front of her computer, a knock sounded at her door. When she opened it, she found Reid holding two cups of coffee.

"Good morning." Reid held out one of the to-go cups for her. "I picked up coffee for us."

Kaiah took the cup. "Thanks."

"It's a vanilla latte. They even spelled your name right."

She turned the cup to the side and found "Cayenne" written in black magic marker, and she snorted. Then she clasped her hand to her mouth to shield her yawn.

His face clouded with a concerned frown. "Uh-oh. You still tired?"

"I was up most of the night writing my article, but I got it done. I sent it to my editor around five."

"Oh, wow." Disappointment and concern covered his face. "You need rest. I'll let you go back to bed."

She grabbed his arm and tugged him toward her. "No, no, no. Come on in. We have a lot of work to do."

Reid didn't look convinced. "Uh, you have dark circles under your eyes. I don't think 'a lot of work' should be on your agenda right now."

"Fine. How about this," Kaiah began. "If I start to fall asleep, I'll take a quick nap, and then we can get together later."

Reid considered her words. "Okay." Then he lifted his eyebrows. "Any chance I can read your article?"

She hesitated before slowly nodding her head. "Sure."

He gestured to the sofa, where her laptop was sitting on the coffee table. She opened the article file and set the computer on his lap, holding her breath while his dark eyes scrolled across the screen. When he finished, she froze, waiting for his reaction.

"It's perfect," he said. "I love how you describe our town."

Relief coursed through her body as she closed the computer and set it on the coffee table. "Thanks." She leaned back against the arm of the sofa.

"Seriously, it's awesome. Thank you, Ky."

"It was my pleasure, truly." She let out a small breath she wasn't even aware she'd been holding. "So what's the plan for today?"

"Well, I had an idea while I was getting dressed this morning. There are so many organizations that host marathons. What if we have a walk or a run that tied to the festival?"

"I love it!" Kaiah pulled out her notebook. "We could have the start and finish line at the lighthouse."

He rubbed the dark scruff on his neck. "Exactly. We'll map out a route that goes in a big circle and comes back to the lighthouse. The participants could get sponsors to pledge donations based on their performance."

"I think it's a great idea. I'll add it to the list," Kaiah said while writing in her notebook. "So we need to start planning a race. What's our first action item for that?"

"How about we talk to the PE teacher at Piper's school?" Reid offered. "He has experience with this sort of thing and can tell us what to do next."

She pushed her notebook into her backpack. "Good point. Let's go."

After checking in at the front office at Coral Cove Elementary School, Reid and Kaiah ambled through the long hallways until they came to the gym. The scent of rubber and sounds of laughter breezed over him as he watched a class playing kickball.

Kaiah's blue eyes sparkled as they darted around the hallway and then back at the large gym. "You and Becca went to school here?"

"Yeah. Not much has changed."

She hugged her notebook to her chest, and when she smiled, a happy current raced through his veins. "It must be special raising your daughter in the same town where you grew up. You can share all of your memories and traditions with her and enjoy seeing her experience some of those same traditions, like the festival."

"Yeah." He nodded. "It is special."

A bell trilled in the hallway, announcing the end of class. The students lined up before a young woman led them out, reminding him of a mother duck leading her ducklings to a pond.

"Reid?" Coach Emmerson rushed over and shook Reid's hand. "What a nice surprise!" The middle-aged man's hair was more gray than dark brown, but he still had the same smile Reid remembered from his school days.

"Coach Emmerson, this is Kaiah Ross. She's a reporter with *The Traveler*." He made a sweeping gesture to Kaiah, who also shook the coach's hand. "We were hoping to talk to you about an event for the spring festival. Do you have a few minutes?"

"I do. Let's go to my office."

They followed the coach to an office located beside the gym, where Reid and Kaiah sat in front of his desk.

Coach Emmerson leaned back in his chair, which squeaked under his weight. "My wife attended the meeting last night and came home excited about the festival. How can I help?"

"We're planning some events to raise money for the school, and we want to have a mini-marathon," Reid began. "It would be a walk and run that could start and end at the lighthouse."

Coach Emmerson folded his hands over his middle. "I like it."

"I've been thinking about names, and I think Beacon of Hope Run and Walk would tie in well with the theme of the festival," Kaiah suggested.

"Perfect," Reid said, and she shot him a smile that melted his heart for a moment. He turned back to the coach. "Could you help us plan it?"

Coach Emmerson sat forward, and his chair groaned in protest. "I sure can. We have walk-a-thons at the school sometimes, so I can design the forms participants can use to ask for sponsorships and pledges."

"Fantastic," Kaiah said. "How about ribbons or trophies?"

"We have a closet full of them. If you send me the logo for the festival, I can take care of decorating them for you." He tapped his finger on the desk. "I bet Piper would love to give out the trophies and ribbons to the winners."

Kaiah touched Reid's arm. "I'm sure she would."

Reid nodded, unable to think of much else but the weight of Kaiah's warmth pressing on his arm.

Coach Emmerson discussed the forms and the awards before they exchanged email addresses and phone numbers.

Soon Reid and Kaiah were heading down the hallway.

Kaiah had a spring in her step. "That went great."

"It did." He came to a stop at the end of the hallway and grabbed her hand. "Want to visit Piper's classroom?"

Kaiah's blue eyes sparkled. "Of course."

He led her to the temporary first-grade section and stopped at a door with "Ms. Mason" written on it.

"Reid, look," Kaiah gasped, gripping his bicep and tugging him toward a wall of artwork beside the classroom, featuring seascapes and lighthouses. "What are the chances?"

He pushed his hand through his hair and perused the display until he found his daughter's picture. Piper had colored a seascape. The careful crayon lines showed a lighthouse with a bright rainbow stretched across a construction-paper sky. He imagined his daughter concentrating on her drawing, biting her lip with her brow furrowed. Pride swelled within him.

Kaiah sidled up and tapped the bulletin board where the drawings hung. "You know what this means?"

"That we need to have a lighthouse craft booth for the kids?"

"Exactly," she told him. "The kids can make lighthouses out of different materials or even draw them." She lifted her gaze, locking her eyes with his. "This is going to be amazing, Reid."

"Yeah." He stared down at her, and when his eyes lowered to her mouth, a heat began to wash over him as his heart pounded wildly in his chest. For a moment he imagined how soft her lips would feel on his, and he yearned to find out.

His chin dipped, and her eyes fluttered shut.

And just before his lips touched hers, a door opened down the hall.

Reid jumped back and did a mental headshake. He was about to make out with Kaiah. In his daughter's school. Not the *best* idea, but could he really help it? Once again, he felt an invisible magnet pulling him toward this woman. He seemed powerless to resist her.

"Hello, Mr. Turner." Ms. Robertson, the principal, headed down the hall, her heels clacking on the worn, polished concrete floor. "Are you here to visit Piper's classroom?"

Reid cleared his throat. "Hi, Ms. Robertson. Yes, I am. This is my friend Kaiah Ross. She's a reporter doing a story on Coral Cove, and we were here discussing an idea for the upcoming festival with Coach Emmerson." He made a sweeping gesture between the women. "Ms. Robertson is the principal."

The principal nodded a greeting.

"Hi." Kaiah pointed toward the bulletin board. "We were admiring the students' artwork."

"I heard about the festival from members of the PTO. The theme is perfect."

Reid shared their ideas about the marathon and the arts and crafts tent.

"The kids will love both of those events. You should tell Piper's class about it," Ms. Robertson said. "I'm sure the kids will get their parents involved in each of them. The PTO is going to work on flyers to send home with all of the students."

"That's perfect," Reid said.

While Ms. Robertson continued down the hall, Kaiah grabbed Reid's arm as excitement flashed over her features. "Getting the elementary school involved is such a great idea. I'm sure the other schools will want to participate too."

"Definitely." He peeked into the window of Piper's classroom door and spotted her sitting in the front row. All of the students were working with their heads bent. He tapped lightly on the door, and the teacher hurried over.

"Mr. Turner," she said.

Across the room, Piper waved and called, "Daddy!"

"Hi, Piper." Reid waved to his daughter and then addressed the teacher, "I was wondering if I could visit. My friend and I were here talking to Coach Emmerson about the upcoming spring festival." He introduced the teacher to Kaiah. "We were hoping we could tell Piper's class about it."

"Of course," Ms. Mason said. "Now is the perfect time. We're just working on a project, and we have some free time before music."

Reid and Kaiah entered the room, and the nearly three dozen students greeted them from their desks, which were cramped in the small classroom. The classes had doubled in size due to the closed wing.

Piper rushed over and hugged Reid's waist.

"Hi, Daddy!" She gazed up at him. "I didn't know you'd be here today." She turned toward the class. "This is my daddy and my friend Miss Kaiah."

Reid touched her nose. "We have something exciting to share with you guys."

Piper threaded her fingers with Reid's and then with Kaiah's. "I'll help you tell your stories." She led them to the front of the room. "Everyone, my daddy is a fireman. He has lots of stories he can share. If you have questions, raise your hand."

When nearly all of the hands in the classroom shot up, Ms. Mason made her way to the front. "Okay, class. Let's have our guests speak before you ask questions, okay?"

Kaiah shot Reid a grin, and he bit back a laugh.

Ms. Mason turned to Reid. "Why don't you tell the class about the festival?"

Reid glanced at Kaiah, and she nodded at him as if telling him to speak while she stood off to the side with Piper and the teacher. "Hi, everyone. I'm Piper's dad. My name is Reid, and my friend Kaiah and I are helping to plan the spring festival. It's going to take place in a week and a half, and the theme is Light the Dark."

A little boy in the front row waved his arm in the air. "Oh! Oh! Like a lamp! Or a lighthouse! We drew some of those the other day."

"Exactly," Reid said. "What can you tell me about the Coral Cove lighthouse?"

For the next several minutes, Reid discussed the history of the lighthouse and then shared the plans for the festival. He ended his talk by sharing about the arts and crafts tent as well as the mini-marathon.

A little girl in the back raised her hand, and Reid pointed to her. "Can we walk in the walk and run?" she asked.

"Of course. If you're interested, you can ask an adult to find the festival's website and then sign up for it. We'll have information out soon, and we'd love for you to participate." He turned toward Kaiah. "Did I miss anything?"

She shook her head. "Nope. You did great."

"Mr. Turner," a little boy called. "Tell us about being a firefighter!"

"Do you see a lot of fires?" a girl asked.

Reid leaned against the board. "No, we don't see many fires."

"What do you do then?" a boy asked.

"We help out in other places," he said. "The other day one of the homes on the beach had a deck that collapsed."

"Oh no!" a few students said.

"Were the people okay?" another asked.

"Thankfully the people at the house only had a few small injuries." He motioned for Kaiah to join him in front of the classroom, and she complied. "Ms. Ross is a journalist. That means she learns about things happening in the world and writes stories about them for people to read. Do you have any questions for her?"

Nearly a dozen hands shot up in the air, and Kaiah chuckled before calling on a little girl.

"Why did you want to become a . . . a journalist?" she asked.

"Because I've always loved to read and tell stories," she began. She talked about writing stories when she was around their age, then shared some of the fun places she'd visited for her stories.

When she finished, Ms. Mason walked toward them. "Let's thank Mr. Turner and Ms. Ross for joining us today."

A chorus of thank-yous followed before Piper took Reid's hand again. "Can I show you and Miss Kaiah my project before you go, Daddy?"

"Of course," Reid said.

Piper guided them to her desk, where a stack of stapled construction paper with the words "Piper Turner's Book" sat decorated with rainbows, the sun, clouds, and a couple of cats, all drawn in colorful markers.

She pointed to the cover. "It's my storybook." She turned the page to a drawing of a house with smoke billowing out of the chimney, a colorful cat peeking out the window, and plenty of flowers smiling in a garden. "That's our house." She pointed to the window. "Ariel is watching those cats that like to run past."

"Nice job," Reid said while sharing a smile with Kaiah.

The next page featured a drawing of two stick figures, a tall one and a short one, along with a cat. The words "Daddy," "Piper," and "Ariel" were written under them while they stood by the ocean. Birds flew in the bright blue sky while clouds and the sun smiled down. "That's me and you at the beach, Daddy."

"You did a great job," Kaiah told her.

"I agree," Reid chimed in.

"There's more." Piper flipped to a page with more people on it. "Here we are with Nana, Auntie Becca, Uncle Cash, and Astrid." She flipped to the next page, featuring what looked like a stick figure holding a baby with the words "Mommy and Piper" written beside the picture.

"And that's me and Mommy."

Reid focused on the picture while tears burned the backs of his eyes.

After four years, sometimes grief punched him in the gut nearly as hard as the day of Brynn's memorial service. For a moment he couldn't speak. He hoped Piper and Kaiah wouldn't notice the tears filling his eyes.

A hand rested on his shoulder, and he looked over to where Kaiah's face formed a sympathetic smile, sending warmth straight to his heart.

"Here's the end," Piper said, showing him a page covered with flowers, rainbows, Ariel the cat, and a few hearts. "Do you like it, Daddy?" she asked, her dark eyes pleading.

He cleared his throat to tamp down the expanding lump and pulled his daughter in for a hug. "Of course I do, sweetheart," he said, his voice sounding rough. "Your book is perfect. Thank you for showing it to us."

"I love it too," Kaiah said before hugging Piper. "We'll see you later."

They waved to the class, then headed for the door.

Chapter 12

"THAT WAS SO FUN," Kaiah said while Reid steered the SUV out of the elementary school parking lot. "And the kids loved you. If this whole firefighting thing doesn't work out, you could totally be a teacher."

His grin sent a shiver dancing up her spine. "You think so, huh?"

"Yep." She glanced down at her phone and checked her email. "I got a message from Libby. My article is live on the magazine's website." She found another email from Clint at the local paper. "Oh! And Clint said he's going to include it in tomorrow's edition of the paper. I'm hoping it gets picked up by the wire and goes national."

"I have a sneaking suspicion it will." He rested his elbow on the door and steered with his right hand. "I had another idea for an event. My mom loves to garden, and she has prize-winning roses. What if we hosted garden tours as part of the festival?"

"Oh, I love that!" Kaiah declared.

"Since we have names for all of our other events, we could call it something like Coral Cove Brightening Blooms and give out a prize for the best garden and different kinds of flowers."

"Yes." She snapped her fingers. "And we could sell tickets for the tours as a fundraiser."

He grinned. "Yup. Great minds think alike. I'll mention it to my mom, and she can get her garden club involved. I know they'll want to volunteer."

Her phone dinged with a message.

Becca: Hi! Do you like to bake?

Kaiah: Hey yourself! Do break-and-bake count?

Becca: LOL! The PTO is hosting a bake sale to raise awareness for the festival. We're calling it the "Light the Way Home Bake Sale," and we'll run it in the cafeterias at each Coral Cove school. With every purchase, we'll include a flyer asking for festival volunteers.

Kaiah: Wow, that's awesome! I'm guessing you're desperate for bakers if you're asking me.

Becca: That obvious, huh? You nailed it. The bake sale starts tomorrow, and we need nautical-themed baked goods, like, yesterday. Any chance I can convince you to bake some cookies and drop them off at one of the schools?

Kaiah glanced at Reid, who was humming along with the nineties country song on the radio and tapping the steering wheel along with the music. A vision of an apron stretching taut across his chest and his biceps flexing as he stirred cookie dough filled her mind—and made her mouth dry.

Oh yes, she *definitely* wanted to bake with him.

She texted: Sure thing! I'll get Reid and Piper to help me this afternoon. Send me details about where to drop them off tomorrow morning.

Becca: Great! Brenda Jones and I are working on the website too. I'll call you later so we can talk about what events we want to feature.

Kaiah: Perfect.

She glanced at the clock on the dashboard. "What time do you have to pick up Piper from school?"

"Two thirty."

"That means we have time to go to the grocery store."

He lifted his dark eyebrows. "And why are we going to the grocery store?"

"Do you like to bake?"

He studied her for a moment. "Why are you answering a question with a question?"

"Why are you?"

He held her gaze for a beat, and then they both started to laugh.

"Fine, fine!" she sang. "Becca said the PTO is going to host a bake sale starting tomorrow to promote the festival, and they need nautical baked goods. So this afternoon we're going to bake some lighthouse cookies, and we'll drop them off at one of the schools in the morning. We can get the supplies now and start baking when Piper gets home."

He stopped at a red light and turned to face her. "You're telling me that you want to make lighthouse cookies today so that the PTO can have a bake sale tomorrow?"

"That's exactly right." She gave him palms up. "What do you think?"

A ghost of a smile played on his lips. "Sure."

Kaiah smiled to herself. She was *going* to get him in that apron.

After picking up supplies at the grocery store, including two lighthouse-shaped cookie cutters, Kaiah got to work mixing the dough while Reid picked up Piper from school. By the time father and daughter arrived home, Kaiah had the oven preheated and the dough ready to shape.

"Miss Kaiah," Piper announced as she scurried into the kitchen, "Daddy said we're going to make cookies and I can help. I love making cookies. This is gonna be great!"

Reid set Piper's backpack on a kitchen chair. "She's a little excited." His warm expression sent Kaiah's pulse quickening.

Kaiah chuckled. "I can see that."

She touched Piper's shoulder. "Why don't you wash your hands at the sink, and then you can help cut out the lighthouses?"

Piper climbed up on her stool and scrubbed her hands before moving her stool over to the counter. "I'm ready."

Reid leaned on the doorframe while Kaiah showed Piper how to cut out the lighthouses and then set them on the cookie sheets.

"Aren't you going to help, Daddy?" Piper asked him.

"Yeah, Reid." Kaiah rested her hand on her hip and made a face. "Why are *we* doing all the work?"

He held up his palms. "We only bought two cookie cutters, and there's no room for me at the counter." He pointed to the oven. "I'll be in charge of putting the cookie sheets in the oven, setting the timer, and taking them out."

Kaiah looked at Piper. "What do you think?"

"I don't know." Piper shook her head. "I think he needs to help us decorate too."

"Good idea." Kaiah and Piper shared a high five. Then she studied Reid again. "By any chance, do you have an apron?"

His eyebrows knitted together. "What?"

"Never mind," she mumbled. She could let that dream go.

After cutting out the cookies and placing them on the baking sheets, Reid set the pans in the oven. Soon the scent of warm, buttery sugar cookies permeated the kitchen.

Once the first batch had cooled, Piper and Reid set to work decorating them with colorful icing and sprinkles.

Piper pointed to a rainbow-colored lighthouse. "Look! Isn't it beautiful?"

Kaiah peeked over from where she rolled out more dough. "It's perfect, Piper."

"I agree." Reid motioned toward his lighthouse, which was striped with black and white icing. "What about mine?"

"Kinda boring," Kaiah teased.

Reid clucked his tongue. "Excuse me?"

"I'm sorry, but I'm being honest," Kaiah continued. "Piper's is much more creative."

Piper's expression was somber. "Yeah. Yours just looks like the regular old lighthouse."

Reid reached over and dabbed white icing on Piper's nose.

Piper screeched and then brushed icing on his nose.

Kaiah laughed just as Reid took her arm, pulled her to him and rubbed icing on *her* nose. She gasped as she looked up at his handsome face. Suddenly, she was yanked back to the moment they'd stood together outside Piper's classroom and his eyes had stayed laser-focused on her lips. The air around them had seemed electrified, and she'd almost been certain he was going to kiss her—and boy, had she wanted him to. But the moment had been ruined by the principal.

Now as she looked up at him, she couldn't stop the joy—or the heat—flooding through her.

Piper appeared and brushed icing over Reid's chin and Kaiah's cheek before cackling.

Reid's dark eyes danced. "You know what this means, Kaiah?"

"War!" Kaiah cried before they each grabbed a tub of icing and chased Piper.

For the next several minutes, they raced around the kitchen, flicking icing at each other and doubling over with laughter.

When the timer on the stove began to beep, Reid stood up and made a T with his hands. The pink icing dotting his shirt and face made Kaiah giggle. The image was such a contrast for the masculine firefighter.

"Time-out! We don't need burned cookies." He pulled on an oven mitt and opened the stove.

"Let's get him," Piper whispered.

Kaiah nodded and bit back a laugh. She and Piper snuck up on him, and after he set the cookies on the cooling rack and put the baking sheet in the sink, they pounced, caking his face with icing.

"Whoa! Whoa!" He hollered with a laugh. "I called time-out."

He wrapped his arms around Piper and lifted her up in the air while she shrieked. Then he eyed Kaiah. "You're a bad influence."

"It was her idea!" Kaiah squeaked.

Reid snorted and shook his head. "We need to get back to using the icing on the *cookies* instead of our faces."

"Okay, Daddy," Piper mumbled. She climbed up on her stool and returned to her artwork.

"Let me see your face, pumpkin," Reid said before brushing a napkin across her cheeks and cleaning up the icing. "We sure made a mess."

Piper lifted her chin. "But it was fun."

"Yes, it was," he agreed with another chuckle.

Kaiah ripped a paper towel off the roll and wiped her own face.

Reid appeared beside her. "You missed some." He pointed to her cheek before he ran a paper towel under the faucet, wrung it out, and then gently wiped her cheek.

His gentle touch sent her heart jumping into her throat, and for a moment she lost herself in his bottomless brown eyes. When she realized she was staring at him, she broke eye contact and moved to the sink, washing her hands. "I-I've never been part of a food fight before."

"I don't believe that for a second."

"How come?"

"You have eight siblings, right?" he asked, and she nodded. "Someone must've started a food fight at some point."

"All nine of us never lived together at the same time, and I can honestly say none of us started a food fight. It was noisy but never that rowdy." She paused for a second, lost in a memory. "But I remember a food fight breaking out in the school cafeteria. Of course, *I* wasn't a participant."

He tilted his head. "Is that right?"

"Uh-huh. I never got into trouble." She reached up and wiped icing off his eyebrow, and she longed to move her finger down the length of his angular jaw.

"I believe you." He tossed the paper towel in the trash can, glanced down at her shirt, and then grimaced. "I'm sorry for the mess."

She took in the splotches of yellow and black icing on her purple top. "It was fun. Actually, this icing fight was the most fun I've had in a long time."

"Me too," he whispered.

He moved his gaze and locked eyes with hers. And when an intense expression—was that . . . longing?—overtook his face, her breath seized in her chest.

"Daddy?" Piper said.

And Reid's posture went rigid.

"Yeah, sweetie?" He returned to the counter beside his daughter.

"Is this enough icing?" She pointed to her lighthouse cookie, which was smothered in a rainbow of colors.

"I think it's beautiful." He moved it to the rack with other cookies that were drying. "Let's get started on another one."

Kaiah tried her best to remember how to breathe while she returned to rolling out dough and cutting out cookies.

A couple hours later, they had four dozen lighthouse cookies tucked into ziplock bags and stacked in boxes, ready for the bake sale. Kaiah set the last cookie sheet in the dishwasher, placed a detergent packet in the slot, and started the humming machine to life.

Piper wiped off the counters she could reach with a paper towel before running off to play with Ariel, and Reid stowed the baking supplies.

"I think our lighthouses will be a hit at the bake sale," Kaiah said while surveying the boxes.

Reid rested a hip against the counter. "I do too."

"We can take them to the office when we drop off Piper at school."

"Yup." He pointed to the clock. "It's about time to eat. Would you like to stay for supper?" he asked.

She shook her head. "I don't want to impose."

"Is that right?" he asked, tossing a dishrag into the sink. "You forced me to spend my afternoon baking and decorating cookies, but *now* you're worried about imposing?" His lips twitched.

She opened and closed her mouth. He had her there.

"Kaiah, I'm kidding." He rubbed her arm. "You're not imposing." His expression became serious. "Stay for supper. Please."

Piper popped her head in the doorway. "Can we have chicken nuggets and french fries?" she asked. "Please, please, *please*, Daddy?"

Reid gave Kaiah an apologetic expression. "What do you think, ma'am?"

"A food fight, cookies, and now chicken nuggets and fries?" Kaiah asked. "I can't think of a more perfect evening."

"Yay!" Piper sang before dancing on her way to the family room.

Reid shot Kaiah a look that sent her pulse jumping. "Thank you. Seriously."

"For what?"

"Just for being you."

While he opened the freezer door, Kaiah hugged her arms to her chest, hoping to slow down her racing heart. She had a sneaking suspicion that Reid felt their connection deepening the way she did.

Whew. Talk about a detour.

Later that evening, Kaiah flopped onto the sofa, found *You've Got Mail* on a streamer, and settled under a blanket. She was worn out from the day, but she also couldn't stop smiling. She'd had such a good time with Reid and Piper. She couldn't remember the last time she'd laughed so much.

Before the movie got too underway, she pulled out her phone to check on her Coral Cove article. She pulled up *The Traveler*'s Instagram feed, and she saw her article already had more than—

Oh my goodness!

Ten thousand likes?

When she clicked on the Coral Cove hashtag used by *The Traveler*'s social team, she found that her article had been posted on other news feeds. It was starting to go viral!

"Go, little article, go," she whispered. She peeked at the names of the people who liked *The Traveler*'s post, and when a familiar name caught her eye she groaned.

"Oh no," she muttered. "This cannot be real."

On closer inspection she realized she'd read the name right.

Hayes Walker had liked the post.

Her ex-boyfriend. The man who had destroyed her heart and her faith in love. The jerk who had taken George away.

She clenched her jaw. The sooner she forgot about him, the better. And he needed to leave her alone.

Her phone began to ring, and she was grateful to see her sister's name on the display.

"Hey, Kam," she said.

"Hey, sis! I haven't heard from you in a couple of days. Whatcha been up to? Anything new with Mr. TDH?"

Kaiah hugged her knees to her chest. "He's fine. We've been busy planning the festival. It's really coming together." She summarized their last few days, all the events they'd coordinated for the big event, even the icing fight she'd just had in the kitchen with her two favorite bakers.

"Whoa, whoa, whoa," Kam said. "Let me get this straight. You just made cookies tonight with a widower and his six-year-old. And you had a food fight? With icing?"

"That's right."

"Wow. You guys are one big happy family now, huh?"

Kaiah's cheeks reddened. "Um, I wouldn't call it that. It wasn't—I mean, I'm not trying to be—"

"Hey, relax. I think it's really nice you guys have kinda bonded while you're there. That's all."

While you're there. The words echoed in Kaiah's mind. "Yep, it's been fun to be here." She moved her hands over the dark blue microfiber blanket, determined to switch topics. "So how are things with you and Devon?"

"Good. Busy." She paused for a moment. "And you'll never guess who called me today."

"Who?"

"Dad."

"Wow, really?" She pressed her lips together. She couldn't remember the last time she'd spoken to her dad and Veronica. Maybe Christmas?

A familiar ache radiated in her chest. She longed for the family she'd had before they'd lost Mom. Maybe she could find that kind of family again someday. But after her breakup with Hayes, she'd lost hope. On the other side of love was heartache, no matter what. So why even bother?

"Yeah, I was surprised too," Kam replied. "It's still weird to me that we live in the same state yet only talk to each other a couple times a year. Whatever. He said he was thinking of me. He even put Veronica on the phone."

"And how are they doing?"

"Fine. He talked about the grandkids and how Veronica is going to be a grandmother again. Stuff like that."

"That's nice." Kaiah yawned. "Sorry, Kam, you're not boring me. I didn't get much sleep last night. I was up all night writing. My new article is posted on *The Traveler* website and the local newspaper here. It's getting tons of likes and shares on social."

"That's amazing, Ky! You need to send me the link."

"I will." She hesitated. "Oh, and do me a favor, sis. Don't text and ask about Mr. TDH. I think Reid saw your text on my phone the other day. It was *mortifying*."

Kam laughed. "Did he ask you about it?"

"No, but I'm sure he's curious."

"It's good to keep him guessing," her sister joked. "Good night."

"Night, Kam. Talk to you soon." Kaiah hung up and then settled on the sofa to watch Tom Hanks and Meg Ryan fall in unexpectedly but completely smitten love with each other and form their own little family—complete with Brinkley the golden retriever.

Chapter 13

"HAVE A GOOD DAY, pumpkin," Reid told Piper as he hugged her the next morning. He and Kaiah had dropped her off at school before they carried the cookies in for the bake sale.

As Kaiah hugged Piper next, he smiled as he remembered how much he'd enjoyed baking cookies yesterday. He couldn't remember the last time he'd laughed so much. And for a moment he'd found himself longing to kiss this woman again. She'd somehow managed not only to become his friend but also to bring his heart back to life. He hadn't felt this alive since—

"Where do we take these cookies?"

Kaiah's question broke through his thoughts. She pointed to the boxes full of lighthouse cookies while Piper scampered down the hallway, disappearing into the sea of students on their way to class.

He picked up the stack of boxes. "I'm assuming we take them to the office."

"Hold on there, Lieutenant," she scolded while reaching for a box. "Let me take a few of these."

He nodded in the direction of the office. "Just get the door, please."

"Yes, Lieutenant." She gave him a salute and grinned as she opened the door, making a sweeping gesture for him to enter.

"Are those for the bake sale?" Misty Rodriguez, one of the PTO members, asked from an office doorway.

Reid set the stack of boxes on the counter. "They sure are." He motioned toward Kaiah. "We made them yesterday—with Piper's help, of course. Kaiah, this is Misty. She's a member of the PTO."

"You have to see our lighthouses." Kaiah opened the box and handed Misty a bag of cookies.

"Oh my goodness." Misty examined the bag. "These are so perfect." She set the box down and disappeared into the office. "Let me show you what we put together last night." She handed Reid a flyer with details about the festival, including the website where volunteers could register.

Kaiah came to stand at his shoulder, and he breathed in the scent of her flowery shampoo. "They're dynamite." She touched the flyer. "We should give these out in town. We could encourage people to sign up for the marathon too."

"Hang on a minute." Misty slipped into the office and returned with a stack of flyers. "You can blanket the town with these. And if you need more, I can print more."

Kaiah took the flyers. "Thank you. Let's head to Main Street."

Kaiah slipped on her pink sunglasses and held up a flyer. "This is fabulous. We need to pass these around."

"I agree. But first, let's check in with the electrician," Reid said while merging onto Main Street. "I'm concerned about the lighthouse. Becca told me Mr. Johnson got a key from one of the historical society members and researched what kind of wiring would need to be done. He's been trying to find someone who can fix the lamp. We have exactly a week now before we'll need to illuminate it, and we want to keep our theme."

Kaiah took in his profile while he sat in the driver's seat beside her, and she couldn't help but notice that he was looking good today—like, *really* good. Once again she imagined what his kiss would've felt like if the principal hadn't interrupted them.

A hot, kind, and caring man wanted to kiss her. A happy thrill skittered in her belly.

He peered over at her. "Why are you staring at me?"

"You look good. I mean, um . . ." *Oh no!* Just like that, her cheeks reddened and felt like they were going to spontaneously combust. "What I meant was, you look like you're well rested." *I don't know how you managed to make it more weird, Ky, but you just succeeded. Great job.*

He flicked on his left blinker and then merged onto the road leading toward the bay side of Coral Cove. After merging, he grinned at her. "And you look like you 'slept well' too."

She swallowed a groan and sank down in the seat. She thought she might drown in embarrassment.

"Hey." He rubbed her shoulder. "All Piper talked about last night and this morning was how much fun she had baking cookies. Thanks again for that."

Kaiah gave him a weak smile. "You're welcome."

"I'm serious. Piper had a great time. That means a lot, Ky."

The warmth in his kind brown eyes made her soul take a leap. "You're welcome. I had fun too."

Reid parked his Suburban in front of Johnson's Electric, a storefront a few blocks from the beach, and then killed the engine. "Let's go see if we're actually going to have a lighthouse brightening the sky next week."

Kaiah followed him to the door, and he held it open for her. A bell rang announcing their entrance, and a young man wearing a shirt with *Rob* sewn above the breast pocket met them at the front desk.

"How can I help you?" Rob asked.

"We're looking for Duke," Reid said. "Is he around?"

"One sec." The young man disappeared through a doorway, and a few moments later Duke appeared.

"Reid, right?" Duke asked, and Reid nodded. Then he pointed at Kaiah. "And you're the journalist."

"Kaiah Ross." She shook his hand. "We wanted to check on the lighthouse."

Reid relaxed against the counter. "My sister said you got a key from Jimmy Barnes so you could check out the wiring in the lighthouse. Have you found a contractor who could help you fix the wiring issues?"

Duke's grim expression sent worry threading through Kaiah. "Not yet. I've been calling around, and I've done a bunch of research, but no luck so far."

"Is there anything we can do to help?" Kaiah offered.

"Not unless you know some electricians," he said, but both Kaiah and Reid shook their heads. "I'm not giving up yet. I have some calls in to the union, and I'm also reaching out to some old friends on the West Coast. I'll let you know when I find something out."

Reid stood up straight. "We want to kick off the festival with a lighting ceremony, so we only have a week to get it done."

"I know." Duke nodded. "I'll do my best."

"Thank you," Kaiah said. "We appreciate your help."

Reid shook his hand, and Duke promised to keep in touch.

They were silent while Reid drove down the road. The only sound came from the rumble of the SUV's engine and a country song playing through the speakers. Reid's stiff posture and the crease in his brow illustrated his worry.

"I think it's going to be fine," Kaiah told him. "Duke has contacts, and I'm sure there's someone out there who will want to help us."

Reid sighed. "I know." He moved his fingers over the steering wheel. "But if the lighthouse isn't lit up . . ."

"It's going to work out, Reid," she said. "Have faith."

He smiled at her. "You're right. We'll concentrate on talking to the merchants for now. Let's swing by the graphic designer and talk to them about donating banners too."

Reid drove to the oceanfront, and after he found a parking spot, they went into Stuart's Signs and Print Shop, where the owners, Daphne and Dan Stuart, agreed to donate banners for the event. They gave them flyers for inspiration and stopped by Baudo's Trattoria to leave a few flyers and discuss featuring the lighthouse-shaped calzones at the Light Snack food event.

They walked outside, and Kaiah breathed in the fresh scent of the ocean while the sun kissed her cheeks.

She grabbed Reid's hand and tugged. "Let's go to the boardwalk."

He allowed her to tow him down the sidewalk, past a group of young adults who left the scent of sunscreen in their wake. When they reached the boardwalk, Kaiah took in the row of storefronts, along with the clusters of people moving in and out their doors. Out on the beach, she found knots of people sunbathing and playing in the sand.

She faced Reid and said, "Last one in is a rotten egg!" Then she jogged down the steps and stopped when she realized he wasn't chasing her. She tented her hands over her eyes and studied him standing on the boardwalk. "Are you coming?"

"Where are you going?" he asked with a chuckle.

She pointed toward the waves. "To dip my toes in the water."

"It's April. The water's still cold."

"But we're at the beach, Lieutenant Turner!" She ran down to the water, dropped her sandals on the sand, and stood by the waves lapping on the shore.

Reid came up behind her and pulled off his shoes. "It's going to be cold," he declared. "I'm warning you."

"I know." She walked out to where the water reached her ankles, and she closed her eyes, enjoying the cool water rushing past her toes and up to her ankles. When she opened her eyes, she found Reid watching her with an intensity that sent heat rushing through her veins. She held her hand out to him. "Humor me, Reid."

He took her hand, and they stood in the waves together. "It *is* cold," he grumbled. "I told you it would be."

"Don't be such a sourpuss," she deadpanned, and he laughed. "You must have loved every moment growing up at the beach." She looked out toward where the waves broke.

"Honestly, I don't think I really appreciated it until after high school. I love it now. I would hate waking up someplace where I didn't have the option to come out here and do this. Even when the water's freezing."

"I can understand that." She watched a few couples plodding past in the sand.

"Would you ever consider living in a small town like this?"

His question caught her off guard, and her gaze collided with his. "I-I don't know. Maybe," she said.

He nodded.

Kaiah took in the scene around her. "Say, what if we had a beach cleanup day during the festival? We could combine it with picnics at the beach."

"You're on a roll, you know that?" He snapped his fingers on his free hand. "We once made kites in Boy Scouts, and it was fun. Instead of just having an arts and crafts booth, we could also hold a whole arts and crafts *day*. Kids could make kites and then have a kite-flying contest. I bet we could ask the owner of Crafty Creations to sponsor it."

"I love it!" Kaiah said.

"Let's go talk to some more business owners," he said. "We can get them to help out."

Kaiah held his hand while they traveled back toward their parking spot, and her heart felt light. She was certain the festival was going to come together, and she hoped Reid believed it too.

~

"You two have been busy," Becca said later that evening as she examined the list of store owners Reid and Kaiah had visited and convinced to participate in the festival.

They were gathered around Reid's kitchen table, and they had just finished eating spaghetti and meatballs while the girls jogged up and down the hallway, singing songs and playing with Ariel, who trotted along with them.

"That's true," Reid told his twin. "We have banners in the works, and Trisha Witherspoon, who owns Crafty Creations, is sponsoring the kite-making day." He touched Kaiah's arm, and she smiled at him while he rattled off the other merchants they visited.

"What about the lighthouse?" Cash asked.

Kaiah's smile wobbled.

"It's not looking good," Reid said. "Mr. Johnson is reaching out to other electricians, but so far no one has the right equipment. That means we may not have a lit-up lighthouse at the opening ceremony."

"Hey, Daddy!" Piper called from the doorway. "Why don't you put Christmas lights on the lighthouse?"

Reid scanned the kitchen table, and the three adults surrounding him appeared to be just as stunned as he was. After a few moments, they all grinned at one another.

"It's the obvious solution." Cash chuckled. "Why didn't we think of that?"

"Because our intelligent niece did it for us," Becca said.

"She sure did," Kaiah agreed.

Reid pointed toward the doorway. "And she got her brilliance from Brynn." He made a note on his list. "I'll call Duke and see what he thinks."

"You don't need to call him," Cash said. "We could do it."

Reid's eyebrows careened upward while he studied his brother-in-law. "What do you mean?"

"Let's get the town's Christmas decorations. We could do it with one of the ladder trucks." Cash gestured around the kitchen. "I mean, we put up the other decorations in town, so what's the difference?"

Reid grinned. "And since you're the fire chief, I'll make sure everyone knows that *you* condoned this."

Cash shrugged. "I'll talk to the mayor. No big deal."

They spent the next couple of hours discussing other items on the festival's punch list. After a while, Piper came to sit on Reid's lap while Astrid curled up on Cash.

"I guess we'd better get this one home." Cash nodded toward a sleepy Astrid in his arms.

Reid glanced at Kaiah and saw a soft expression painted on her face. For a moment he wondered if she could ever imagine having a family like this one. With him.

The idea sent a whirlwind of emotions through him.

Cash stood, and Astrid shifted before snuggling deeper into his shoulder. He patted his daughter's back and whispered something to her before kissing her head.

"Do you want Piper to stay over tonight since you're working in the morning?" Becca asked.

"No," Piper whined. "I want to stay with Kaiah tomorrow."

Reid turned to Kaiah, and a sheepish expression spread over her features. "I understand if you'd rather Piper spend tomorrow with Becca."

"No," Piper hissed before motioning for Kaiah to lean down. "I want to play with Kaiah tomorrow. Please, Daddy."

Reid lifted his eyebrows while Kaiah seemed to watch him, awaiting his approval.

"It's okay with me," Reid said. "I'll set up the spare room for you. That way you don't have to wake up too early to come over before my shift starts at seven."

Kaiah beamed. "Great."

Becca stood and touched Kaiah's shoulder. "If you need me, I'll be around tomorrow. Feel free to text me." Then she hugged Piper. "Good night, sweetie."

After Becca, Cash, and Astrid were gone, Reid got Piper into a soapy bubble bath.

Kaiah stood in the bathroom doorway. "I'll go pack some things for our day tomorrow."

"Okay," he told her.

"I'll see you in the morning, Piper, okay?" Kaiah said.

"Good night, Miss Kaiah," Piper sang.

Kaiah blew her a kiss and then lingered in the doorway for a moment before she disappeared. Her soft footsteps sounded in the hallway before the front door opened and then clicked shut.

Since Piper couldn't stop yawning throughout her bath, Reid got her dressed in her pajamas and tucked in bed.

"Be good for Miss Kaiah tomorrow," he told her after reading her a story.

"I will, Daddy." Piper touched his cheek. "Thank you for letting her stay with me."

"You're welcome." He kissed her cheek. "Good night, pumpkin." He scratched Ariel's chin. "And good night, Ariel."

He quickly put fresh sheets on the double bed in the spare room. He couldn't believe he hadn't had a guest in this room since his in-laws had come up from Florida to see Piper two years ago. It boggled his mind that they didn't want to see their granddaughter more often, but that was their choice. When they decided to move shortly after Brynn's death, he'd made it clear they were always welcome.

After the bed was made, he walked out into the hallway and heard a soft knock at the front door. He yanked it open and found Kaiah standing on the porch holding a large tote bag. "You don't have to knock."

"I didn't want to impose."

"I think we already established that you're not imposing." He waved her in. "Get on in here." He pulled a set of keys down from the hook by the door. "These are yours."

She studied the key ring and then blinked up at him. "I don't understand."

"There's a sedan in the garage. You're welcome to use it if you'd like. It should have a full tank."

She studied him. "Thanks, Reid."

"No, thank *you* for wanting to spend time with my daughter."

"Are there any rules?"

He rubbed his chin and chuckled. "If I had any, Piper would enforce them. She's good that way." He pointed down the hallway. "The spare room is ready. I even put new sheets on the bed. Make yourself at home."

"Thanks."

As he watched her walk down the hallway, he wondered what it would be like if Kaiah stayed in Coral Cove.

Even better, what would it be like to have her by his side forever?

Chapter 14

KAIAH ROLLED OVER AND stretched, rubbing her eyes as she took in the room. A three-drawer wood dresser with a mirror filled the wall across from her while four paintings of the same beach scene, representing each of the seasons, adorned the opposite wall. A light-colored desk with a chair sat on the third wall.

For a moment she didn't know where she was, but then it all came back to her in a rush—Reid setting up the spare room for her, watching a movie with him on the sofa, talking until they were both ready for bed.

A lazy smile filled her face as she remembered his muscled frame sitting beside her smaller one. They'd laughed through *Miss Congeniality* (which he watched without complaint!), and when the movie was over, they swapped stories about their childhoods. Everything seemed so simple with Reid. Easy. They never ran out of words. She never felt uncomfortable with him. It was the total opposite of what she'd experienced with Hayes.

Kaiah groaned. The *last* thing she wanted was to let Hayes live in her head rent-free. She rolled to her side before she reached for her phone on the nightstand. It was eight fifteen. Time to get up and make breakfast before Piper came running out.

She pulled on a pair of jeans and a T-shirt, then scooped her hair up in a ponytail before heading out to the kitchen. By the time Piper came scampering out in her mermaid-theme pajamas, the table was set with two plates of scrambled eggs, toast, and bacon.

"Bacon!" Piper exclaimed. "That's my favorite!"

Kaiah sat down beside her, and they dug in. "So what do you want to do today, Miss Piper?"

"Can we play outside for a while?"

The young woman smiled. "Sounds like a plan."

After breakfast, Kaiah took Piper outside, where she played on her elaborate wooden swing set. Kaiah pushed the six-year-old on the swing until, after a few minutes, Piper grew bored and decided to play in her sandbox.

Kaiah sat on the deck with a glass of sweet tea and watched the girl lift a small shovel filled with sand and slowly let the grains drift down like a waterfall. Truthfully it was mesmerizing. Piper sang to herself as she lifted the sand in clumps with her hands and patted them together, smoothing the formation to make an igloo. Kaiah lost herself in the moment, watching the girl create in the sand. Her revery was broken when her phone dinged with a text. Instantly her heart rate bumped up. Was it Reid? She glanced down at the screen, and her face clouded with a glower.

Hayes: Hey. We should talk.

Kaiah's stomach twisted. She hadn't expected to hear from him again. In fact, she hoped she wouldn't. She squeezed the bridge of her nose and debated what to do. Part of her wanted to delete his text and block him. And wouldn't that feel good? It was something she'd thought about a hundred times since their breakup.

But the same dilemma tripped her up every single time.

What if George was sick? Or what if Hayes wanted to bring George to her?

If George needed her, then she'd jump at the chance to have him back. So, no. She couldn't block Hayes. Not as long as she knew George was alive.

She peered across the yard to where Piper was drawing ice blocks on her sand igloo. She'd be okay if Kaiah was distracted for a minute or two. Kaiah poised her thumbs over her phone and responded.

Kaiah: Is George okay?

A few moments passed without a response, and Kaiah held her breath. Finally, the dancing dots appeared on the screen.

Hayes: He's fine.

She blew out a breath. *Thank goodness.*

Kaiah: Do you need a freelancer to help with a story?

Hayes: No. Although I've been reading your Hidden Gems series. Really good stuff.

She rolled her eyes. That was all she needed to know. If her dog was fine and Hayes didn't have any business to discuss, then she was done with him.

Kaiah: Then there's nothing for us to talk about.

Hayes: Kaiah, I need to explain to you why I left.

Her head swam with dizziness. Had she stopped breathing too? Her heart was thundering in her chest when she forced herself to look back down at the screen.

Hayes: I never would've let you go if I hadn't gotten that job. You have to believe me. I'm still trying to convince Global Media they need another travel reporter. Once I do, you can move out here and we can be together again. We can be a family with George. Please, Kaiah. You have to understand why I left. I took this job for us—for you. I still love you.

Kaiah rolled her eyes before she locked her phone. Hayes was still the narcissist he always was, and that would never change. She was better off without him.

"Miss Kaiah." Piper trotted over to the deck, and Kaiah was happy for the distraction. "Can we watch *The Little Mermaid*?"

"You got it, sweetie."

Later that evening, Reid walked out behind the fire station where a couple of his fellow firefighters were playing basketball. He sat on the curb to relax for a minute and watch the game. They'd had a calm day with only a couple of nonurgent medical calls.

He'd done his best to focus on work, but he also kept wondering how Piper's day was going with Kaiah. He especially couldn't stop thinking about his not-a-date-but-kind-of-a-date with Kaiah the previous evening. He craved more quiet nights with her but knew those nights were numbered. He'd just have to enjoy every minute he could manage to steal away with her.

"Lieutenant," Cash called from the bay.

He joined Cash by the trucks. "Did you need me, Chief?"

"Have you talked to Piper and Kaiah today?"

"Yeah," Reid said. "I checked on them earlier. They've been playing outside for a lot of the day. Sounds like they're having fun."

Cash nodded slowly. "It seems like you and Piper have gotten close to Kaiah."

Reid sat down on a stool. *Here we go.* "We have. And Becks has too."

"She's mentioned that to me." Cash paused for a moment. "Honestly, bro? I'm just gonna come out and say it. Kaiah seems great for you and for Piper."

Reid nodded. "I agree. But there's one problem: She's not staying in Coral Cove. Once the festival is over and she finishes her articles about Coral Cove, she'll be long gone."

Cash didn't look convinced. "I don't know about that."

Reid arched an eyebrow. "What do you mean?"

"I just have a feeling that you and Kaiah might remain friends after all of this is over. If not more than friends." Cash looked right into his eyes. "I'm sure you're lonely. And Piper could sure use a mom."

Reid let his brother-in-law's comment settle over him. He couldn't ignore the small feeling—was it hope?—that began sprouting in his heart. He cared deeply for Kaiah, and more than ever he felt compelled to ask her to stay. Was that a huge step? Absolutely. Was it too much too soon? Maybe. But seemingly overnight, his heart had been overtaken by this smart, beautiful, compassionate woman. He knew enough by now that if he wanted a shot with Kaiah, he had to take it, even if the circumstances weren't what he'd choose.

But his thoughts were cut off as a long, shrill tone screamed through the loudspeakers. At the same time the fluorescent lights above them automatically flipped on and off.

"All available units respond to accident with injuries at Fifth Street and Ocean Boulevard," the bodiless voice over the radio blared. "Repeat. All available units respond to accident with injuries at Fifth Street and Ocean Boulevard."

A switch flipped in Reid's brain. Gone were any thoughts of emotion, replaced with a cool head and the muscle memory of emergency response. Adrenaline pumped through his veins as he and his team pulled on their turnout gear and piled into the fire truck. Soon they were on their way with the siren wailing and the diesel engine roaring down the road.

When they reached the scene of the accident, the fire truck parked in the center of the street. Reid and his team jumped out of the truck, and when his eyes focused on the scene of the accident, he froze.

A blue Hyundai sedan was lying on its side, a door crunched in, the hood smoldering. And a large pickup truck with its front smashed in sat on the side of the road.

Immediately Reid was yanked four years back in time when he'd responded to a similar accident. Only the sedan wasn't a Hyundai. It was a Toyota. And the driver hadn't survived.

Brynn wasn't supposed to be there. Reid should've picked up Piper that day. It was his turn, but he backed out at the last minute for a work meeting that he could've skipped.

No, that he *should've* skipped. If he had, Brynn would be alive today. She'd be here to celebrate her birthday tomorrow.

Bile burned his throat. He wanted to turn and run, but his feet were cemented in place. He was stuck there—forced to face the deadly mistake he'd made that had changed his and Piper's life forever.

Cash and the rest of his team were already checking on the occupants in the vehicles. Reid pushed his hands down his face. A hot sweat broke out on the back of his neck, and as memories of that day scrolled through his mind, he feared he was going to be sick. He could smell the gasoline. He could see the smashed metal.

And he could see . . . Brynn.

She could've been sleeping. Her expression seemed so serene, so at peace.

Stop it! Stop it!

Sirens wailed in the distance and moved closer, slicing through his painful thoughts as he struggled to breathe. A couple of police cruisers pulled up to the scene, and the officers jumped out and quickly began to direct traffic.

"Lieutenant Turner!"

Reid spun to where Cash waved at him. "We need you over here."

Reid forced himself to swallow the bile in his throat and take a deep breath. "Yes, Chief."

He managed to propel himself forward, and stuffing down his agonizing memories, he focused on the passengers in the sedan, who were banged up but alert. He spent the next two hours tending to the victims, removing them from the vehicles and loading them into the ambulances.

Once the patients were gone, the team focused on cleaning up the scene.

Every muscle in Reid's body was sore by the time they returned to the firehouse. After a debrief session with his captain and his chief, Reid started toward the showers. He wanted just to stand under the hot water and wash the painful memories and exhaustion down the drain.

"Lieutenant Turner," Cash called after him.

Reid froze. He knew what was coming. Cash had witnessed his breakdown, and a lecture was certain to follow. He took a cleansing breath and then returned to face his brother-in-law, who was also his boss's boss. "Yes, Chief?"

"Could you give us a minute please, Chris?" Cash asked Captain Ward.

Captain Ward stood. "Of course." He nodded at Reid on his way out the door.

"Come into my office and close the door," Cash told Reid.

Reid did as he was instructed and sat across from Cash at his desk. "You want to discuss how I froze at the accident site earlier."

Cash steepled his hands. "You were remembering Brynn's accident."

Reid let out a heavy sigh. "I know I messed up today." He could hear the strain in his voice. "I can assure you it won't happen again."

"Reid, I didn't call you in here to reprimand you. I wanted to offer to listen."

The younger man shook his head and tried to ignore how his throat thickened. "I'm fine, Chief. Really. I just had a moment."

Cash seemed to study him.

"I'm telling the truth, man. I'm fine. I just had to regroup. I mean it when I say it won't happen again."

"All right." Cash paused and studied him. "If you needed to talk, would you tell me?"

Reid brushed his hand over his throat. "Yes. I would." He swallowed. "I haven't had a . . . a moment in a long time. I saw that sedan knocked over with a truck sitting beside it, and I think it all hit me at once. The memory of the accident. And that tomorrow is Brynn's birthday." He held up his hands. "But I promise this was an isolated incident. I won't let my emotions interfere with my performance again, Chief. You have my word."

"Reid, I'm talking to you as your brother-in-law and friend, not as your chief." Cash rested his hand on the wooden desk. "Sometimes you're going to have a moment. You're human. It happens. If you need to talk, I'm here. Becca is always available too."

Reid nodded as his eyes started to sting. He'd learned as a rookie to compartmentalize his emotions.

But the accident. And Brynn's birthday. It all just felt so overwhelming.

Cash tilted back in the chair. "Listen, it's okay to talk to someone. If you don't want to talk to me or your sister, I get it. Please know you can always reach out to one of the staff counselors. They're here to help you. You are never alone."

"Yes, sir." Reid nodded.

Cash gave him a small smile. "Dismissed."

As Reid headed out of the office, he squared his shoulders. He would get his emotions under control. He had to. His job and his sanity depended on it.

Chapter 15

REID UNLOCKED THE FRONT door and stepped inside his house. The soft patter of feet sounded before Ariel appeared in the foyer. She uttered a quiet meow before rubbing up against the corner of the wall.

"Mornin', Princess Ariel," he whispered. "Are you the only one awake?"

She meowed again and then skedaddled toward the kitchen.

He left his large duffel on the floor before joining the cat in the kitchen. Ariel walked circles at his feet, singing her usual morning chorus of meows while he filled her bowl with fishy canned food. Once she was settled with breakfast, he padded down the hallway and stopped at Piper's door, which had been cracked open enough for Ariel to escape.

Reid pushed on the door and leaned his shoulder on the doorframe. Piper was snuggled on her stomach, holding her favorite mermaid doll in her arms while her soft snores punctuated the hum of the air conditioner.

He bit back a yawn and glanced toward his bedroom across the hall. He considered crawling into bed and trying to get some sleep before Piper woke up, but he'd already struggled through a sleepless night at the station. Surely he wouldn't get any sleep at home either. For years he'd managed to bury the memories and guilt that haunted him after Brynn's death, but the accident yesterday had unlocked it all. He'd worked so hard to move forward, to push through life with his sole focus on being the best father he could be, but his resolve had started to crack yesterday. And that terrified him. He needed to find a way to cram the ugliness back down, deep in his soul, back into the locked box. He had to ignore the pang that was radiating through him—especially today, on Brynn's birthday. It was always one of the toughest days of the year, along with the anniversary of Brynn's accident and Mother's Day. He missed his best friend.

Pushing off the doorframe, he turned to leave, but something on his daughter's dresser caught his eye. He walked softly across the room and found a card made out of construction paper. In Piper's adorably messy six-year-old handwriting, "Mommy" was scrawled, and the paper was decorated with flowers, rainbows, and mermaids. His heart constricted as he pictured her working hard on it.

Opening the card, he found a stick figure drawing of what looked like a woman with long, light brown hair standing by a little girl with dark brown pigtails and a multicolored cat. Below it, Piper had written:

Mommy,

Hapy brthday! I luv u sooooo much. I mis u. Ariel dos to.

Luv,
Piper and Ariel

The backs of his eyes began to burn, and his throat closed around the lump forming inside it. His daughter would always miss her mother. And he would never forgive himself for what happened to her.

Taking a deep breath, he gingerly laid the card back on her dresser before walking out to the hallway. His eyes focused on the closed guest room door, and he imagined Kaiah asleep in the double bed. He'd hoped she would've been up when he arrived home, but he couldn't blame her for sleeping past seven. He just looked forward to seeing her.

In fact, part of him wanted to knock on the door, wake her up, and tell her about his shift, including his emotional breakdown. If he felt comfortable talking to anyone, it was definitely her.

But he didn't want to overwhelm Kaiah. It wasn't fair of him to take his trauma and dump it at her doorstep. She didn't ask for that.

But he couldn't help it. He was tired of having no one to trust with his heart. In fact, his heart was screaming for him to dive in headfirst and see where this friendship could lead. But at the same time, he had Piper's feelings to consider. If he dove in headfirst and things didn't work out, Piper's heart would be broken for sure, and he'd already done enough damage to Piper when she lost her mom.

Shaking his head, Reid retrieved his duffel and headed into his bedroom. He retreated into his bathroom and took a long hot shower before pulling on a pair of athletic shorts and a plain gray T-shirt. Then he returned to the kitchen and began to cook, losing himself in the task of making French toast.

When he heard footsteps behind him, he craned his neck to where Kaiah stood in the doorway, her purse and bag thrown over her shoulder. Her wavy blonde hair was swept up into a thick ponytail with wisps falling around her face, and her bright blue eyes sparkled in the morning sunlight. He couldn't take his eyes off her.

"Well, good morning," he said. "How'd you sleep?"

"Great. Thanks." She pushed an errant lock of hair behind her ear. "How was your shift?"

"Fine," he said, but he averted his eyes, not wanting to pour his heart out to her—not now. Instead, he pointed to a platter of French toast. "Hope you're hungry."

She waved off the offer. "Oh no, none for me. I need to get started on my next article. I'll see you and Piper tomorrow." She shouldered her tote bag and backed out of the doorway.

"Kaiah," he called, his voice sounding more urgent than he'd intended. "Wait. Please."

She whirled around, her expression full of curiosity.

"I just— Stay for breakfast. You can work on your article later."

She raised an eyebrow and set her bags down in the foyer. "Okay." When her eyes focused on him, he could feel concern coming off her in waves. "Is everything all right, Reid?"

He shrugged, hoping he looked casual. "Yeah." He pointed to the coffeepot. "Would you mind pouring us a couple of cups?"

"Sure," she said, but worry flashed across her face.

Piper scampered into the kitchen, and they all sat down to eat. After they ate breakfast and cleaned up the kitchen, Kaiah hefted her bags onto her shoulder. "That was delicious. Seriously, though, *now* I need to get started on my article. I'll see you tomorrow."

"Wait, Miss Kaiah," Piper said. "You should come with us to go see Mommy."

Reid's lips pressed into a flat line. The last thing he wanted to do today was take Kaiah to the cemetery. That kind of macabre field trip might push her out of his life faster than she'd planned.

Against his better judgment, he chose to ignore Piper and instead force his lips into a thin smile. "I can't wait to read your article."

"Daddy?" Piper asked, and when he didn't respond, she shook his arm. "Daddy! I want Miss Kaiah to meet Mommy. Can she come with us? Please?"

Reid's spine stiffened. Closing his eyes, he brushed his hand over his mouth as he worked to form a response. A hand on his bicep startled him.

Kaiah had moved to his side, and her blue eyes were soft with concern. "Are you okay, Reid?"

He tucked his stress away with a bit of a smile. "I'm fine," he fibbed. "She wants to take you to the cemetery," he muttered. "It's Brynn's birthday."

Kaiah blinked. "Oh. That's why she said something about making her mommy a birthday card. She showed it to me, but I didn't make the connection."

"You don't have to . . ."

She hesitated, and his stomach knotted. The last thing he wanted to do was make her feel uncomfortable.

"I don't want to interfere," she offered. "You two go, and I'll show you my article when I finish it."

"But I want you to come with us, Miss Kaiah," Piper said.

Reid couldn't stand the whine in his daughter's voice. "No, Piper," he said, gruffer than he meant to, and his daughter winced at his tone. "Miss Kaiah needs to work on her article about the festival."

"Can't you work on it later?" Piper offered.

The small, patient smile on Kaiah's face nearly stopped Reid's heart. She looked up at him. "Are you okay with me going with you? I feel like I'm stepping on your private family time."

"Listen, I know this isn't exactly a normal outing. But you could never intrude, Kaiah. Really." Their gazes held, and he felt something warm and palpable pass between them. "You're more than welcome to join us. But if it feels too weird, I completely understand."

"Are you sure?"

He nodded at her.

Kaiah closed the distance between her and Piper and then bent down to her level. "If you want me to go, then I'll go."

Piper clapped. "Yay!"

After stopping at the grocery store for a bouquet of spring flowers, Reid drove to Coral Cove Memorial Gardens. Moments with Brynn washed over him as he steered through the quiet cemetery. But his mind settled on the worst one. He remembered the day they had laid his beautiful young wife to rest and the service their pastor had held at her graveside. He couldn't recall a word Pastor Deborah had spoken, but he did remember his twin's tight grip as she held his hand and sobbed.

Reid parked by the row that led to Brynn's grave, and he surveyed the headstones. Flowers, balloons, and toys signaled that other folks had recently visited their loved ones, and more regret pummeled him. He should make an effort to visit Brynn's grave more often instead of only on Mother's Day and her birthday.

Piper scrambled out of the back seat. "Let's go, Miss Kaiah! You can meet my mommy."

Reid glanced over at Kaiah beside him. "You don't have to do this."

"It's okay." Kaiah lightly placed her hand on his before pushing her door open just as Piper appeared. His daughter held the birthday card she'd made in one hand, and she grabbed Kaiah's hand with the other. The young woman retrieved the bouquet of flowers he'd bought at the grocery store. Something in her eyes told him that she truly wanted to be here, and the gesture touched him deep in his soul.

"C'mon, Miss Kaiah." Piper yanked Kaiah toward the grave.

Reid walked slowly behind them. He breathed in the fresh April air and the scent of freshly cut grass mixed with blooming roses as he scanned the nearby headstones. Piper and Kaiah reached Brynn's grave, and Kaiah helped Piper unwrap the flowers before they arranged them in the permanent vase in front of Brynn's headstone. Then they laid the homemade card next to the flowers.

His eyes began to sting as he took in the scene. Kaiah crouched down beside his daughter and nodded with interest while Piper seemed to be in the middle of another elaborate story. They looked like they belonged together. Like his shattered family . . . could be mended after all. The thought sent the air whooshing out of his lungs.

When he joined them, concern filled Kaiah's face as she studied his, and she reached for him. He hesitated for a moment before allowing her to thread her fingers with his.

"Oh look!" Piper exclaimed. "A butterfly!" Then she took off, skipping while she followed the butterfly to the next row of headstones.

Kaiah tilted her head and gave Reid's hand a gentle squeeze while she studied him. "I know you keep saying everything is all right, but I could tell the moment I saw you in the kitchen this morning that something was wrong."

For some reason, he couldn't lie to her. He was tired of keeping everything locked up so tightly inside. He was ready to let it all out. But he couldn't—he just couldn't. She was leaving soon, and he didn't need to keep trying to hitch her to a relationship that was destined to stay a dream.

He took a shuddering breath and shook his head. "You're right. Something is definitely wrong."

She pulled him toward a bench across from the headstone. Then she sat down and brushed her hand over the spot beside her. "Sit and talk to me, Reid."

He did as he was told while keeping his eyes focused on the headstone and the words inscribed on it: *Brynn Elizabeth Hawkins Turner*, along with the date she was born and the date that changed everything.

Reid and Kaiah sat silently for several moments while she held his hand. Piper continued to dance around while singing to herself several yards away.

Finally, Reid faced Kaiah. The gentle warmth of her skin caressing his hand whispered that she might be a soft place to land. He longed to give in to that warmth, to let it envelop his whole being. So he did. "Yesterday we were called to a scene of an accident, and it brought it all back to me," he began, his voice sounding hoarse. "It was like I was reliving Brynn's death over again."

Kaiah shifted toward him and rested her free hand on their entwined fingers. Her expression was open, ready to listen.

"The car . . ." He paused and tried to swallow against his thickening throat. "The car was on its side, and that was what happened the day Brynn died."

"Oh, Reid," she whispered.

"When I saw it, I froze." He studied their hands. "I couldn't move. I've been a firefighter for almost fifteen years, and I've never had that happen before. I learned in training to compartmentalize, to leave my emotions behind when we go on calls. But yesterday I couldn't do it. When I saw the car on its side, everything came rushing back."

She nodded, encouraging him to continue.

"The day she died, it was my turn to pick up Piper at day care. We took turns depending on when I was working. I was off that day, and she had planned to stay late at school to finish up some projects. But I was selfish." His tone was throaty, hoarse. "I wanted to go in for a meeting at the fire station because I was trying to earn brownie points with my captain. I was so determined to impress him and get promoted as soon as possible. It was all I cared about. I had taken Piper to day care since my mom couldn't keep her, and I told Brynn to pick her up. I didn't even ask. I *told* her that I was going. I was arrogant and thoughtless. It was like I had something to prove, which was so ridiculous."

He took a shaky breath. "Brynn was furious, and we argued a bit. She was angry with me, and she had every right to be. I ruined her plans." He shook his head, disgusted with himself. "I went to the meeting, and while I was there, we got a call about an accident a few blocks from Piper's day care. And I had this feeling, this sick, horrible feeling deep in my gut. It was like I knew."

Kaiah shifted closer to him. She rested her shoulder against his side, and the sweet gesture gave him the strength to keep talking.

"When we got there," he whispered as the vision filled his mind, "I saw her car, and I fell to my knees, and . . ." His words sounded raspy, and his eyes were wet. "It was all my fault. If I had gone to pick up Piper, my wife wouldn't have been there when that dump truck swerved into head-on traffic. Then my daughter would still have her mother. Then maybe I would've been the one—"

"Shhh. Don't say it." Kaiah interrupted him, cupping her hands to his cheeks. Her blue eyes glistened with tears. "Don't, Reid," she told him softly. "Don't blame yourself. It's not your fault that driver came across the centerline. And don't you *ever* say that you deserve to be the one in the ground. It's not true. The person to blame is the one who hit your wife's car."

He sniffed, and she wiped his tears. The feeling of her fingers brushing across his face was almost too much for him. He longed to take her in his arms and hold her close.

"You're such a good dad," she continued. "Piper is blessed to have a dad like you, and it's not your fault Brynn is gone. Stop torturing and blaming yourself. Just forgive yourself. You're allowed."

He blew out a shaky puff of air, and she traced her fingers down his cheeks. At that moment, he felt closer to her than to anyone else. He sniffed and studied her beautiful face.

"What are you thinking right now?" she asked.

"How is it that I've only known you eight days, but I feel like I've known you my entire life?"

"I was just wondering the same thing," she told him softly.

He cupped her cheek with his hand, and he stared down at her lips. Once again, he longed to kiss her, and he yearned to know if she would kiss him back. He dipped his chin, and he was certain he heard her breath hitch.

"Daddy!"

Reid froze, and his eyes snapped over to Piper as she skipped toward him. "See that grave over there?" She pointed out in the distance. "It has Elizabeth on it, just like Mommy's."

"Oh wow." Reid wiped his eyes and smiled. He hoped his daughter didn't notice the tremble in his voice. "No kidding."

Out of the corner of his eye, he was almost certain Kaiah was working to catch her breath.

"Why don't we go pick up something for lunch?" Reid offered.

"Pizza!" Piper announced while racing toward the car.

Reid held his hand out to Kaiah. "Care for more pizza?"

"Why not?" Kaiah took his hand, allowing him to lift her to her feet.

~

Later that evening, Kaiah walked down the hallway from Piper's bedroom toward the den. She'd read the girl a few bedtime stories and tucked her into bed. She stopped in the doorway and found Reid watching the evening news.

It had been quite a day for the three of them. Kaiah couldn't imagine the stew of feelings that must have been bubbling up in Reid earlier that day. Grief. Guilt. Anger. He'd opened his heart to her at the cemetery, and even now her chest squeezed as she remembered the raw emotions that clouded his eyes.

But she'd also found something else in his gaze.

Longing. For her. She saw it in his eyes as he leaned in to kiss her—at least she was pretty sure he was going to. How many times would she have to wait for his kiss, to feel his mouth claim hers?

He glanced over at her and muted the television. "How's Piper? I appreciate you doing bedtime with her. I know she was pretty insistent."

"That's okay, I was happy to do it. She's fine. We just read a few bedtime stories. Who knew there were so many kids' books about mermaids?" She read the clock on the wall. "Oh, wow, it's after eight. I need to work on my story."

"Go get 'em, tiger. Thanks for spending the day with us. You sure you don't mind staying with Piper again tonight?"

"Of course not." She jammed her thumb toward the doorway. "I need to get my bags, and then I'll shower and repack before I come back down." She jogged to the guest room, retrieved her bags, then returned to the den.

When her phone chimed with a text, she glanced around before spotting it on the coffee table in front of Reid. His brow puckered as he glanced at the screen.

Hmm, that's weird.

When Kaiah made her way to the phone, she found a text from Kam on the display, and her stomach dropped.

Kam: Soooooo how are things with Mr. TDH?

Kaiah gritted her teeth as her cheeks burned. *Really, Kam?* She peeked over at Reid.

"You okay?" he asked.

"Uh-huh." She stood and smoothed her hands down her jeans. "I'm going to run up to the apartment. I'll be back soon."

"Hold on."

She froze in place, then turned to face him. His handsome, chiseled face was looking at her with something that looked like confusion or possibly concern. Her hands began to shake.

"Kaiah," he began, "who . . . is Mr. TDH?"

Oh no, no, no. She wished she could just melt into a puddle right there.

Reid tucked his hands into his pockets, appearing sheepish. "I'm sorry, I shouldn't have read your text. It's none of my business, but it was on the screen and—"

"You!" she blurted.

He paused, and then his brow puckered. "What?"

"Reid, it's *you*." She pointed a trembling finger at him.

He moved his hand over the stubble on his neck. "Sorry, but I don't—"

"Mr. TDH is short for 'Mr. Tall, Dark, and Handsome.' That's how my sister and I talk about you in texts," she said, her voice sounding thin and reedy while he studied her. "I started calling you that when I first saw you in the coffee shop. I thought you were, well, *hot*. And, um, I didn't know your name . . ." Her words trailed off while her embarrassment flared. "And well . . . it sorta stuck."

Reid's mouth formed a perfectly circular O. His jaw ticked, but no words came out.

Certain her face would burst into flames, Kaiah ran out his front door.

~

The front door slammed shut, and Reid stared at the spot where Kaiah made her mad dash. A mixture of shock and something he couldn't quite identify—pride? flattery?—rolled through him while he tried to process the last two minutes.

Kaiah and her sister referred her him as Mr. Tall, Dark, and Handsome.

Apparently she was just as attracted to him as he was to her. And when she admitted it, she seemed mortified, while he couldn't have been more pleased.

Kaiah was beautiful, smart, thoughtful, compassionate, and successful. And she was attracted to *him*. Only hours ago he'd opened up to her, showing her the demons he'd been fighting for the past few years. She'd responded by consoling him, holding his hands and wiping his tears. Her kindness was more than he could've asked for.

There was no denying it, not anymore.

He was falling for her. And he longed to ask her to stay.

Plus, she'd looked absolutely adorable with her cheeks rosy from embarrassment.

It was time he told her how he felt.

Chapter 16

MONDAY MORNING, KAIAH WAVED as Piper and Astrid climbed out of Becca's SUV and scrambled up the sidewalk toward the school's front door.

While Becca navigated out of the school parking lot, the events of the night before washed over Kaiah, the familiar embarrassment creeping back into her belly. She was grateful she'd somehow made it through the evening without another horrifying incident. She had (strategically!) taken her time showering and packing another round of clothes before she returned to Reid's house. When she finally got there, he was getting ready for bed. They briefly discussed his Monday schedule, she said good night, and that was that. Thankfully, Reid hadn't mentioned Kam's text again.

But still, Kaiah couldn't sleep. She stayed up half the night working on another festival article and replaying the Mr. TDH conversation on a loop in her head. She was going to give Kam a piece of her mind when she spoke to her again.

She mercifully fell asleep around midnight and woke up in time to get Piper ready for school. She also sent her article to Libby, and she was on pins and needles waiting to hear what Libby thought about it. Till then, she and Becca were running festival errands.

"Let's stop by the bakery and check on the lighthouse pastries. Then we can head to the historical society to see who else we need to call," Becca suggested. "Sound good?"

Kaiah nodded. "Yep. Do you think they'll get the lighthouse lamp fixed before Friday?"

"I don't know." Becca pressed her lips together. "But I sure hope so."

~

The fire truck rumbled down the street after Reid and his team finished responding to a minor traffic accident. The morning had been busy with a couple of medical calls before they'd received this one. Thankfully the folks in the accident were fine and the cleanup was quick. A busy day, but at least it was a manageable one.

Reid looked out the window at the clear afternoon sky, and his thoughts turned to the festival. It was Monday, and the lighthouse needed to illuminate the sky Friday night. They were running out of time. He had to do something—and quick. He shot off a text to his brother-in-law.

Reid: Hi, Chief. Has Public Works found the white Christmas lights for the lighthouse?

After a few moments, the dancing dots appeared before Cash's response came through:

Cash: No luck. Jerry couldn't find them.

Reid: Bummer. They've only been in storage a few months. Wonder what happened to them.

Drumming his fingers on his lap, Reid tried to come up with another solution. He turned to Toby, who was driving the fire truck.

"Toby," he called over the radio, "can you go by town hall?"

Reid's captain tapped his shoulder. "Why, Lieutenant?" Chris asked.

"I'd like to go by the Public Works office. Chief checked to see if we could borrow the white Christmas lights for the lighthouse, just in case we need a backup way to light it up on Friday night. They told him that they couldn't find the lights, but I want to have them just in case."

"Christmas lights, huh? That could work," Chris said. "The Public Works guys already owe us a favor. The mayor asked if we could help 'em hang festival banners in between calls. We can get started on the banners while you check on the lights, Turner."

"Perfect."

Reid smiled as he looked out the window and turned his attention to the next problem he needed to figure out. He wanted to do something sweet and romantic for Kaiah, something that maybe, just maybe, could convince her to stay. He just needed to figure out what that might be.

"Good deal," Becca said as they walked out of Crafty Creations. "We're all set for the kite-making session and the contest. Trisha also agreed to help with a second arts and crafts session next Monday. Let's see where we should go next." She studied her clipboard.

Kaiah stepped onto the sidewalk and stopped when she spotted a crew of firemen hanging banners and decorations for the festival. Colorful shells, starfish, and lighthouses—all made out of strings of lights—decorated the lampposts, while banners advertising the Light the Dark Festival stretched across the street.

When Kaiah's eyes found Reid standing on a ladder and attaching a lighthouse to a lamppost, her heart leapt. Clad in his blue uniform, with his biceps straining against the sleeves of his shirt and his clean-shaven face showing off his cheekbones carved from marble, she couldn't stop staring.

Oh, I love a man in a uniform!

His eyes collided with hers, and his handsome face lit up with a smile. "Hey, Ky." He climbed down from the ladder and jogged over to her and Becca before he gestured around the street. "What do you guys think?"

Of Mr. TDH in uniform? Oh yes, I do indeed approve!

It took her half a second to realize he was talking about the decorations, not how fabulous he looked.

She took in the banners stretched across the street. One said "Light the Dark Festival," while another said, "Coral Cove Lighthouse, established 1805" and featured a photo of the beloved black-and-white-striped structure.

"They look excellent, Lieutenant Turner," she told him.

He grinned, and she thought her heart might explode. He nodded at his twin. "Becks?"

Becca divided a look between them and then gave them a coy expression. "Looks good, bro. But I've gotta dash. I need to see if the bookstore wants a booth at the festival. Callie was still thinking about it when I talked to her a few days ago." She took off in a light jog toward Beach Reads.

"How has your day been?" Kaiah asked, her cheeks turning pink. Try as she might, she was still mortified about the Mr. TDH incident. Would she ever move past that humiliation?

He leaned against a newspaper stand. "Okay. We had a few calls this morning, but nothing too bad. Then the captain told us we were hanging decorations and banners this afternoon." He paused for a moment. "Did I tell you I'm off work tomorrow? Then I won't work again until Friday."

"Really?"

"Yup." He pointed to her clipboard. "How are plans going?"

"Great." As she rattled off action items on her clipboard, she could feel his intense gaze settle on her, sending a tingle of heat up her spine. She'd felt the same way yesterday when she touched his face, and she couldn't wait for another chance to feel his dark stubble and chiseled jaw against her fingers. A flush of longing washed over her.

"How was Piper when you dropped her off at school?" he asked.

Kaiah tried to calm the storm of emotions raging inside her, doing her best to answer in an even voice. "She was happy and excited as always."

"Good." His eyes flitted to the banner swaying in the gentle breeze, and then his gaze slid down the street before returning to her. "I'm going to check with Mr. Johnson about the lighthouse. I'm hoping he found someone who can fix it."

"Do you want me to go with you?" she offered, hoping to spend more time with him.

"Sure, if you want to," he said.

A radio crackled before a voice announced, "All available units respond to accident with multiple injuries at Sixth Street and Laurel Avenue."

Reid gave her a sad smile. "Duty calls." He touched her hand. "I'll see you in the morning."

"I'll be there, Lieutenant Turner."

He grinned. "Let's go," he called to his team.

Kaiah stood by the curb while Reid and his crew climbed into the fire truck. He waved as the truck rumbled to life. The siren wailed, and the lights flashed as it motored off toward the oceanfront.

Becca appeared at her side. "Callie's going to have a book booth by the lighthouse."

"Oh," Kaiah said, a goofy smile plastered on her face.

Her friend smirked at her. "What's the grin for?"

"Nothing in particular."

Becca turned toward the taillights of the fire truck. Then she looked back at Kaiah. "You and my brother are so cute together."

Heat filled Kaiah's cheeks, betraying her embarrassment yet again. Why, oh *why*, was she constantly blushing?

Becca's phone began to ring. "Oh! It's Candice Counts from the chamber of commerce." She answered the phone, "Candice, hi. What's up?" A smile spread across her lips while she listened. "That's great news." She beamed at Kaiah. "Yes, I'm sure it is because of Kaiah's articles. She's standing right here. I'll be sure to tell her. Thanks for calling me." She hung up and put away her phone. "Candice said that all of the hotels and inns are filling up because of the festival. You're bringing in the visitors! You're a genius!"

They shared a high five.

"I'm so glad it's working out," Kaiah said.

"I've been keeping tabs on your second article. Seems like it was shared even more than the first," Becca said. "The festival is going to be a hit." Her posture sagged. "My big worry is the lighthouse, but Reid said he was working on that today."

"It'll work out."

"Yeah, maybe. But if we don't have those Christmas lights, I don't know what we're going to do." Becca looped her arm around Kaiah's shoulders while they walked toward her car. "Let's go get the kids."

On Tuesday morning Kaiah wrapped her hand around Reid's and steered him down Main Street. "I can't wait for you to see these cupcakes. You're going to love them."

Reid was curious about the cupcakes, but he was much more excited to spend the day with Kaiah. He didn't care what kinds of small tasks they needed to do for festival prep. Just being with her put him in a good mood, like yesterday. He wasn't expecting to see her when he was putting up decorations, but there she was, looking cute and casual, and his breath caught in his throat. He was bummed that their time together had been cut short by the call he'd received, but just getting to see her for a few minutes had been a treat. A whole day with her felt like a Christmas present.

"Becca and I stopped by the bakery yesterday to see the cupcakes," Kaiah continued, "and I knew I had to show you in person how cute they were." They reached the Beachside Bakery, and she yanked open the door. "You're going to flip!"

He loved the joy vibrating in her voice. As they walked in, the bell rang above the door, and Reid breathed in the delicious scent of pastries.

"Kaiah," one of the Watson twins called—Reid could never tell who was talking if he couldn't see her name tag—"you're back."

"I am! I just had to bring Reid to see those cupcakes." She towed him to the counter. "Do you have any you can share?"

Jenni held up her pointer finger. "I'll be back in a sec." She disappeared into the back and then returned with a tray of cupcakes decorated with lighthouses, shells, life preservers, and starfish. "What do you think?"

Reid picked up a cupcake that looked like it had a real lighthouse lying on top of it. "Are these plastic?"

"Nope!" Jessica laughed as she joined her twin sister behind the counter. "I promise they're edible."

"How did you make them?" he asked.

They shared a knowing look and then said in unison, "Magic."

Kaiah laughed. "Trust me, they're much more professional than the ones we made for the PTO bake sale." She unlocked her phone and shared a photo of the infamous icing-fight cookies they had donated to the school.

The twins examined them and nodded slowly.

"Not bad," Jenni said.

"Okay, you're just being nice," Reid declared, and the group shared a laughed.

Jessica folded her hands and leaned on the counter. "I'm sure the kids enjoyed them."

"We hope so," Kaiah said with a chuckle.

Jenni pointed to a pile of flyers by the register. "We've given a flyer to each customer and have one hanging in the window. We heard quite a few families have already signed up for the mini-marathon."

"That's fantastic," Reid said before turning to Kaiah. "I spread the word at work yesterday. The fire department is going to support the Run and Walk too. Most of the guys have signed up, and Coach Emmerson has teams registering at the schools. And he's an early bird on those awards too. He already has them ready to hand out."

"Really? That's great news!" Kaiah pointed to the tray. "Seriously, I've got to have a couple of those cupcakes before they sell out." She pulled out her wallet. "How much are they?"

The twins shared another look and smiled.

"Free for you two since you're working so hard to get this festival off the ground," Jenni said.

"Absolutely," Jessica chimed in. "It's going to be great for our little town."

"Well, I'm not going to fight you too hard on that." Kaiah bumped her shoulder against Reid's arm. "Pick one."

"Okay." He chose a lighthouse cupcake while Kaiah took one sporting a life preserver. He took a bite and closed his eyes, savoring the light, fluffy cake. It reminded him of the birthday cakes his mom made him growing up.

When he opened his eyes, Kaiah asked, "Well, what do you think?"

"Definitely better than our cookies," he quipped, and they all cracked up again. He turned to Jenni and Jessica. "You guys have outdone yourselves. These are going to be a *hit*. Could I buy some to take home to Piper?"

Reid purchased one of each design, and Jenni packaged up the cupcakes before he and Kaiah headed back out to the street.

"I *told* you the cupcakes were good," Kaiah said.

"You weren't kidding." He unlocked his Suburban and stored the box in the back seat. When he turned around, he caught Kaiah snapping photos of Main Street. He leaned against the SUV and enjoyed seeing her expertise in action. She'd line up a photo and push the shutter button, her face clouded with concentration. Somehow she seemed even more attractive while he watched her work.

She pivoted to face him. "I wanted to get a few shots of Main Street with the banners stretched across and the lighthouse in the background. Talk about Americana. It's going to look adorable in the next article." She cocked her head to the side. "Are you staring at me?"

He grinned at her. "Who, me? Nope. Nuh-uh. No way."

Her eyebrow flew up, and she placed a sassy hand on her hip. "You're staring at me, Reid. How come?"

"No reason." He pushed off the Suburban. "You know what we haven't done yet?"

She hung her camera around her neck and adjusted the straps on her backpack purse. "What's that?"

"Booked musical groups for the stage."

She studied him, and an amused expression flickered over her face. "I can't say I know any musical groups around here. That's the locals' job. So do *you* know any musicians around here?"

"Actually I do." He lifted his chin. "I went to high school with a group of brothers who formed a country band. The Sandy Boots Brothers."

She giggled. "I love it. Are they still around?"

"They sure are." He joined her on the sidewalk. "They own the pet store a couple of blocks over. Let's go talk to them."

Kaiah snapped a few photos while they made their way to the Best Friends Pet Shop. Reid found flyers advertising the festival on the door, and when they walked inside, Kaiah rushed over to a young woman with a black cocker spaniel.

"Ohhh," she gushed, bending down to meet the dog. "What's your puppy's name?"

The young woman beamed. "This is Patrick."

"How are you, buddy?" Kaiah held out her hand. "Is it okay . . . ?"

The woman nodded. "You can pet him. He loves attention. He's a sweetie."

Kaiah stroked the dog's head and asked Patrick's owner all about him. Every time she glanced down at the spaniel, her face radiated her affection for animals. Reid yearned to capture the moment. He pulled out his phone and took a few photos while she was completely unaware.

After a minute, Kaiah stood. "Thank you for letting me meet Patrick."

The woman chuckled. "No problem. You made our day."

Kaiah sighed and looped her arm through Reid's. "I miss my dog so much." When she rested her head on his arm, he melted into her touch. "I hope Georgie is healthy and happy."

"Reid?"

Turning, Reid spotted Brad Duncan waving on his way down the dog food aisle.

"Hey, Brad." He shook his friend's hand, then turned to Kaiah. "Brad is the lead singer and oldest brother in the band. This is Kaiah. She's a journalist who's working on a story about the festival."

"Great to meet you, Kaiah." Brad folded his arms over his chest. "Are you guys here for cat food?"

"Actually, we're wondering if the Sandy Boots Brothers would be interested in performing at the festival."

Brad's face lit up. "The festival? Now *that's* a good gig. Count us in." He pointed to the store's front window. "We've been talking to customers about the festival, and my brothers and I were just thinking about what we could do to help. We're forming a team for the marathon, for sure. I'd heard that there was going to be a market and a stage. Sounds like we might be a fit for both of those."

"Right on," Reid said.

Kaiah wrote in her notebook. "What kind of music do you and your brothers play?"

"Mostly classic country, but we have a few of our own songs. We're working on an album."

"That's so cool! I can't wait to hear you play."

Reid patted his old friend's shoulder. "I'm sure you have some contacts in the local music scene. Could you spread the word that we need some folks to perform? We're putting out feelers for other acts."

"Sure thing. I'll text you some folks to reach out to right now."

After Brad shared the details, Reid and Kaiah headed back out to the Suburban.

"I'd say we've had a successful day," Kaiah said as she climbed into the passenger seat.

He smiled over at her. "Me too."

And when an idea for a romantic evening began to form in his mind, his pulse sped up.

Chapter 17

KAIAH HIT SEND ON her email and then collapsed back on the sofa later that evening. After helping Reid with more festival planning, she'd retreated to her apartment after supper to finish her third Coral Cove article. She wanted this one to give more details about Coral Cove's rich history, including the lighthouse, and highlight how the community was coming together to make the festival a reality. She still couldn't believe how many people were donating their time and resources. Talk about the perfect hidden gem! Hopefully her article would encourage more visitors to check it out.

When her phone rang with a FaceTime call, she wasn't surprised to find Kam's name on the screen. Kaiah hadn't responded to her text Sunday night, which she was now calling "Mr. TDH-gate." Her cheeks still burned hot whenever she thought about having to explain it all to Reid.

"Hey, Kam." Kaiah tried to make her voice as neutral as possible and wasn't sure she succeeded.

Her sister eyed her with annoyance. "Um, where have you been? Why haven't you called me or texted me?"

"I've been busy. It's Tuesday, and the festival starts Friday night."

"Riiiiight. Well, I'm glad I didn't have to call the cops—I was getting worried. So have you been busy *only* with the festival?" her sister asked with a grin.

"Yes, *only* with the festival. We've had to coordinate with vendors, plan live shows, make plans to set up markets, and get permits for events on the beach. It's a ton of work. So yeah, I've been MIA."

"Cool, cool, cool." Kam's expression dimmed, and she seemed . . . preoccupied?

"You're being weird. What's going on, Kam?"

"What do you mean?"

"You seem distracted. Do you have something on your mind?"

Kam hesitated for a moment. "I . . . have news."

"Oh?"

Kamryn's usual bright smile filled her pretty face. "You're going to be an auntie again."

"What?!" Kaiah exclaimed, and any thoughts she had about a stern talk flew out of her brain as excitement buzzed through her. "When did you find out?"

"Today! I wanted to tell you first." Kam sniffed. "Devon and I have been praying for this for so long, Ky. I can't believe it finally happened."

Tears pressed against Kaiah's eyes. "That's amazing, Kam. I'm so happy for you."

Kamryn started crying, and Kaiah did too.

"What's wrong with us?" Kam swiped her fingers over her eyes, then laughed.

Kaiah dabbed her face with a tissue. "We're just really, really happy. And you're really, really hormonal."

A knock sounded on the door, and Kaiah popped up from the sofa.

"Is that Mr. TDH?" Kam's grin was back.

Kaiah shushed her. "You need to stop calling him that. You got me in trouble."

"Oooh! Sorry, not sorry. I need to hear that story."

Kaiah looked through the peephole and found Reid standing on the deck. "It's Reid. Behave or I'm going to hang up on you."

"I promise I'll behave. I want to meet the babe who's stolen my sister's heart."

Kaiah groaned. "You're so dramatic. Now don't embarrass me." She unlocked and opened the door before sniffing and wiping her eyes. "Hi."

Reid's forehead creased with concern. "Hey, have you've been crying? What's wrong?"

Kaiah smiled. "Everything's great. My sister just told me some good news." She held up the phone.

"Oh, I'm sorry. You're busy. I'll come back later." He started toward the stairs.

"Hold on. Wait." Kaiah held the phone up toward him. "Kam, this is Reid."

Reid grinned at the phone. "Hello, Kam. I'm also known as Mr. TDH."

Kamryn burst out laughing. "And the name certainly fits," she managed to say between cackles.

Kaiah's face was hot again—*Kam!* But when Reid snickered, she couldn't help but laugh along with them.

"It's great to meet you, Reid," Kam said. "I'm Kaiah's favorite sister."

Reid nodded. "That's what I hear."

"Kam just shared that she's expecting," Kaiah explained.

Reid's smile was warm and genuine, and it sent a thrill through Kaiah. "Congratulations! That's the best news."

"Thank you," Kam told him. "I'll let you two go. Talk to you later, sis."

"I'll call you soon. You take care of yourself—I guess I should say 'yourselves.' Wow, that's going to take some getting used to." Kaiah ended the call and turned to Reid. "Hey, you. What's up?"

He rubbed the back of his head. "I was wondering if you wanted to see something."

"Sure," she said. "What is it?"

He started for the door. "Be downstairs in fifteen minutes. We're going for a ride."

"Okay . . ." She watched him descend the stairs, curiosity threading its way through her. What was that man up to?

She had no idea, but she couldn't wait to find out.

~

Reid met Becca in the driveway as she parked her SUV. After tossing his daughter's overnight bag in the truck, he helped Piper get buckled into the booster seat. "Now, have fun with Astrid and listen to your auntie, okay?"

"I will, Daddy." Piper kissed his cheek. "Love you."

"Love you too." Reid waved at his niece. "Have fun."

Piper immediately began telling Astrid a story about her cat, and Reid shut the door.

He spotted the lights glowing behind the shades in the apartment over the garage. Kaiah was probably getting ready for their date.

Date.

He almost laughed out loud. As if he remembered how to go

on a first date. How long had it been? Seventeen years? Did he even know how to do this anymore?

He met his sister's curious expression. "Thanks for picking up Piper. I figured you guys would go out for supper." He pulled his wallet from his back pocket and opened it. "Here's some cash to cover it."

Becca held up her hand and rolled her eyes. "Keep your money, but I want all the deets later." She rested her hands on her hips "What are you guys up to?"

He shrugged. "I'm taking Kaiah out."

Her brows shot up to the moon. "On a date?"

He sighed and then nodded.

"Reid! Finally! I *knew* you two liked each other."

"I'm pretty sure we do. And tonight I'm going to make it pretty clear how I feel about her."

"Good. You should. At least have a DTR talk with her."

"DTR?"

"It means *define the relationship.* She's leaving in a couple weeks, at most. If you want this thing to have a chance, you need to tell her exactly how you feel."

"*Exactly* how I feel? That might be . . . a bit much."

"Right . . ." She paused for a second. "Listen, we're twins. I can tell you have some really intense feelings for her."

That was true, but he wasn't going to talk about them with her. There were some things he just wanted to keep to himself—no twin ESP allowed.

"Uh-huh. Well, Becks, I appreciate you helping me out last minute."

"You know we love having Piper stay over." Becca's dark eyes focused on something behind him, and her expression lit up. "Hey, Kaiah. You look nice."

Reid whirled around, and he could've sworn the air stood still.

Kaiah was captivating, clad in a dress the color of a ripe peach, with her hair pulled back and falling in soft curls past her shoulders. Whatever makeup she'd done made her blue eyes sparkle. For a moment he couldn't take his eyes off her.

Kaiah's eyes flittered to her dress and then back to him. "I thought I'd dress up. Too much, right?" She took a step back. "I'll change into a pair of jeans."

She turned to head back upstairs, but he clasped her wrist before she could get too far.

"No," he said. "You're . . . you're perfect."

Her adorable cheeks turned the color of her dress almost instantly. He'd never get tired of seeing her blush.

"You two have fun!" Becca sang before winking at Reid and climbing into her SUV. A moment later, she backed out of the driveway.

Reid smiled at Kaiah. "You ready?"

She nodded, and he opened the passenger door for her.

~

Reid navigated the winding town roads, the setting sun casting a symphony of colors across the horizon.

"Where are we going?" Kaiah asked, her gaze fixed on the shifting hues outside her window.

"You'll see." Reid's response was paired with a mischievous grin, his casual attire of khakis and a gray button-down lending a boyish charm.

Her mind echoed with the memory of his appreciative once-over when they'd met in the driveway. Butterflies took flight in her stomach as she remembered his eyes grazing her dress, then settling on her face. Then she turned her attention back to the world racing past her window. She had no idea where they were going. An intimate dinner, perhaps? A movie? Either way, why the mystery?

"How about Kamryn?" Reid asked.

A rush of joy swept over her at the memory of Kam's news. "They've been trying for a while. I'm thrilled for them," she confessed, her hands smoothing the fabric of her dress in a nervous gesture. "And she wanted to tell me first. What an honor."

"Definitely. She seems great," Reid observed, his grin pulling at the corners of his lips. "She has a good sense of humor."

"I think you two would really like each other."

As Reid turned onto the familiar road leading to the cove, a newfound excitement surged within her. "Wait. Are we going to the lighthouse?" she ventured.

His lips curved into a knowing smile, but he didn't answer.

Pulling into the lighthouse parking lot, he climbed out and hurried to open her door. He extended his hand, and Kaiah took it, brushing his strong, calloused palm as their fingers intertwined. They began to walk down the long boardwalk leading to the lighthouse, passing the vibrant flowers dancing in the breeze.

"Are we having supper here?" she asked.

"Nope." He released her hand while he unlocked the gate, which squealed in protest as he pushed it open. Then he took her hand again and led her to the beach beside the lighthouse. "Wait here, okay?"

She nodded at him.

He started toward the lighthouse and then turned. "I'll be right back. I promise."

"I'll be waiting." She faced the beach and lifted her eyes toward the sky, where the sunset had begun to fade and stars were sparkling in the clear night. Tiny waves lapped onto the sand, and the silhouette of slow-moving ships glided across the horizon.

A shower of white lights suddenly illuminated behind her. Kaiah turned around and saw the lighthouse was glowing, wrapped in a dotted blanket filled with thousands of small white lights.

She cupped her hands to her mouth and swallowed a gasp of air. Footfalls sounded, and Reid loped down the stone steps toward her.

"What do you think?" he asked.

"Reid," she whispered, "it's the most beautiful thing I've ever seen."

He laughed. "And to think it was my daughter's brilliant idea."

"It's amazing!" She grasped his hands and pulled him to her. "When did you do this?" she asked, her eyes searching his.

Reid pushed a lock of her hair behind her ear, his touch leaving a trail of heat in its wake. "The guys and I took care of the lights yesterday after that call we had when I saw you downtown. Jerry over at Public Works finally found the lights. We got the crew at Station 3 to help us, and still it took hours. I was grateful we didn't get any calls so we could finish it. Just in case Mr. Johnson isn't able to fix the wiring, this will be a pretty good solution, I think. Especially based on your reaction." He traced his fingertip along her jawline. "I couldn't wait to show you. That's why I called Becks and asked her to keep Piper."

Without thinking, Kaiah threw her arms around his neck and pulled him close. "It's perfect, Reid. Just perfect."

Reid rested his hands on her lower back and his cheek on the top of her head as he relaxed against her. "I can't thank you enough for all you've done for this town. And for me."

"It's my pleasure," she whispered.

The only sound she could hear was the rhythmic beat of waves against the beach as she held on to him. She savored his familiar scent—soap and sandalwood—along with the joy of being in his arms.

"I really like you, Kaiah," he said. His voice was husky, and suddenly the spring breeze wasn't enough to cool the heat of her skin. "I like you *a lot*."

She let his words settle over her before she answered, the corners of her mouth curving up. "I like you too, Reid."

When he pulled away, Reid's smile had smoothed out. His soft expression turned into a smolder, and she held her breath as her nerve endings stood on end.

He gently angled her chin toward his, and when his lips met hers, her knees buckled. Happiness blossomed in the pit of her belly as he cradled the nape of her neck, and she melted against him. She closed her eyes, savoring the feel of his muscled frame leaning against hers as she lost herself in his kiss.

Wow.

That was like nothing she'd ever experienced before. When he shifted away from her, she grasped his shoulders for balance.

"I've wanted to do that ever since we went to the elementary school to talk to Coach Emmerson."

"What took you so long?" she whispered, her voice breathy.

With that, he lowered his mouth to hers and kissed her again, and this time she looped her arms around his neck and pulled him closer. He leaned in to deepen the kiss, and the feel of his body under her fingertips, the way it pressed against hers, made her feel as if all her cells were on fire.

When he pulled away, he rested his forehead against hers and grinned. "I'm sorry I waited so long, but I can't say I'm disappointed."

She laughed. "Me neither."

"I'm glad to hear it." He stood up straight, linked his fingers with hers, and turned toward the lighthouse. "So, now that we've figured out how to light up the lighthouse, I was thinking I could give tours during the festival," he said. "But it really needs to be cleaned up. Would you help me get it ready?"

She nodded while trying to find her voice. "Yeah. Of course."

"Great. Let's go inside."

As he pulled her toward the lighthouse, she hoped they'd repeat that kiss soon.

~

Reid guided Kaiah through the lighthouse, showing her where he was thinking about placing booths for the historical society to sell souvenirs and take donations. Then he led her up the stairs to the lantern room.

Although he prattled on about his plans for the lighthouse, his mind was still stuck on the moment they'd shared on the beach. Holding her felt like a dream. He hadn't felt such a rush of emotions—comfort, desire, joy, and hope—since he'd been with Brynn. Kaiah had awakened something deep inside him, something he'd tried to lock away nearly half a decade ago. Holding her against him had felt right. It was as if she belonged in his arms, and he needed to find a way to convince her to stay so that he could kiss her again. Thoroughly. And often.

"Mr. Johnson said he's still working on getting the lamp repaired," Reid told her while they stood in the lantern room. "If he gets it fixed on time, we'll have extra ambience."

Kaiah took his hand and motioned toward the gallery deck. "Let's see the view from out there."

He followed her outside, and a cool breeze fluttered over them.

She rested her head against his shoulder. "It's beautiful up here."

He nodded, but his eyes were focused on her gorgeous profile, taking in her high cheekbones, ocean-blue eyes, pink lips, and sun-kissed skin, while doing his best to commit to memory how she seemed to glow in the light of the sunset. He wanted his mind to document this moment forever. And more than anything, he wanted to convince this woman to stay in Coral Cove and build a life with him and his daughter.

Her phone dinged, yanking him back to reality as she plucked it from her purse. She studied the screen, and her brow furrowed before she locked the phone and dropped it back into her bag.

"Everything okay?" he asked.

She huffed out a breath. "It's my ex. He won't take a hint."

"Hayes?" he asked, and she nodded. He tried in vain to banish the jealousy worming its way through him. She'd made it clear that she was done with him, so why did he care if the guy was still reaching out to her?

But it bothered him. Badly.

They stood in silence for several moments, both of them unsure how to move the night forward.

Kaiah acted first. "Listen, let's just forget him," she said. She leaned against him, kissed his cheek, and released a happy sigh from her pink lips. "I can't believe it's Tuesday and the festival is Friday. I feel like everything's coming together."

"And that's because of you, Ky." He pulled her against him and enjoyed the feeling of her soft, warm skin on his. "We can tie up loose ends tomorrow. I have to work Friday, but Cash already told me we'll be stationed at the festival."

"That means I'll get to see you," she said.

They enjoyed the view for a few more minutes before they

started down the stairs. When they walked outside, Kaiah motioned toward the lighthouse. "I need to get more photos. I might use them for my write-up after the festival."

She snapped several photos with her phone and then grabbed his arm. "We should take a selfie with the lighthouse in the background."

She handed him the phone, then snuggled up to him, and he held the phone up high before snapping several photos.

"Send me those," he told her.

"I will." She held his hand while they descended the steps. "I'm going to write another article tonight and include the winner of the photo contest. I can't believe we had a thousand folks vote online for the entries."

After they walked back to Reid's Suburban and climbed inside, he leaned over and brushed his lips over hers. He began slowly, taking his time to explore her velvet lips as the world around them fell away. Her hands moved to the nape of his neck, and her fingertips combed through his hair.

When he broke away, he pulled in air, working to slow the shock waves still rocking his body.

Her lips were a swollen pout as she touched his face. "I could get used to that," she whispered.

He grinned. "I think I could too."

Chapter 18

RAIN DRUMMED ON THE roof above Kaiah Thursday morning. She peeked out Reid's kitchen window. Droplets of rain peppered the windshield of the Suburban while bushes filled with pink and white azaleas danced in the gentle breeze. Dark clouds promised that the storm would last throughout the day.

Reid came to stand beside her, and the aroma of fresh coffee filled her nostrils as he sipped from his mug. Then he leaned over and brushed a java-flavored kiss over her lips. She would never get tired of kissing him.

"Any idea how we're gonna set up the market tents and that huge music stage while it's raining?" she asked.

He shrugged and sipped more coffee. "We'll figure it out."

Kaiah pulled her phone from the back pocket of her jean shorts and consulted the forecast. Her shoulders sagged when she saw rain clouds dotting the weather grid for the next six days. "Oh no, it's supposed to rain until *next Thursday*. It's going to ruin all of our plans. How on earth will the festival happen in the rain?"

"We'll go with the flow. It can still work."

She took in his bright smile. "But what if no one comes?"

"It's going to be fine, Ky. I just know it."

The front door opened and shut with a bang before Becca came into the den. "It's raining!"

Reid and Kaiah shared a smile before he addressed his twin. "It's not a problem."

"How can you be so calm, Reid?" Becca demanded. "It's a mess out there." She pointed toward the window.

"It's going to be fine, sis. I promise you."

Becca narrowed her eyes at her brother.

"Look," he began, "since I have to work tomorrow, we're going to get as much done today as we can. We'll roll with the rain as we need to."

"If you say so," Becca said. She started toward the door. "Let's go, guys. We've got a lot of work to do."

A few hours later, Kaiah stood under the large tent while rain continued to fall. She glanced around at the different booths where vendors had begun to set up. The wind blew the flaps of the tent open, and a cool breeze rushed over her before a cold river of liquid began streaming down her back. *Why don't I ever pack my rain jacket on these reporting trips?* she thought. *Sheesh!* She shivered and wiped her hand across her neck before craning her neck upward just as more rain snuck in between the seams of the tent.

The rain hadn't let up all day long. In fact, the rain and the wind had only gotten worse as the day progressed. Kaiah moved through the large tent where merchants were stacking product and readying displays. Her phone dinged with a text, and when she found Hayes's name on the screen, she groaned. She hadn't responded to his text on Tuesday.

Hayes: Kaiah, please. Can we talk?

Instead, she'd told Reid about their breakup, and it had felt good to get it off her chest. Reid had been so kind to her. And she had nothing else to give to someone who'd taken so much from her.

But after two days of silence, Hayes had reached out again:

Hayes: Ky, come on. I really want to talk to you.

Hayes: I know you're working on a story in NC. I've liked your articles.

Hayes: How long will you be there? Can I come see you?

Hayes: We need to talk, Ky. Please!

"Can't you take a hint?" she said, glowering at her phone.

"Who are you talking to?"

Kaiah whirled around to find Becca, who watched her with confusion. "Sorry. I got a text from my ex."

"What does that jerk want?"

Kaiah angled the screen toward Becca.

"Ugh," Becca said. "Time to block him."

Kaiah shook her head. "I can't, just in case something happens to George. Or if he has a lead on a story."

"Listen, I know you're a freelancer and jobs are hard to come by sometimes. But Hayes doesn't deserve to stay in contact with you or know where you are," Becca said. But when Kaiah hesitated, she threw her arms up in the air. "He took your *dog*, Kaiah. The one you cared for together. Who does that?" She waved him off. "Forget about that guy. He's not worth your time." Then her expression became clandestine. "As long as we're being real right now, tell me this: Are you dating my brother?"

Kaiah pocketed her phone, staying quiet for a beat before answering. "Um, yeah. Sort of. How did you know?"

Becca scoffed, then smiled. "Uh, anybody who's seen the goo-goo eyes you give each other would know. Plus, I saw you kiss him before we left his house earlier. That was a pretty good clue." She elbowed Kaiah in the side. "I approve, by the way."

Kaiah beamed. "Thanks. I do too."

"Rebecca," a woman called from a nearby booth. A sign beside her read *Beach Collectibles*. "I'm starting to wonder why we're bothering to set up this market when it's going to rain until next Friday. Who's gonna come out for this?"

"You know what? I was thinking the same thing," a man called from the Carolina Jewelers booth. "This is a waste of time, not to mention manpower. We should load it all up and take it back to the store. At least people can park in front of our buildings and shop in the rain. Who's gonna trudge through all that mud?"

"Y'all, don't be a bunch of Debbie Downers. It's all going to be fine," Reid called while he walked toward the man. He held up his arms, and his face was the picture of calm. "I have a feeling the weather is going to pass us over and the weekend is going to be perfect."

"What forecast are you reading?" the man from the jeweler's booth asked. "The one from the Pie in the Sky channel?"

Becca's phone started to ring, and she answered it. "Hi, Mayor Whittington." Her tone was sunnier than her expression. "Yes, absolutely. I'll spread the word." She hung up the call and glanced around. "We're having an emergency town meeting tonight at seven to discuss the festival."

Worry drenched Kaiah's spirit like the pouring rain.

Reid rested his hand on her shoulder. "It's going to be fine," he whispered in her ear. "You'll see."

Although she was certain the weather was against them, she hoped Reid was right.

~

A rumble of conversations echoed around the large town hall later that evening while rain pounded on the roof. Kaiah stood in the back of the hall beside Cash while Reid and Becca walked up to the podium with the mayor.

She wrung her hands while she glanced around the full room. She couldn't stop herself from wondering if the festival was going to fall apart, if the elementary school kids would ever leave their crowded classrooms and get the attention they needed to thrive. She wondered if the stories she was writing were making a difference at all for this town that had grown so dear to her, mostly because the people who made it their home had opened their hearts to her.

"Good evening," Mayor Whittington said into the microphone, pulling Kaiah back to the present. "Let's get started. I called this meeting so that we can firm up our plans for the festival."

"There isn't going to *be* a festival if this rain doesn't stop," a man called from the back of the hall.

"We've spent all this money," a woman yelled, "and now it's going to be a washout!"

A chorus of voices agreed with her.

Kaiah turned to Cash beside her. "I don't have a good feeling about this meeting."

"I don't think I do either," Cash agreed.

"And what about the school?" another woman hollered. "We were going to save the school, and now we're just going to lose money."

"That's the truth!" a man exclaimed. "We have guests arriving tomorrow. If they look at the weather forecast, they're going to cancel their reservations, and we'll lose all that revenue."

"Why are we having the festival this early anyway?" another hollered. "It would make more sense to have it in summer when it's warm and you can actually swim!"

A murmur of conversations swept around the hall again, and the dissatisfied buzzing grew louder and louder.

The mayor spoke into the microphone, but her voice was lost in the crescendo of complaints echoing around the hall.

Reid came up behind the mayor, touched her shoulder, and whispered something before she moved to the side and he took command of the microphone. His mouth moved, but his words weren't audible over the angry protests. His gaze slid around the room before he stuck two fingers in his mouth and blew out a whistle that pierced over the loudspeaker, instantly silencing the voices.

"Thank you." Reid's smooth voice was calm despite the heightened stress in the room. "Now, I know everyone is concerned about the weather, but I need you to listen." He rested his hands on the podium. "I've seen the forecast. I know it's supposed to rain until late next week. We can't control the weather, but we *can* control our attitudes. If we keep up our enthusiasm for the event, then our excitement will spread to others. Energy is infectious. People *want* to be somewhere others want to be. Our festival is still going to be dynamite, even if it rains. Think about it: We can still have our lighthouse illumination ceremony. The tents are set up for the market, and the vendors are ready to go. The stage is covered, and we can play up the rainy concert as having a 'music fest' vibe—the weather never drowns out the crowds at Bonnaroo or Lollapalooza, does it?

"Y'all, I know this isn't the festival we expected," Reid continued. "But if we're excited about this event, people will show up. We can show guests a good time and encourage them to come back to see us again. If we keep our spirits up, I promise this festival is not going to be a waste of time or money."

He paused, and his wide chest rose and then fell. "Someone asked why we plan this festival for April instead of closer to summer. I think we all need a reminder about our town and its history. Some of you may have forgotten why we have this festival every year. It's about Coral Cove and why we live here. It's because of our beloved lighthouse, the symbol of our town, that was built in 1805. One windy day in early April, it saved a ship full of sailors from running up on the shoals during a storm. One of those sailors was my ancestor. So if it weren't for that lighthouse, I wouldn't be here. My sister, Becca, wouldn't be here. My *daughter*, who I love more than anything in the world, wouldn't be here. I'm sure some of y'all are in the same boat."

Reid's gaze darted around the room until his eyes collided with Kaiah's, and a slow smile lifted his lips, accelerating her pulse. "The lighthouse represents light through the darkness. That's why someone much smarter than I am suggested we name the festival 'Light the Dark.' That lighthouse has been a beacon of light for our community for more than two hundred years. We need to honor what it represents and be a light for folks in our town and beyond. So I say we see this thing through. It's who we are as a community."

His dark eyes roved over the crowd again. "We can't give up now. We've come this far. So let's put everything we have into this festival. If we all believe in it, I think—no, I *know*—it'll be a success."

Reid stood at the microphone, scanning the crowd. Kaiah could've heard a pin drop as the crowd absorbed his words. Her stomach crackled with nerves. *Please, please go for this, you guys.*

"He's right," someone called from the middle of the room.

A waterfall of relief cascaded through her head to toe.

"We can't give up now," another voice said.

A woman stood. "I'm putting everything I can into my market booth. We can't shut this thing down. Not yet."

"Let's do this!" a man called.

Claps started at the back of the room and then spread out until every pair of hands was sounding their agreement. Pride surged through Kaiah's chest as she took in the way Reid's words had changed the tide.

She tapped Cash's arm. "He's good."

"I told him that he needs to run for mayor, but he always laughs at me," Cash said. "Seriously, people respect him."

Becca moved to the microphone. "Thank you, Reid," she told her brother before facing the crowd. "I think we can all agree we should move forward with our plans for the festival." She began reciting the schedule of events before taking questions from the crowd.

At the end of the meeting, Kaiah and Cash moved to the side of the hall while the townsfolk filed out and into the pouring spring rain. Turning toward the podium, Kaiah waited while Reid and Becca spoke with the mayor before they made their way off the stage.

Before brother and sister arrived, Kaiah turned to Cash. "Do you really think we'll be able to pull this off?"

"Knowing those two," he began, nodding at the twins, "it's going to be just fine."

Reid could feel Kaiah's eyes watching him while he drove through the gusting wind and pounding rain to his house. The windshield wipers swished as he slowed to a stop at a red light, and he gave Kaiah a sideways glance. "You look like something's on your mind. Wanna talk about it?"

Kaiah tilted her head and rested her hands on her lap. "I want to know when you're launching your campaign to run for mayor."

He barked a laugh. "I can tell you've been talking to Cash. I can't tell you how many times he's told me to hang up my uniform and go into politics."

"He's not wrong." She moved her fingers over his shoulder. "You could do both, right? You only work ten days a month, so you could be Lieutenant Turner for ten days and then Mayor Turner the others."

"I appreciate your confidence in me, but I'm not sure I'm cut out for that."

The light turned green, and he finished the short journey to his driveway, where he parked in his usual spot in front of the garage. He killed the engine, and the soothing sound of rain drummed on the roof and sent small streams rolling down the windshield.

Kaiah angled her body toward him and crossed her ankles. "Becca and I are going to firm up last-minute tasks while you're at work tomorrow."

He unbuckled his seat belt. "The lighthouse still doesn't have an actual lamp that works. Mr. Johnson called me earlier, and he hasn't had any luck with the wiring kits he's tried." His head fell backward and thumped against the headrest on the driver's seat. "I told the entire town that everything would be okay. But truthfully?

I'm not so sure. The weather forecast is dismal. Who wants to walk around a festival in the rain?"

Kaiah's warm hand held his. "You said it's all going to be okay, and I believe you. The whole town believes you. You gave them all a gift tonight, Reid. You gave them hope."

His eyes lingered on their enmeshed hands as a heavy sigh escaped his lips. "Maybe. But I'm afraid we may have done all of this work for nothing. I may have roped you into promoting an event that's going to be a total bust." The familiar churn of guilt began lashing through his stomach. "It'll be my fault if your journalistic credibility suffers because of me."

For a moment all he could hear were the beads of rain hitting the roof.

"Look at me, Reid."

When he met her gaze, her lips were softly curled up into a bow, and his heart thumped against his rib cage. "The lighthouse is going to illuminate tomorrow night, whether it's lit by the Christmas lights or Mr. Johnson gets the lamp to glow again. Either way, tomorrow night the lighthouse is going to glow. And then the fireworks are going to explode in the sky, and the festival is going to start with a bang, and we're going to raise enough money not only to rebuild the damaged wing of the school but also to buy all new desks, computers, and books for the kids. We're even going to fix up the lighthouse and make it look brand-new."

"You think so?"

"I *know* so."

He searched her kind blue eyes. "How did I get so lucky to meet you, Ky?"

Her mouth opened and closed as her cheeks blushed the color of a spring rose. "I-I don't know," she whispered. "But I do know I've been wondering the same thing about you."

He gently rested his hand on the side of her face, and she leaned into his touch. He cupped his other hand to her shoulder, and as her eyes met his, a tendril of her golden hair floated in front of her forehead. He reached out and brushed it away.

She traced a finger along his jaw before pulling him closer and planting her satin lips on his. He groaned as she slid her fingertips down his back, every nerve ending catching fire at her touch. Right then and there he knew: He was crazy about this woman. As she parted her lips and pressed herself firmly against him, he knew there was nowhere else he'd rather be. He'd never grow tired of tasting her.

When he pulled away, he felt an overwhelming urge to tell her he wanted her to stay forever. He opened his mouth and tried to form the words, but just as he was going to speak, his phone rang. He and Kaiah both jumped before she pointed to his phone sitting in the cup holder.

"It's Piper," she said.

With his heart still pounding, he answered the FaceTime call, trying desperately to look unrattled. "Hey, pumpkin." His words sounded as if he'd just swam from the Coral Cove oceanfront to the Outer Banks. "What's up?"

"Nana said I could call you and say good night," Piper told him. She immediately launched into a story detailing everything she'd done since arriving at his parents' house earlier that day. That gave his heartbeat enough time to slow down and the tremble to exit his voice.

"Sounds like you're having fun," he told her.

"Uh-huh," Piper said. "Nana is going to take me and Astrid to school tomorrow and pick us up." She moved her head as if trying to see behind him. "Are you in the car?"

"Yes," he told her.

"Is Miss Kaiah there?"

Kaiah leaned on his shoulder and waved at his daughter. "Hi, Piper. What are you up to?"

Reid sighed as Kaiah rested against his shoulder. The woman grinned and listened patiently as his daughter once again summarized her evening, as if Kaiah hadn't already heard her.

"Wow, that sounds like a blast!" Kaiah told his daughter after she'd finished her stories. "I'm so glad you're having fun. Can't wait to see you tomorrow, kiddo."

"Me too. Good night, Miss Kaiah. And good night, Daddy," Piper sang before blowing each of them a kiss.

Reid waved to her. "Good night, sweetheart." He clicked his phone off and then turned to Kaiah. "Are you ready to run through the rain?"

She picked up an umbrella from the floor. "As I'll ever be."

He pushed open the door, and they met at the front of the SUV.

Kaiah pulled him close, planted a quick kiss on his nose, and then loped toward the steps leading to the apartment. "See you tomorrow!" she called while pounding up the wet steps.

Reid stood in the downpour and watched her disappear, oblivious to the rain.

Chapter 19

"I CAN'T BELIEVE THE rain finally stopped."

Kaiah wiped the beads of sweat clinging to her forehead. She and Becca had spent the day tying up loose ends, pitching in where they could: helping vendors set up display tables, coordinating light technicians rigging the stage, answering all kinds of questions from all kinds of volunteers. She'd been moving her body a hundred miles an hour, and she was exhausted. But she scanned the market at the base of the lighthouse and grinned when she found booths filled with handmade crafts, paintings, photography, and jewelry. She took a deep inhale and nearly groaned from the aroma of cinnamon pecans mingling with buttery popcorn and freshly baked pretzels. The air felt moist and humid, leftovers from the band of showers that had made their way through. But when Kaiah peered up at the sky, she saw no evidence of the storm. Instead, the setting sun transformed the blue expanse into bands of oranges and purples melting into each other.

Becca patted Kaiah's shoulder. "My brother was right. I usually hate to say it, but this time I really wanted him to be. This festival's going to work out after all."

The nearby stage was set and waiting for the live bands to start. Across the way, Mr. Johnson and a crew from his electrical company buzzed in and out of the lighthouse carrying bags of tools, giving Kaiah a grain of hope. Maybe, just maybe, the lighthouse would shine for the first time in decades.

"Everything looks fantastic," Mayor Whittington said as she sidled up to them. She held up a handful of note cards. "I'm ready to start whenever y'all are."

Becca looped her arm around Kaiah's shoulders. "It's going to be great."

"I think you may be right," Kaiah agreed.

The mayor divided a look between them. "Thank you both for making this day a reality. Truly, it's a small miracle we're all standing here right now."

"It was all Kaiah's idea." Becca gave Kaiah's neck a squeeze in a half hug. "Without her, this never would have happened."

Kaiah smiled. "It's been fun."

The mayor's assistant took her arm. "We should get you ready for the ceremony," the young woman said.

"I'd better go," the mayor told Becca and Kaiah. "I'll see you after."

"Miss Kaiah! Auntie!" Piper called while she and Astrid held hands and raced toward them with Becca's parents, Blake and Sue, following closely behind them.

"Hi, Mommy!" Astrid hugged Becca's waist.

Kaiah took Piper's hand. "Are you two ready to see the lighthouse glow? And watch those fireworks?"

"Yes!" Piper and Astrid hollered in unison while bouncing up and down.

Becca and Kaiah shared a smile. Then Becca pointed behind Kaiah. "Look at the crowd."

A swarm of folks had begun to gather near the lighthouse and the marketplace. The sun had dipped under the horizon, and with darkness setting in, there was a hum in the air. Everyone was waiting for the main event.

"Where's Daddy?" Piper asked.

Kaiah stared beyond the crowd to where a fire truck was parked, but she could tell that it wasn't from his station. "I'm sure he'll be here soon."

And she hoped so. She couldn't imagine watching the opening ceremony without Reid at her side—not after all their planning. It only seemed right that they'd experience the festival together.

For the next several minutes Kaiah stood with Becca and her parents, along with Astrid and Piper, while the crowd continued to grow around the lighthouse. Darkness deepened over the cove, and the buzz of the chattering crowd, along with the tide rolling on the shore in waves, filled the air. Piper held on to Kaiah's hand while they waited for the ceremony to begin.

Once the streetlights began to pop on one after the other, Mayor Whittington took the stage.

"Good evening. And welcome, everyone, to Coral Cove's first Light the Dark Festival. I'm Susan Whittington, and I'm honored to be the mayor and to have the opportunity to welcome you to our festival. For the next six days we're going to come together to celebrate our town's rich history, and whether you've lived here your whole life or you're visiting us for the first time, I'm so glad you've come to join us. Many years ago, this lighthouse saved the lives of a group of sailors during one fateful, stormy night . . ."

A hand on Kaiah's shoulder startled her, and she turned to find

Reid standing behind her, clad in his uniform and wearing a wide smile.

"Reid," she whispered. "You made it!"

"Daddy!" Piper yelled.

People around them turned to stare.

Reid shushed Piper and pulled her into his arms. "Listen to the mayor, okay?" Then he met Kaiah's eyes. "Sorry I'm late," he whispered. "We had to take care of a few things before we came out here."

"I'm just glad—" she began, but her words were cut off when the lighthouse suddenly lit up with thousands of white lights.

Then the lamp atop the black-and-white frame suddenly burst with light, and in an instant, the historic structure was brought back to life.

Kaiah gasped as the crowd erupted into a chorus of applause. She couldn't believe what a majestic sight it was, watching the light sail miles into the ocean, cutting through the darkness. She could only imagine how those sailors must have felt that night with nothing to guide them but the light from this very structure.

Reid's strong hand massaged Kaiah's shoulder. "We did it, Ky," he whispered in her ear. Would hearing his deep voice say her name *always* send a zip of heat racing through her body? She hoped so.

She took in his dark eyes. "Yes, we did, Reid. Yes, we did."

"And now I'd like to declare the Light the Dark Festival officially open," Mayor Whittington called into the microphone. "Let's celebrate Coral Cove!"

Just then a *whoosh* of color sailed into the air and was followed by a cracking *boom*. Kaiah jumped and then laughed at herself as fireworks exploded in the sky. Reid pulled her against his side as Piper's hands flew to her face, her mouth agape as she watched fireworks of red and blue, green and purple fill the sky and reflect on the water.

"Oh!" Piper exclaimed as more fireworks flared. "Look at that one! And that one! Oh *wow!*"

Kaiah's eyes found Reid as he whispered to his daughter, who balanced in his arms. He was so dashing with his dark eyes reflecting the sparkling light. She wrapped her arm around his trim waist, leaning her head on his shoulder and wishing the moment could last forever.

All too soon, the grand finale filled the black canvas with hundreds of colored lights streaking and exploding in the air, causing everyone on the shore to gasp with delight. When the colors faded away and smoke and silence were all that was left, they all clapped and cheered—especially Piper and Astrid.

Kaiah stepped away from Reid. The fireworks had come to a close too quickly. She pulled out her camera and captured the lighthouse, lit up in all its glory against the dark sky.

A local band had set up on the stage during the fireworks show and now began the twangy opening chords of "Boot Scootin' Boogie" by Brooks & Dunn. The crowd instantly gravitated toward the honky-tonk tune, and a few couples began to break into a line dance. Others moved toward the shops, pulling out their wallets as they perused the wares.

The Light the Dark Festival was officially open for business.

"Do you want to get some popcorn or ice cream?" Reid's father, Blake, asked the girls, and they both responded with happy cheers. "Let's go," he said.

Becca reached for Piper. "Come with me, Piper," she told her niece.

Reid set Piper down, and Becca took her hand. "Have fun."

Kaiah watched Becca head for the market with her parents and the girls while the enticing scents of hot coffee, fresh waffle cones, and creamy red velvet funnel cakes wafted over her.

Reid took her arm and led her toward the fence that lined the path to the lighthouse. She studied the beautiful structure, admiring how it stood against the clear, dark sky speckled with bright stars.

"Did you know the lighthouse lamp had been repaired?" she asked Reid.

He shrugged, but Kaiah saw his lips twitch ever so slightly.

She swatted his muscular bicep. "You goof! Why didn't you tell me?"

"It was a surprise." He rested his arm on her shoulder and craned his neck to take in his handiwork. "What do you think?"

She lifted her fingertips to the side of his face and gently pulled until his gaze met hers. "It's perfect. Everything is. Did you call in a favor to get the weather cleared up?"

His eyes held a mischievous glint. "I may have folded my hands and put in a request or two. However it happened, I'm just thankful we're blessed with this incredible weather tonight. We'll worry about the weather for the beach cleanup and the picnic tomorrow. Maybe I'll submit a couple more requests."

They leaned against the fence and glanced over at the marketplace, which was bustling with activity while the band continued to play.

"Thank you," he told her, looping his arm around her shoulder.

She looked up at him, searching his face. "You keep saying that, but I really didn't do anything."

He chuckled. "Right." Then he pointed to the market. "You just made this happen. That's all."

She smiled and threaded her fingers with his. "*We* did."

"Lieutenant Turner," the mayor called as she walked over to them. "Looks like everything's off to a great start. Everyone's buzzing about the lighthouse and the fireworks. Plus the shopping that's happening—it's off the charts!" She shook Reid's hand and then Kaiah's. "Thank you for your help with the festival. Truly."

"You're welcome," Reid said.

Kaiah nodded. "I'm relieved it all came together."

The mayor made a sweeping gesture toward the vendors. "You guys have put in the work, and now's the time to enjoy it. Go have some fun," she said before moving on to talk to more folks milling about near the lighthouse.

Kaiah grinned up at Reid. "You heard the mayor. Let's go."

They wandered through the market and soon found Sue and Piper. The six-year-old was holding a giant bag of popcorn in one hand while licking a chocolate ice cream cone in the other. Reid laughed and shook his head as he admired his daughter's palate.

Piper held the bag up to Kaiah. "Want some kettle corn?"

"Absolutely I do." Kaiah took the bag. "Kettle corn is my favorite." She pointed to a nearby bench. "Let's sit down while you finish your cone."

Piper handed her kettle corn to Kaiah, and the foursome sat on the bench and ate their treats, watching people walk and talk, dance and shop.

After snack time Reid visited different vendors with Becca and Astrid, and Kaiah spotted him paying for something before he rejoined them at the bench. He sank down beside Piper and began wiping her hands with a napkin. "It's almost eleven, kiddo. It's way past your bedtime."

Piper shook her head and yawned. "But I'm not even tired."

Kaiah and Reid exchanged smirks.

Kaiah had almost forgotten Reid was still working his shift. "Becca and I will take her home," she offered.

"Thanks. I owe you one," he said before tossing the napkins into a nearby trash can.

Becca and Cash walked over to them. Cash held a sleeping Astrid in his arms.

"I think it's time for us to head home," Becca said.

"Yeah," Kaiah agreed. "This night went by too quickly."

"I'll carry her to the car." Reid lifted Piper into his arms, and she rested her head on his shoulder while they waded through the sea of people toward the parking lot.

When they reached Becca's SUV, she unlocked the doors, and Reid and Cash loaded the two girls into their booster seats. Instantly Piper closed her eyes, and both girls' heads lolled to the side as they slept.

Reid kissed his daughter's head, and she snored softly.

Kaiah smiled at the two of them. She loved watching Reid interact with his daughter.

When Reid straightened up and started toward Kaiah, his radio crackled.

"All available units respond to 1742 Glenn Avenue, Coral Cove, seventy-four-year-old man," the voice over the radio blared. "Head injury. Possible concussion."

Cash kissed Becca. "Duty calls. See you tomorrow, babe," he told her before giving her a quick peck.

Reid said good night to his sister and parents and then turned his attention to Kaiah. "I'll see you bright and early for the beach cleanup." He pulled something out of his pocket and folded it into her palm.

"What's this?"

"Something to help you remember Coral Cove." He kissed her, and her heart skipped a beat as he and Cash double-timed it toward the fire engine.

Kaiah slipped the little bag into her pocket. She couldn't wait to open it after she tucked Piper into bed.

~

"Thank you for the ride," Kaiah told Becca after she'd parked in Reid's driveway.

Becca swiveled toward the back seat where the girls were fast asleep. "Do you need help carrying Piper in?"

"No, I'll just wake her up." She climbed out of the passenger seat and opened the back door. She rubbed Piper's arm as she unbuckled her. "Hey, Piper, time to wake up. We need to walk into the house."

Piper groaned and snuggled deeper into the seat.

"Come on, sweetie. I need you to walk into the house, and then we'll get you in bed, okay?"

"Nooo," Piper groaned.

Becca shut off the SUV. "You carry her, and I'll unlock the door."

"Good idea." Kaiah hoisted the sleepy girl into her arms and then carefully walked up to the house, where Becca had the door unlocked and opened. "Thank you."

"No, thank *you*," Becca said. "You made this festival happen." Then she paused. "And thank you for helping my brother smile again."

Kaiah shuddered as a quick thrill slipped down her spine. Then Piper shifted in her arms and moaned in her sleep.

"You'd better get her in bed. See you tomorrow." Becca jogged down the front steps and out to her SUV.

Kaiah carried Piper to her bedroom, where she managed to pull on her pajamas before tucking her into bed. Ariel curled up in her usual spot at Piper's feet, and Kaiah rubbed the cat's ears before ambling across the hallway to the guest room.

She hopped onto the bed and pulled the small bag from her pocket. Inside she found a dainty beaded bracelet with the words "Coral Cove" spelled out in beads.

Her eyes stung as she pulled the bracelet onto her wrist. Then she flopped back on the bed, held her arm up over her head, and studied the piece.

"I could never forget this place," she whispered.

Chapter 20

PIPER RAN OVER TO Reid and dropped a handful of wrappers into the bag before dashing toward the water once again.

Reid pushed his sunglasses on top of his head, and his eyes roved over the beach. It seemed the entire town had come out to clean up the beach. He bent down and picked up a disposable smoothie cup and dropped it into the trash bag, which was already half full.

Beside him, Kaiah plucked an empty soda bottle and added it to the bag. When she moved her wrist, he caught a flash of beads out of the corner of his eye. She'd worn the beaded bracelet he'd purchased for her. The realization made his chest tighten.

"You like the bracelet?" he asked.

She touched it. "I love it. Every time I see it, I'll think of this wonderful place and all the wonderful people I met."

"Good. I'm glad. I wanted you to have something to remind you of Piper and me."

It was Saturday, and Kaiah had been in Coral Cove for two weeks now. He expected Bill from Coral Cove Car Care would call any day to tell her it was time to pick up her car, and he was planning to find the perfect time to ask her to stay.

"Daddy, look!" Piper held up a take-out bag from a local restaurant. "Why can't people just put their trash in a trash can?"

"That's a very good question, pumpkin." Reid held the bag open, and Piper tossed in the trash.

He turned to look at the sand, cupping his eyes to shield them from the strong morning sun (and *wow*, had the weather forecast been wrong!). They had started their beach cleanup a few hours ago, and he could already see a difference in the shoreline. Although the beach had always been appealing, now it was almost pristine.

"How'd the rest of your night go?" Kaiah asked while adding a handful of cigarette butts, along with an empty carton, into the bag.

"It was fine," he said. "We had a couple of emergency medical calls, but then it was quiet. I did some paperwork and filed a few reports."

"Glad to hear it."

He added a couple of empty cans into the bag.

Kaiah pulled out her camera. "Smile, Reid."

"Wait!" Piper ran over. "Can I be in the picture?"

"Of course you can. Now stand with your daddy. I might put it in the article I'm going to write about the festival after it's over."

Reid squatted down next to Piper, and she wrapped her arms around his neck before Kaiah took more photos.

"Oh no!" Piper announced. "I see more trash over there." She trotted across the sand.

"Don't run," Reid told her before shaking his head. "Why do I even bother?"

"At least she'll have a soft landing," Kaiah quipped, and he laughed. "We have the kite-making class later. I'm sure she'll enjoy that."

"I bet she will. And there's a kite-flying contest and lots of games for the kids."

"I'll have to get some photos of you and Piper with her kite." She pointed toward the booth where a local restaurant owner was handing out basket lunches. "They're selling the baskets for the picnic now. Should we get one?"

"Of course." He had carried a few towels and a large blanket in the backpack he'd brought along. His mother had insisted he and Kaiah have some time to themselves, so she invited Piper to eat lunch with her. He couldn't wait to have a quiet moment with her by the water.

Reid bought a basket and they chose a spot on the sand for lunch. He and Kaiah spread out the large blanket, then took a seat.

~

Kaiah smeared brown mustard on her turkey sandwich and looked out toward where Piper ate with Becca, Cash, Astrid, and Reid's parents across the beach. Beside her, Reid seemed relaxed while he sipped from a bottle of water.

She studied her beaded bracelet and turned it on her wrist while she munched on her sandwich.

"I see Brynn in Piper," Reid said.

Kaiah looked up from her bracelet and saw Reid's face soften as he watched his daughter. "The bigger she gets, the more she looks like her."

"Becca told me that you grew up with Brynn."

He nodded. "She was Becca's best friend since we started school.

She always hung around, and when we were kids I didn't think much of her. I saw her on the playground and at church. She was at our house all the time and practically lived in Becca's room. She was always just Becca's friend. Until high school."

"Becca said Brynn had a crush on you."

"She did, but I was oblivious." He laughed. "Somehow she changed the summer before we started high school. Or maybe I changed. I don't know." He popped a potato chip into his mouth. "Either way, I noticed her—like, *really* noticed her. And when the homecoming dance came around, I took a chance and asked her to go. I expected her to reject me, and then she and Becks would make fun of me for the rest of the year. But she actually said yes." He held his hand up. "No, she said something like, 'I thought you'd never ask.' And I was like, 'What do you mean?' and she said, 'Reid, I've had a crush on you since fourth grade.'" He laughed, and Kaiah joined in.

Reid crunched on another chip. "I thought she liked my friend Cody. He was captain of the football team. She said she thought he was cute, but what can I say? Apparently she couldn't resist the Turner charm."

He waggled his eyebrows and she swatted his arm, laughing.

"Did you play football?" she asked.

"I was more of a bench warmer, but that didn't bother her at all. We started dating freshman year, and we stayed together from then on. We had a few rocky periods when she went away to college—which, I mean, everybody does—but we worked through it. And then I proposed after she graduated from college. Just your typical high school sweetheart kind of stuff. I thought we'd be together forever."

Kaiah nodded and tried to imagine what it must've felt like to know you'd found your forever person. She'd always dreamed of having a life partner, someone she could text inside jokes to, someone to decorate the Christmas tree with, someone who would pick up orange juice on the way home because he knew it was her favorite. But it just didn't seem to be in the cards for her.

She took a bite of her sandwich, and while she ate, she peered out toward the water where Cash played with Astrid and Piper in the sand.

"People like to tell me that Piper needs a mom, and I've been alone long enough." He kept his focus on the waves. "It's so easy for people to tell me what my daughter and I need."

"What do *you* think you need?" Kaiah asked.

Reid studied her. "I want to find someone to share my life with, but it's not something I can force. It has to happen naturally. I need to find someone who can love my daughter as much as they love me."

Kaiah nodded slowly, and a chill rushed over her skin despite the warm spring sunshine. "Piper's a happy little girl. Does she need a mother when she has your sister and your mother, and they're so good with her?"

"That's true," he said. "She has my sister and my mom. She also has you. For now. Whatever that's worth. You're the only other woman I've seen her bond with."

Kaiah touched her bracelet while the weight of his words settled on her heart.

"What do you think of my kite, Daddy?"

A couple hours later, Piper held up her colorful kite with its long tail.

"It's beautiful," he told her. "Why don't we fly it now?"

After lunch, Reid and Piper attended one of the kite-making workshops Trisha Witherspoon, the owner of Crafty Creations, held at her booth by the beach. Becca, Cash, and Astrid also attended, but they'd already finished their kite and were running on the beach, participating in the kite-flying contest.

Reid and Piper trudged out onto the warm sand, and Reid spotted Kaiah taking photos of the kites dancing in the air. She was gorgeous yet casual, wearing a gray tank top and jean shorts, with her thick golden hair pulled back in a ponytail and small hoops dangling from her ears. But what he couldn't stop staring at were her long, lean legs, tanned by the sun.

"Let's stand here, Daddy."

Piper yanked him out of his daydream, hopping on the spot where she'd chosen to launch her kite. Reid held the kite in his hands, and on the count of three, he thrust it upward. The gentle spring breeze carried the kite as it sailed toward the sky.

"Hold on to the string, pumpkin," Reid told her.

Piper bit her bottom lip as she held on to the spool with all of her might.

Reid pointed. "Look at it go, Piper. You made that glorious kite!"

"Piper! Reid!" Kaiah pointed her camera toward them. "Smile!" she ordered.

Reid tapped Piper's shoulder and gestured toward Kaiah. "Look over there, honey. Kaiah wants to take our photo."

They both grinned for the camera. "This is so fun, Daddy," Piper said.

"It is, isn't it?"

"I'm so glad Miss Kaiah came to see us. I'm having such a great time with her."

Reid smiled. "I am too."

That evening Reid's eyes flickered to his rearview mirror to where Piper slept in her seat. Her second-place ribbon was stuck to her shirt, and she hugged her kite against her chest. "She's tuckered out," he said.

Kaiah rotated toward Piper in the back seat and grinned. "She had an exciting day. I'd be more surprised if she *wasn't* fast asleep."

Reid looked over at Kaiah. They'd spent the day swimming, laughing, and eating together, the three of them. He'd only known Kaiah for two weeks, and he knew it was fast, but he didn't care. It felt like the three of them belonged together.

Kaiah dipped her chin toward the screen on her digital camera. "I'll have to show you the photos I took of the kids flying their kites. I may be biased, but I think they're pretty good. I'm going to include them in my article, as long as it's okay with you and the other parents."

Reid steered down the street toward his house. "If you say they're good, then I know they're good. You'll have to show me after I get her settled into bed."

Kaiah flipped a few buttons on her camera, staring at the screen. "I wish you didn't have to work tomorrow."

"I know. But after tomorrow I'm off five days in a row."

"Hmm." She rested her finger on her chin, her mouth curved in a smirk. "I get why you took this job. You're off more than you work."

He chuckled as he parked in the driveway. "Let's get her inside."

Reid carried Piper while Kaiah brought in their bags.

When he set Piper on her bed, she yawned and rubbed her eyes. "Can Miss Kaiah give me a bath tonight?" she asked.

"I'll ask her." Reid slipped out into the hallway. "Kaiah?"

"Yeah?" she called from down the hallway.

"Miss Piper has requested that you give her a bath."

Kaiah appeared in the doorway, smiling. "No problem."

Reid went out to the kitchen where Ariel rubbed against his shin and began her usual repertoire of meows. Giggles filtered in from the hallway, and he smiled while he fed the cat. When he heard a phone ding with a text, he found Kaiah's phone sitting on the counter. He held his breath, debating if he should investigate it.

What was on Kaiah's phone wasn't any of his business. She had a whole life outside of him. She was allowed to share only what she wanted.

But when the phone dinged again, he couldn't help himself. He glanced down at the screen.

Hayes: Hey, I miss you.

Hayes: Kaiah, I messed up. I love you. Call me. Let's work this out.

A giant pit began to expand in his stomach.

Then her phone dinged again with a third text.

Hayes: Let's be a family—you, me, and George.

The pit was the size of the Grand Canyon now. Suddenly he realized he wasn't breathing.

Then Reid shook his head, forcing the doom out of his mind. Kaiah had made it clear that she was done with Hayes. And this loser was kidding himself if he thought he had another chance with Kaiah. Yes, they had a history. And yes, they had adopted a dog together. But that didn't mean they were a family. Hayes had left that family behind.

Still, the idea of her reconciling with that guy jerked a knot in his gut.

"Daddy!" Piper called. "Come listen to my story."

Reid grabbed the phone off the counter. "Coming, sweetie." He carried the phone to Piper's bedroom, where she sat on the bed wearing her favorite mermaid pajamas. He held the phone out to Kaiah. "You got a text."

She took the phone. "Thanks." She glanced at the screen and kept her expression blank, but as she read the screen, her brow wrinkled. She pressed her lips together, locked the phone, and shoved it into the back pocket of her jean shorts.

If only he could read her thoughts. Though again, Hayes was her business. If she wanted to talk to Reid about it, she would. He wasn't supposed to see those texts anyway. Still, he wondered, was she going to say anything to him?

Kaiah sat on the end of the bed and began rubbing Ariel's chin. The cat responded by closing her eyes and purring—loudly.

"How about you both read me a story?" Piper held up her favorite book, *The Littlest Mermaid*. "You can take turns."

"Sure." Kaiah reached for the book. "Want me to start?"

Piper patted the bed on either side of her. "Yeah, but I want you both to sit with me. Here."

Kaiah snuggled up to Piper in the space between the girl and the wall, while Reid balanced on the edge on the other side. For the next half hour, Reid and Kaiah took turns reading the book, passing it back and forth while Piper beamed and held her favorite mermaid doll. When they reached the end of the story, they kissed her on the cheek at the same time, prompting laughter.

"Let's do this every night forever!" Piper held up her doll.

Kaiah gave Reid a sheepish smile. "It was fun, wasn't it, Reid?"

"Yeah." His heart turned over as he turned his attention to his daughter. "Be good tomorrow, pumpkin." He kissed her forehead and then followed Kaiah out to the hallway.

"Good night, Reid," Kaiah said before wrapping her arms around his neck and kissing him. "Maybe I'll see you at the festival." She smiled and held up her finger. "In a nonemergency capacity, of course."

"Right." He kissed her forehead and then her lips. "Sleep well, Kaiah," he told her before she slipped into the guest room.

Chapter 21

KAIAH SNAPPED A FEW photos of the long line snaking down the sidewalk as she and Becca walked to the first of the garden tours. "It's official, Becca. Coral Cove Brightening Blooms is gonna be a huge success! Just look at that line." She pointed toward the few dozen people waiting to tour Mrs. Gordon's rose garden.

"That's not even the best part." Becca rested her hand on Kaiah's arm and lowered her voice. "We've already raised more than five thousand dollars for the school, and it's only Sunday. I think we're going to exceed our goal."

Kaiah grinned. "That's amazing news. I bet that means you guys can renovate the lighthouse too."

She took a few more photos before they took their place in line. "Your dad was so sweet to keep the girls today so we could tour the gardens."

"My dad loves to have the girls to himself. He likes to show them 'boy things,' as he says." Becca made air quotes with her fingers.

"What are 'boy things'?"

"Oh, you know," Becca began, waving her arms around. "Taking them to car shows, showing how to use a screwdriver, stuff like that. I walked in on him once with the hood of the car open. He was showing them how to change their oil."

Kaiah laughed. "It's never too early, I guess. I'm definitely not good at keeping up with car maintenance. Maybe your dad can show me a thing or two."

Becca laughed too. "I think my dad was hoping for a grandson, but he won't admit it." She faced the front of the line, and her smile flattened for a fraction of a second.

Kaiah held her breath. The journalist in her wanted to ask her what she was thinking about, but the friend in her wanted to respect her privacy. "My sister Kam just found out she's expecting."

"That's awesome news." Becca's wide smile was back. "Her first?"

Kaiah nodded. "They've been trying for a while now. I'm so happy for her."

"I love that for her." Becca fiddled with the large diamond and gold band on her ring finger. "Brynn always said she wanted a dozen kids, but Reid said he'd only agree to a half dozen."

"A half dozen, huh?"

Becca chuckled. "You don't like kids?"

Kaiah held her hands up. "I didn't say that. But as the middle of five, along with another four stepsiblings, I can assure you big families can be chaotic. And sometimes . . . sometimes kids get lost in the shuffle."

"That makes sense." Becca pulled out a tube of lip balm and smoothed it over her lips while the line inched up a few steps. "I'd just like a couple more."

Kaiah felt a twinge in her chest for her friend. "Don't give up hope."

"I won't." She stuck the lip balm in her pocket. "I've gotten all kinds of advice. *It happens when you least expect it*, blah, blah, blah." Her lips tipped downward. "I just hope it *happens* at some point."

Kaiah rubbed her shoulder.

"Now that I've brought the conversation down . . ." Becca gave her a somber smile. "What's new with you?"

"Hayes texted me again." Kaiah blurted the words out without thinking.

Becca's dark eyes narrowed. "For real? What did he say this time?"

Kaiah grimaced and summarized the text messages. "He's still trying to apologize, and he's practically begging me to talk to him."

Becca's dark eyes scrutinized her. "Does he know your email address?"

"Of course."

"I know you want him to reach you if he has a story lead or wants to return George. But what if you told him you're blocking his texts? And he can *only* email you?"

Kaiah released a long breath in defeat. "That's a good idea."

"Seriously, block the jerk. If he really needs to find you, he'll email you. And if you see his emails show up in your inbox, you can scan the subject line and delete them if you need to."

"Good point."

They moved forward in line and purchased tickets for the garden tour, along with a map.

"I'm so thrilled with how this turned out." Becca pointed to the map. "This is Mrs. Waterson's garden." She leaned toward Kaiah and lowered her voice. "She's known for her roses. Personally, I think my mom's roses are even more spectacular. But promise you won't quote me on that."

"I won't." Kaiah chuckled. "Let's go through all the gardens, and I'll take photos."

They wandered through the large, picture-perfect yard, and Kaiah took photos of the rosebushes. She marveled at the rows of flowers in every color of the rainbow—even multicolored ones. She knelt down and took several close-ups, capturing tight buds to blooms spreading their petals to the sun, and even a few wide shots to capture the fullness of the foliage. Becca walked through the beds, pointing out the most vibrant blooms for Kaiah to capture. Spectators ranged from ages five to eighty-five, and all were marveling at the blooms sending their perfume into the warm spring sunshine. It was truly a gorgeous day for a garden tour.

"Have you spoken to my brother today?" Becca asked while they moved on to the next garden, which belonged to Mrs. Phillips.

Kaiah sidestepped a group of teenagers who hurried past giggling. "No. Why?"

"Just wondering." Becca shrugged, but her lips formed a grin.

They moved through the gate, and Kaiah spotted a few columns of tall white boxes beside a colorful spray of wildflowers.

Beehives.

They were beehives. With thousands of bees. Right here. In this garden.

She froze while Becca continued to walk farther ahead. After a few moments, Becca stopped and turned around, her expression stoic. "You okay, Ky? Your face is as white as a sheet."

Kaiah's finger trembled while she pointed toward the hives. "I, uh, I don't do bees. Or any flying insects, for that matter. I'm allergic to bees, and wasp stings *hurt* to high heaven. So I'm terrified of all of them."

"Oh?" Becca looked concerned as she glanced toward the hives and then back at Kaiah. "Oh no. I didn't realize that."

"Yeah, I had a bad reaction to a beesting when I was a kid." Kaiah rubbed her arm as the memory flared in her mind, and her entire body started to shake. "I'm sorry, but I just can't."

Becca looped her arm around Kaiah's shoulder in a side hug. "Hey, it's no problem. There are plenty of other gardens to tour. Let's get you out of here."

They continued following the map and touring gardens for the next hour. When they arrived at Blake and Sue's house, they found Astrid and Piper sitting at a table in the driveway, handing out cups of lemonade and homemade chocolate chip cookies to the visitors.

"What's going on here?" Becca asked as she and Kaiah approached the table.

Piper pointed to her grandfather. "We asked Grandpa if we could give out snacks to everyone who came to see Nana's roses."

"We made lemonade and cookies," Astrid chimed in.

"Uh-huh." Becca covered her mouth and whispered something to her father.

Blake, her father, shook his head. "We're not trying to buy votes for best garden. They just wanted to hand out snacks."

Becca seemed unconvinced, but she also helped herself to a cup of lemonade and a cookie.

Kaiah held up her camera. "Would you lovely ladies please smile for me?"

As if on cue, Piper and Astrid threw their arms around each other and sang, "Cheeeese!"

Kaiah captured several photos, including a few with the girls serving their customers. They were going to be an adorable addition to the article. "Thanks, ladies." She swiped a cookie and then followed Becca to a gate that led to the backyard.

They followed the slate path around the large house, then stopped at the edge of the yard. Kaiah glanced around in awe, taking in the two fountains, a row of benches, and the stone pathway leading to a large deck flanked by walls of rosebushes.

"*Wow*," Kaiah gushed. Her eyes could hardly believe how vibrant Sue's flowers were, and the variety of colors. "This garden is phenomenal. Seriously, it should be on HGTV. It must have taken years to get it just right." She grabbed her camera and captured photos of visitors enjoying the view. "These flowers are breathtaking."

"Right?" Becca asked. "Better than Mrs. Waterson's."

"By *far*."

For the next thirty minutes Kaiah walked around the yard and filled her camera roll with Sue's glorious blooms. A couple of bees buzzed by her, and she tried to ignore them, despite the hair standing on the back of her neck.

Just ignore the bees. You're a grown up, Ky! They're here for the flowers, not you.

She took a few more photos of the roses and started back across the yard with Becca. "I think I want to try some of that lemonade," she said. "It looks really—"

Her words were cut off when she felt a sharp prick—a sting?—on her shoulder.

"I . . . I, um . . ."

Kaiah trailed off as she began to sway, her tongue beginning to grow thick and hot in her mouth.

Becca took her arm. "Ky? You okay?"

She felt another prick on her neck, then on her forearm. Pain radiated down her back, continuing to her arm and shoulder.

What was that?

She stopped short, and a wave of nausea washed over her as she felt the color drain from her face.

"Kaiah, you're pale." Becca's voice shook as she led Kaiah to a bench. "Sit," she ordered, and Kaiah complied. Worry fell over Becca's face. "What's wrong?"

"I don't . . ." Kaiah dipped her chin down and found a waterfall of welts cascading down her right forearm. "Becca, I don't . . . feel well."

Her head started to pound, and her throat felt thick. Suddenly she couldn't swallow, and she could hardly breathe. It was as if there was a large knot clogging her throat.

"B-Beck," Kaiah stuttered. "I think . . . somethinth ith . . ." But her voice sounded funny. Her words were slurred. She wilted back on the bench as she suddenly found it hard to breathe. She wheezed.

"Kaiah!" Becca pulled out her phone as her features were frozen in fear. "I think you were stung. Do you have an EpiPen?" Her voice was full of panic.

Kaiah shook her head.

A man rushed over. "Do you need help?"

"Call 911," she said before reciting the address. "My dad is out front by the table. Ask him to come back here."

"Becca?" Sue appeared in Kaiah's peripheral vision. "Oh! Kaiah! What's happened?"

"I think Kaiah's having an allergic reaction to a sting," Becca said, but her voice sounded far away. "We need help!"

"Blake!" Sue called. "Get some ice!"

Kaiah tried to focus, but her vision was fuzzy at the edges. She tried to watch as people rushed around, but nothing made sense. Voices were hollering, and it sounded like a little girl was crying.

What's happening?

Becca knelt in front of her as she punched in numbers on her phone. Kaiah tried to watch her, but her eyes felt so heavy, they kept wanting to close.

And why was it so hard to breathe? Was someone sitting on her chest?

"Reid!" Becca yelled. "Reid! I've been trying to call you. It's an emergency. Get to Mom's house—*quick*! It's Kaiah. She's having an allergic reaction to a beesting. She needs an EpiPen, and I don't have one!" Her voice broke, her breaths grew ragged. "Get here, Reid. *Please!*"

Dots swam in front of Kaiah's eyes, and then everything went black.

Reid rested his hands on his lap. Chris and Cash addressed the crew while they stood in the bay beside the fire engines. It was their usual afternoon debrief.

Nothing too intriguing to discuss. The most exciting call they'd had was when one of Cash's neighbors had accidentally set his yard on fire while burning some trash, but it didn't take long to extinguish it. Reid appreciated dull days when they only had a couple of calls and no one was seriously hurt. Not only were the residents okay, but he also didn't have much paperwork. It really was a win-win for both Reid and the team.

Reid's phone vibrated with a call, and he ignored it. He couldn't stand it when his team studied their phones while he was addressing them. Instead, he expected to receive his team's full attention, and he always did his best to extend the same courtesy to his captain and his chief. Folding his arms over his chest, Reid tried to concentrate on the meeting.

When his phone began vibrating again, Reid assumed it was a spam call. Surely it was someone trying to sell him an extended warranty on the Suburban or some other scam.

But then unease gripped his chest. It was something he only felt when his sister was anxious about something. It was their "twin thing," as they'd called it since they were little.

Something's wrong.

He couldn't stop himself from fishing his phone from his pocket. His eyes focused on his sister's name on the screen. Becca knew better than to blow up his phone when he was at work. She would only repeatedly call him if she had reason to—if it was serious. That anxiety that had been building in his chest morphed into something deeper.

Dread.

His blood ran cold. Had something happened to one of their parents? Or Piper?

Oh no.

He had to call her back—*now*—whether or not his bosses considered him rude or, worse yet, insubordinate. He unlocked his phone just as a shrill tone screamed through the loudspeaker, startling him. At the same time, the fluorescent lights above him in the large bay flickered.

"All available units respond to 250 Little Island Road. Female, mid-twenties. Multiple insect stings and possible anaphylaxis."

Reid's eyes snapped to Cash's. "That's my parents' house."

"Right." Cash waved at the team. "Let's go."

Just as the voice began to repeat the call, Reid's phone vibrated, indicating that his sister had left a message.

A sick feeling washed over him. She rarely left him a message, and she'd never leave one just to chat, especially when he was at work. His fingers shook and adrenaline pulsed through his body as he listened to her message, and her frantic voice filled his ears.

"Cash!" Reid's body shook as he listened to the message. "Cash! We gotta go. It's Kaiah!"

Cash's eyes were swimming in puzzlement. "How do you know?"

"Becca called me, and it sounds like she's going into shock. Let's go!"

Reid grabbed his gear and raced to the engine. He jumped into the passenger seat, his body continuing to vibrate while worry coursed through him.

What if they didn't make it in time? What if she . . .?

No, no, no! This is not happening again!

Cash, Chris, and the rest of the crew joined him, and the engine roared to life, siren blaring.

As Chris steered the truck down the street, Reid switched on the radio and waited for more information to come through. He drummed his fingers on the door of the truck as worry and fear clashed within him. His pulse sounded loud in his ears.

"Reid," Cash said, speaking over his headset. "She's gonna be fine, man."

Reid waved off his brother-in-law's platitudes. "Do we have an EpiPen?"

"Of course we do," Cash told him. "The ambulance will meet us there, and they'll have one too."

Hang on, Kaiah. Please, just hang on.

"Units are responding to a female, approximately mid-twenties, with at least three beestings," the voice continued. "Patient is unconscious and unresponsive. She's pale, and areas around the stings are covered in hives."

Reid felt like the wind had been knocked out of him. Kaiah was unresponsive. Would they arrive in time to help her? He turned to Chris as the fire truck approached an intersection. "Can we hurry?"

"We're almost there." Chris kept his eyes trained on the road ahead as they roared onto Little Island Road. "It's all going to be fine. We'll help her."

Reid braced the door handle, ready to launch himself from the truck when they arrived. When his parents' house came into view, his heartbeat spiked. Flashing lights from two ambulances reflected off the house.

"EMTs are here," Cash said, stating the obvious. "She's in good hands."

As soon as the truck slowed, Reid wrenched the door open and jumped from the moving truck. He took off running across the driveway past curious onlookers.

He had to save Kaiah. He just had to.

Chapter 22

REID BOLTED THROUGH THE open gate to the backyard. His heart pounded against his rib cage as he approached four EMTs standing over Kaiah. She was lying on a gurney, and when he saw her eyes were open, a thin ribbon of relief rushed through him.

"How is she?" Reid asked, his voice thready and his heartbeat echoing in his ears.

"Lieutenant Turner." A young EMT he recognized as Taylor Bailey pointed to Kaiah. "We gave her an EpiPen, and she's regained consciousness. Her vitals are coming back to normal. We're going to transport her to the hospital for an eval."

"Thank you," he told Taylor before turning his attention to Kaiah. "Hey, Ky." His words sounded pained.

Kaiah rubbed her eyes. "What happened?" she whispered, her voice shaky. She reached for him, and he cradled her quaking hand in his.

"Just rest," he told her, and his voice caught in his throat. He pushed her hair away from her face. He spotted a rash and hives on her neck, shoulder, and arm. Worry threatened to drag him under and drown him. If the EMTs hadn't reached her in time . . . He wouldn't allow himself to finish that thought.

His team jogged up behind him, and while another EMT gave them an update, Reid focused on Taylor. "I want to ride with her to the hospital."

"Oh?" she asked. "Are you family?"

Reid shook his head. "I'm her—I'm her boyfriend," he said, and he liked the sound of that word. "She doesn't have any family here."

"Daddy! Daddy! Daddy!"

Reid turned just as Piper rushed over and threw herself into his arms. "Hey, baby."

"Miss Kaiah's sick." Piper sniffed and tears trailed down her cheeks. "Is she going to be okay?"

"Yes, sweetie, she is," he told her before kissing her head.

Becca, Cash, Astrid, and his parents appeared behind her.

"Piper's been a mess." Becca wiped her hands over her face and picked up Astrid, who was also wiping tears. "We were so worried." Her voice was hoarse, and Cash pulled her against him. "It all happened so fast. We were talking, and then her face turned white, she said she didn't feel well, and she passed out. Someone called 911, and I called you . . ." Her voice trailed off, and Cash rubbed her back.

"I'm glad you called me." Reid touched Piper's nose. "Miss Kaiah's going to be okay. I have to go now, and I need you to be brave. Can you do that for me, Piper?" His daughter nodded, and he handed her to his father. Then he addressed his brother-in-law. "Chief, I want to ride to the hospital with her and make sure she's okay."

"That's fine," Cash said. "We'll send someone to get you."

Dad rubbed Becca's shoulder. "And we'll come to the hospital too. Kaiah's like family."

"Yeah," Reid said. "She is." He kissed Piper's cheek. "I'll see you soon."

Kaiah watched the IV dripping down from the pole and into her arm. The events from earlier in the day were fuzzy, but now she was at the ER at Coral Cove Regional Hospital. This was definitely not on her bingo card this morning.

"Kaiah? Can I come in?"

Reid's voice sounded from outside the curtain, and she finger-combed her hair. What was her problem? She was in a hospital gown with an IV in her arm. There was no way she was going to look cute. She was still covered in hives.

It is what it is. Now he gets to see me at my worst.

"Yeah," she said, her voice sounding thin.

He pushed open the curtain, slipped inside, and closed it behind him. "How are you?" he asked, his face full of concern.

Ready to die from embarrassment. "Okay."

He pulled a chair over to her bed, empty except for her purse, and dropped himself onto it. Then he set her purse on the rolling table beside her bed.

Kaiah let her gaze travel over him. She would never get tired of seeing that man and his biceps straining the arms of his uniform. Nope. Never. In fact, if she had her phone in her hand, she'd sneak a photo of him right now and cherish it forever. Maybe she should see if her camera was in her purse . . .

"You gave us all a real scare." Reid blew out a sigh that sounded like he'd released it deep in his soul, rested his elbows on his thighs, and shook his head.

"I'm so sorry." She grimaced. "I didn't mean to ruin your day."

He barked a laugh that shocked her. "Why are you sorry? It wasn't your fault. Trust me, you didn't ruin anything." His smile faded. "You'd mentioned that you were stung when you were a kid."

"Yeah, the first time was when I was stung by a bee in first grade."

"What happened?"

She rubbed her neck as the memory swelled in her mind. "I was running my hand along a fence." She rested her arm on the bed rail. "I saw the bee there before my brain could stop my hand. Next thing I knew, it had stung me and left the stinger in. My arm swelled up, and they put it in a sling. Then I was stung again in high school, and the same thing happened—my arm swelled up."

"And you don't carry an EpiPen." It was more a statement than a question.

"I was never stung again, and no one ever told me to carry one."

"I'm sure the doctor will tell you to now. Allergies can get worse when we become adults."

"I know that now." She opened her backpack purse and felt her phone. But there was a big gap in the pocket that shouldn't have been there.

My camera.

She pulled in a gulp of air. All of those photos she'd taken during the festival were gone. Now what would she do? She groaned.

"What's wrong?" he asked.

"My camera," she began. "I'd been taking photos of the gardens and—"

"Don't worry. Becca has it. She's coming up to get you, and Cash is going to pick me up."

Kaiah pulled out her phone and set it on the table. Then she met Reid's concerned expression while she tried to put together the pieces of what had happened. Why were her thoughts so fuzzy?

"It was so strange, Reid," she said. "I remember feeling pain, and then everything went black. The next thing I saw was a couple of EMTs standing over me, and I felt a strange sensation in my body. My heart was racing, and I couldn't catch my breath. And then you were there, and then we were in the ambulance, but I'm not sure how it all happened."

"You were stung three times. Becca said someone called 911, and she called me. When I got her message and she said you were going into shock . . ." His dark eyes sparkled in the fluorescent light, and he sniffed. "If you hadn't gotten an EpiPen in time . . ." He scrubbed his hand over his mouth as his eyes misted over.

The worry in his face was too much for her. For a moment she couldn't speak.

"I'm sorry," she whispered. "I didn't mean to scare you." She reached for him.

"Hey." Leaning over, he took her hand in his. "Stop apologizing. I'm grateful it happened when other people were around, because if you'd been alone . . . I can't even allow myself to imagine what would've happened." He gave her hand a squeeze, and a crooked smile overtook his handsome features. "I kinda like you. I don't want to imagine something bad happening to you."

She laughed. "I'm glad. The feeling's mutual."

Leaning down, he kissed her forehead and then her lips, and she closed her eyes, enjoying how his mouth lingered against hers. "I'm so glad you're okay, Kaiah," he whispered, and his husky tone sent a shiver through her.

The curtain opened, and a woman in scrubs with a stethoscope looped around her shoulders appeared holding a clipboard. "Ms. Ross, I'm Dr. House. How are you feeling?"

"Okay," she said.

"You had a very bad reaction to a few beestings. I see you received an EpiPen at the scene. We're treating you with an IV of antihistamines, and we're going to keep an eye on you for a bit before we let you go. And I'm going to send you on your way with a prescription for a steroid." She set the clipboard down and then picked up her stethoscope. "I'm going to have a listen if that's okay."

Kaiah was aware of Reid watching her while the doctor listened to her heart and lungs.

"Everything sounds good," the doctor said. "Have you had this reaction in the past?"

Kaiah gave her a quick summary of when she was stung as a child. "It hasn't happened again, but I've had a phobia of bees and wasps since then. I try to stay away from them."

The doctor nodded. "I recommend you carry an EpiPen with you in the future."

"Told you," Reid muttered.

Dr. House smiled. "He's right. Are you her husband or boyfriend or . . . ?"

"Oh. Um. Boyfriend," Kaiah stammered, and when she met his stare, his approving expression sent warmth wafting over her body again. Why did this man always cause that reaction in her?

Dr. House smiled. "If you don't mind hanging out a bit, I'd like to make sure you're okay before we cut you loose."

"Okay," Kaiah said. "Thank you."

The doctor left, and Kaiah's phone dinged with a text. She read a message from her sister on the screen.

Kam: Hey, sis. What's up? How's the festival going?

Kaiah locked her phone and met Reid's gaze. "I suppose that's good news from the doctor."

He nodded and rested his right ankle on his left knee. But a strange expression rippled over his face.

What did that mean?

An awkward silence filled the space, and she longed to read his thoughts.

"Did Hayes text you again?" he finally asked.

Her eyes snapped to Reid's, and she was shocked to find worry in his eyes. "Hayes?" she asked. "Why . . . ?" She swallowed a gasp as understanding filled her mind. "You saw his texts last night."

He swallowed, his Adam's apple bobbing. "Yeah, I did. I didn't mean to," he said. "You were in the bathroom with Piper, and your phone dinged. I saw it light up on the screen, and, well." He licked his lips. "Did you answer him?"

"No. I didn't."

He remained silent, and he seemed more anxious than before he'd asked the question. Was he jealous? But why would he be?

"You can look at my texts from him. I don't mind." She unlocked her phone, pulled up Hayes's texts, and held the phone out to him. "Here. Take it."

"It's none of my business."

"I have nothing to hide, Reid." She continued to hold the phone out to him. "Go ahead and look. I didn't respond to him last night, and he didn't text me now. It was Kam just checking in." She paused, but he didn't move. "Reid, you can read it. I trust you."

He hesitated and then took her phone, glanced at the screen, and handed it back. Shame flickered over his face. "I'm sorry." He raked his hand through his short hair. "I shouldn't have done that. I guess I'm just a little jealous."

"Listen, it's over between us. I mean it." She set the phone on the table and reached for him, and he clasped her hands in his. "He's part of my past, and that's where he'll stay."

Reid's posture relaxed—slightly.

The curtain opened again, and a nurse appeared.

"Ms. Ross, Rebecca Griffin and Sue Turner are here to see you," the nurse said.

"Would you please send them in?" Kaiah asked.

"I will," the nurse said before leaving.

Reid pulled his phone from his pocket. "I should get back to work since they're here," he said. "I'll text Cash." He typed on his phone, and then his gaze met hers. "I wish I could stay."

His words warmed her from the inside out. "I'll be fine," she said.

He leaned down, and when his lips brushed hers, his kiss was slow and gentle. "I'm so glad you're okay," he whispered while his fingertip traced her cheek and her jaw. "Don't scare me like that again, okay?"

"I'll try not to. I promise."

He touched her shoulder. "I'll call you later to check on you." His phone chimed, and he looked down at it. "Cash is on his way to pick me up. Promise me you'll take it easy."

"I will, Lieutenant."

The curtain opened again, and Becca and Sue scurried in as Reid stepped aside.

"We've been so worried," Becca said as she bent to hug Kaiah.

Sue touched her hand. "You gave us quite the scare, sweetheart. I'm so glad you're okay. Piper and Astrid are worried sick. Blake is too."

"I'm sorry for worrying you guys. How was the rest of the garden tour?" Kaiah asked.

Becca jammed her thumb toward her mom. "My mom won the trophy for the best garden. I *told* you her roses were the cream of the crop." She pulled her phone out and flashed a photo of Sue holding a huge trophy, with Piper and Astrid grinning on either side of her.

"I'm not surprised." Reid leaned over to see the photo. "Good job, Mom."

Becca's expression became serious. "I'm so glad you were on duty today."

"Me too." He rubbed Kaiah's arm. "I hate to leave, but I have to get back to work."

"Don't worry about it. Thanks for coming with me. I'll see you tomorrow," Kaiah said.

He pulled her in for a hug, and she held on to him while inhaling his comforting scent. "Take good care of yourself, Ky," he whispered in her ear, and his deep, smooth voice sent a delicious chill shimmying down her spine.

"I will," she promised. She wanted to hold on to him forever.

Reid stood and divided a look between Becca and Sue. "Watch out for her tonight, and get her back to the hospital if she needs to be seen again."

"We will," Becca said. "I'll stay at your house and make sure she's okay."

Reid nodded. "Thanks. Give my love to Piper." He sauntered out of the examination room.

A knowing look passed between Becca and her mother as Reid disappeared through the curtain.

"Thank you for taking such good care of me," Kaiah told Becca later that evening as she relaxed on her boyfriend's sofa. Sue and Becca had taken her back to Reid's house, where Blake and the girls had brought takeout from a nearby sandwich shop. Sitting with these kind people at the kitchen table, cutting up and swapping stories, Kaiah was overwhelmed by how much she enjoyed being with Reid's family. They were the kind of family she'd always wished for but never had: close enough to mess with each other, kind and considerate even in their differences. She was grateful they'd allowed her to be part of their little unit.

Kaiah covered her mouth to shield a yawn. "Sorry, guys. I think all of the excitement from today is taking a toll on me." She stood and gathered up their empty plates.

"Oh no you don't." Becca jumped up and swatted her hands. "You get ready for bed. I'll take care of the kitchen."

Sue stood up. "Let me and your dad clean up the kitchen." She eyed Kaiah. "You get ready for bed." Then she focused on her daughter again. "And you take care of the girls."

"I want Miss Kaiah to tuck me and Astrid into bed." Piper pulled on Kaiah's arm.

Kaiah faced Becca. "Is that all right? I think I can handle sitting during bathtime and reading a couple of bedtime stories."

"Pleeeease, Auntie?" Piper begged. "Me and Astrid will be really good. Right, Astrid?"

"Uh-huh!" Astrid insisted.

Becca's expression warmed. "Fine, fine. But you be gentle with Miss Kaiah. She's had a long day."

Blake set up a cot in Piper's room for Astrid, and Kaiah sat with the girls while they took their bath. After they were dressed in their pajamas, the girls climbed into their beds. Ariel took her usual spot at Piper's feet. After Sue and Blake kissed the girls and told them goodbye, Kaiah read them *The Littlest Mermaid*.

"Now it's time to go to sleep," Kaiah said after finishing the story and tucking them in. "You have sweet dreams." She kissed each of them on the head. "I'll see you guys in the morning."

"Miss Kaiah," Piper called when Kaiah had reached the door. "Are you okay now?"

She smiled at the girl. "I feel much better."

Piper's big brown eyes brimmed with tears. "I was so scared," she said as she started to sob.

"Hey, sweetie." Kaiah rushed over to Piper's bed. Her heart pinched as she rubbed Piper's cheek. "I promise I'm okay." She ripped a few tissues from a nearby box and wiped up the six-year-old's tears. "You don't have to cry, Piper. I'm all better."

"It was so scary," Astrid said, her voice shaking. "Your eyes were closed."

"Yeah," Piper agreed with a sniff.

"I'm so sorry for scaring you." Kaiah worked to keep her voice even despite the guilt rushing through her. "I'm going to carry medicine with me so that if I ever get stung again, I can take care of myself. I'll do my best never to scare you like that again."

Piper held her arms out, and Kaiah pulled her in for a hug. "I love you, Miss Kaiah."

Kaiah swallowed her own sob, and she sniffed. "I love you too, Piper." Then she touched Astrid's arm. "I love you too, Astrid." She dropped the tissues into a nearby trash can. "Now we all need some sleep. We've had a very busy day."

She slipped out into the hallway, leaving Piper's door cracked for the cat to escape if she needed. Then she found Becca in the den.

Becca had changed into gray yoga pants and a red tank top, and she was eating a bowl of ice cream and watching *Runaway Bride*.

A woman after my own heart, Kaiah thought.

"Hey, where are your parents?" she asked Becca.

"They headed home. How were the girls?"

She handed Kaiah a bowl of ice cream and a spoon, and Kaiah ate a spoonful.

"A little teary." Kaiah summarized their conversation before she'd left them. "I had a hard time not crying along with them."

An unreadable expression rippled over Becca's features as she spooned more ice cream into her mouth.

Kaiah waited for her to speak, but when she remained silent, Kaiah set her bowl and spoon on the coffee table. "Just say it."

"What?" Becca gave her feigned confusion.

"Whatever you're thinking. I can tell you're holding something back."

Becca also set her bowl and spoon down. "I'm not surprised about Piper."

"What do you mean?"

"Think about it, Ky. Her mom didn't come home one day." Becca smoothed her hands over her yoga pants. "Yes, she was only two, but she still feels that loss." She hesitated. "And you've become really important to her . . . and to my brother."

Kaiah's nose began to prickle as her eyes welled up with tears. Why was she emotional today? Maybe it was the EpiPen. Yup, that was it. She was having another reaction, but this time it was to the medications.

Kaiah collapsed against the back of the sofa. If she were being honest, she knew the medicine wasn't the culprit for her tears. The problem was that her feelings were mutual. Both Reid and Piper had become important to her too. She would have to leave them behind in a few days. That idea was starting to get a little more real. She and Reid could call each other "boyfriend" and "girlfriend" all they wanted, but the fact was that her life was in New York. Theirs was in Coral Cove, hundreds of miles away. She didn't know how she was going to get along without seeing them every day, let alone if her relationship with Reid would survive at such a long distance.

Picking up her bowl, Kaiah began to eat her ice cream while the ridiculously attractive Richard Gere and Julia Roberts shared a passionate kiss on-screen. All of her own passionate kisses with Reid filled her mind, sending flutters through her chest. He was her boyfriend. This strong, kind man, seemingly filled with integrity, had committed himself to her. She wanted to see where a relationship with him might lead. But was she ready to give up her dreams of traveling the world and writing meaningful stories to settle down in a small town? And was she ready to be somebody's mother?

Oh my goodness. I would be a mother. I don't know how to be a mother.

Kaiah's heart began to beat wildly. She could only manage tiny gulps of air as her vision blurred and her ears began to pound.

Stop torturing yourself, Ky!

"Hey, you okay?" Becca's face was etched with concern, and she began to rub Kaiah's back. "I'm sorry. I didn't mean to overwhelm you. I think I overstepped."

"It's okay," Kaiah said. "They're important to me too. You all are." Her eyes stung, and she wiped them again. "I think I'm just tired." She took another bite of ice cream and then stood. "I'm going to go to bed."

"All right. Call me if you feel like you're having a relapse, okay? I'll be right next door in Reid's room."

"I promise I will."

"You'd better. Reid will have my head if I don't take care of you."

Kaiah laughed. "Thank you, Becca. Good night." She washed her bowl and headed back to the guest room, changing into her pajamas and climbing into bed.

The day's events scrolled through her mind as she stared at the ceiling. Hugging her arms to her middle, she rolled to her side. She suddenly remembered that Kam had texted her but she hadn't responded. Kaiah considered calling her, but she was just so tired.

Closing her eyes, she tried to stop the thoughts swirling through her mind. But she kept replaying Reid's warm presence in the hospital, his arms wrapped around her before he left, and Piper's tears in her bedroom.

They were both so important to her. And now she didn't know how she was ever going to leave them.

Chapter 23

KAIAH EXAMINED HER MAKEUP in the mirror one last time and brushed her hands down her purple sundress. She'd awakened feeling refreshed after her reaction to the beestings yesterday, and after having breakfast with Reid, Becca, and the girls, she had hurried up to the apartment to shower and get ready to spend the day at the festival.

She checked the time on her phone. She had fifteen minutes before they'd planned to leave, which meant she could check her email. Kaiah climbed onto the sofa and opened her laptop. She checked her third Coral Cove article—and was shocked to find thousands of people had shared it, and more than fifty thousand had liked it.

Okay, this has to be some sort of record. Viral again? Am I the Shakespeare of small towns?

Basking in the glow of her success, she clicked around to see if anyone famous had seen it—Simone Biles shared it on her Instagram Stories! Ahh! She clicked around some more, hoping to see another famous name among the shares. But one second later, her blood ran cold.

Under the Likes, near the very top, was Hayes Walker.

Ugh.

"Just go away, Hayes," she muttered before opening her email. She found the usual messages with news updates, ads for clothing sales, and requests for donations. But nestled in the digital junk mail was an unexpected name, Anita Williams. Kaiah read the subject line attached to her message: *Possible Interview*, and she froze. Then, taking a deep breath, she clicked on the message:

Dear Kaiah,

> *A colleague at* US Road Trip *brought your Hidden Gems: Coral Cove articles to my attention. I'm impressed not only with how you've painted a picture of this charming place but also by how you highlighted its small-town community spirit. A deeper dive into your stories further showcased your talent at painting pictures with your words.*
>
> *Needless to say, I'm impressed with your talent, and you might just be what we need here at* US Road Trip. *Our goal at our magazine is to highlight different places around the globe, from the exotic to the ordinary but unknown. We also believe in featuring compelling stories about those living in our global community. Your articles seem to embody our values.*
>
> *I'm excited to share that we have an opening on our staff, and I'd love to discuss this with you. Our home office is located in Washington, DC. We take pride in having our staff writers based on-site to foster a collaborative environment.*

We'd love to have you on our team. If this sounds like something that might interest you, please reach out to me at your earliest convenience. I look forward to hearing from you soon.

Sincerely,
Anita Williams
Managing Editor
US Road Trip*, Washington, DC Bureau*

Oh. My. Word.

It was happening. *US Road Trip* was interested in her.

US Road Trip!

She swallowed a screech. A premier travel magazine wanted *her* to write for them. This was a huge step forward, getting her even closer to writing for *Travel and Culture*. It was the kind of job she'd been dreaming of since she was a little girl, filling notebooks with stories. No more scrounging for freelance gigs. No more endless pitching to land a story. A real travel budget. A 401(k). *Dental!* She was growing giddier by the second.

She skimmed the email one more time, pinching herself to make sure it was real. But something stuck out on her second read.

"Our home office is located in Washington, DC. We take pride in having our staff writers based on-site . . ."

Oh.

Oh no.

She'd have to move to Washington, DC.

Not only would she have to leave New York, but she'd also have to leave the dream of Coral Cove behind. Which meant leaving Reid and Piper behind.

Kaiah pressed her fingers to her temples as her head started to spin. This was too much. She'd gotten so caught up in the business of planning the festival and writing about the town that it hadn't occurred to her what these articles could mean for her career.

A burning sensation bubbled low in her stomach as she processed the tidal wave of emotions roiling through her body. Anger. Fear. Sadness.

Why do all of these dreams have to come with conditions attached? she thought. *Why can't they all just happen for me?* Twin streams of tears began to cascade down her face. *Why do I have to choose?*

What was she going to do? Should she call this Anita Williams and discuss the position? Or should she ignore the email altogether?

She couldn't decide this minute. She needed time to think. She didn't have much time left with Reid and Piper as it was. Maybe she should keep her focus on them. She'd figure out what to do later. Maybe.

A knock sounded on her door.

"Hey, Ky? Are you ready?" Reid's warm voice was a welcome balm, and her heart ached, knowing she may not hear it much longer.

She wiped away her tears and checked her makeup one last time. Then she squared her shoulders and cleared her throat.

"Coming!" she called, rushing toward the door.

"Thank you for coming to see our lighthouse," Reid told a group of visitors. It was midmorning, and he and other members of the Coral Cove Historical Society were giving tours of the lighthouse while other events went on outside.

An elderly couple stopped by the donation box and slipped a few bills inside.

Reid smiled. Although the tours cost ten dollars a person, with all of the money going into the fundraiser, they also had a donation box for folks who were feeling extra generous. "Thank you for helping our school," he told them. He loved how his community had come together for this festival. It was just another reason why he enjoyed living in this place.

The couple shared a smile before turning their bright countenances toward Reid.

"We raised our family here, and we're so grateful our children and grandchildren have chosen to do the same," the woman said. "Do you have a family, young man?"

"Yes, ma'am. A daughter."

"I hope she grows and flourishes here as we all have."

"I do too."

The elderly couple held hands and then headed toward the door.

He watched them go, and his chest felt tight. He'd always imagined he and Brynn would resemble that older couple someday, spending their golden years together while enjoying their grandchildren. But that dream was ripped from his grasp the day a dump truck driver came across the centerline and stole Brynn from Reid and Piper forever.

"Hey, Reid. Wanna take a break?"

He pivoted to where Ashley Humphrey, another tour guide, stood at the doorway leading to the spiral staircase. "You sure?"

"Now's the best time." She pointed to the doorway. "The line for tours has died down. Take a half hour. I'll take a break when you get back."

"Great. Thanks." Reid hurried out into the midmorning sunshine and down the long boardwalk toward the road.

The marketplace was in full swing with people walking in and out of the tents at the base of the lighthouse. Nearby a local historian stood onstage and shared the story of the sailors who were saved by the lighthouse. Reid picked up his pace on his way to the tent across the way where a large sign read "Arts and Crafts, Sponsored by Crafty Creations."

Something inside him shifted as soon as he spotted Kaiah working with a group of children who were creating lighthouses out of Pringles cans. She crouched down next to a little boy who looked to be about five. His tongue was slipped out the corner of his mouth as he concentrated on following Kaiah's instructions for gluing a piece of white construction paper onto the cardboard tube.

Kaiah was lovely in a purple sundress with her hair roped into a braid that hung to the middle of her back. He'd tossed and turned most of the night at the station, worrying about her, and he'd even texted his sister three times to check on her. He grinned recalling his twin's predictable answers.

Becca: She's fine! I got it handled. Now get back to work.

Becca: I told you she's okay, Reid! Stop worrying already!

Becca: It's midnight, Reid. Go to sleep.

The little boy said something to Kaiah, and she helped him finish gluing the paper before she instructed him on what to do next. Reid's heart swelled as he watched her talking with the child. She was always so patient and sweet to Piper, and it was evident that she enjoyed interacting with kids.

Would she consider having a family with me?

The question sent a shudder through him.

Kaiah rotated toward him, and a warm expression overtook her face. "Hey, Mr. TDH."

"Hello, ma'am. I was wondering if I could make a lighthouse." Reid pointed to the little boy's project. "Do you think you could help me?"

A flirtatious smile overtook her lips. "Hmm. Have you done arts and crafts before? This one might be too complicated for you."

"I'll help you, mister," the little boy said.

Reid and Kaiah shared a grin.

Kaiah pointed to the boy. "Noah is happy to help you. Would you like me to get you some supplies?"

"You have to make a donation, mister," Noah explained. "But the money goes to a good cause. Mrs. Witherspoon from Crafty Creations gave all the supplies."

"That's fantastic, Noah. Thanks for telling me," Reid said. Then he held his hand out to Kaiah, and she walked over to him. "Any chance you can take a break?" he asked her softly.

She seemed surprised. "Oh. Let me ask Mia if she can take over." Kaiah scooted over to talk to a young woman with blonde hair with pink highlights and a nose ring. Kaiah said something to the woman, and she nodded before Kaiah hurried back over to him. "I'm free for a break." She touched Noah's shoulder. "You're doing great. Mia is going to help you finish up."

Noah appeared disappointed. "You're not going to try to make one? I think you can do it, mister. You just have to try." He tapped the chair beside him. "Sit by me. I'll help you."

Kaiah touched her hand to her pink lips, trying to hide a smile.

Reid worked to keep his grin at bay. "Thank you, Noah. I'll give it a try later."

The little boy shrugged. "Suit yourself." Then he returned to his project.

Reid clasped his fingers with Kaiah's, and they walked in the direction of the market. "How are you feeling?"

"I'm fine," she said, and then she laughed. "You've asked me that at least a dozen times since I got up this morning. I promise you I'm okay. Really."

He lifted a suspicious eyebrow. "You sure?"

"Ugh!" She playfully smacked his shoulder. "Yes. I'm positive." She pointed toward the lighthouse. "How are the tours going?"

"Great. We've been busy since we opened at nine, but when we had a lull Ashley told me to take a break. And I wanted to check on you." The delicious aroma of popcorn drifted over him. "Hungry?"

"Not really," she said. "It's not lunchtime yet." Her eyes lifted to the stage. "Oh look. The Sandy Boots Brothers are setting up." She quickened her steps, leading him to the stage. "I wanted to hear them play ever since we met the lead singer."

After a few moments, the opening chords of a familiar song started before Brad Duncan and his brothers began a surprisingly good rendition of "Fishin' in the Dark" by Nitty Gritty Dirt Band. Almost immediately couples began dancing in front of the stage while Brad belted out the lyrics.

Reid took both of Kaiah's hands in his. "Dance with me."

"What?"

"You heard me," he repeated. "Dance with me, Kaiah. Please."

"Um, I'm not much of a dancer."

"Me neither. But nineties country is calling us, and we must answer." He pulled her toward him. "Come on."

She gave a nervous laugh. "Okay."

She wound her arms around his neck while he settled his hands on her waist, right above the swell of her hips. They swayed to the music, and he breathed in her flowery scent. Having her so close to him sent his senses spinning.

All too soon, the song ended, and Kaiah gave Reid a shy smile as she stepped away from him. Claps, cheers, and whistles erupted in the gathering crowd. Reid and Kaiah clapped too.

"Thank y'all," Brad said. "We're The Sandy Boots Brothers, and we're locals here."

More whistles sounded.

"We're so happy that you've joined us for this Light the Dark Festival. Now we're going to play one of our favorites." Brad motioned to the crowd. "If y'all know it, y'all sing it with us." He addressed his brothers. "One, two, three," he said before they began playing another song.

Reid recognized it immediately as one of his mother's favorites—Shenandoah's "Next to You, Next to Me." He reached for Kaiah's hand and towed her to him. Once again, Kaiah wrapped her arms around his neck, and Reid held her close while they swayed to the music.

When she rested her cheek against his collarbone, Reid thought he might just float away. Kaiah fit into his arms as if she were made just for him. As he held her, for a moment he imagined what life could be like if she decided to stay in Coral Cove. They could do this at every community concert, swaying to the music, just the two of them. They could go to the festival every year. They could make a donation and smile, sharing that they'd raised their family in Coral Cove. At that moment, he wanted nothing more.

The song ended, and Kaiah held on to Reid's hand and steered him toward the food vendors. "How about some nachos?"

"I never say no to nachos."

He purchased a plate of nachos and two sodas, and they sat on a bench facing the lighthouse. They ate their snack while visitors moved in and out of the historic structure.

Kaiah looked up at the sky, closed her eyes, and let out a long sigh.

"What was that for?" he asked before bumping his arm gently against her.

"It's the perfect day. The sun is sparkling on the water. The sky is blue. The seagulls are singing. And we're here together." She glanced around before her focus rested on him. "I love it here."

"Then stay."

The words slipped out of his mouth before he could think about them. But when he heard himself say it, he didn't care. It was now or never.

Her eyes grew wide as saucers.

"Stay, Kaiah. I mean it." His heart began to pound while she remained quiet. "You can work anywhere, right? Why not make this your home base? You could travel all you want, write any story you want, and then come home to me and Piper."

"I . . ." Kaiah's hands fiddled with a napkin while she kept her eyes trained on the water, staring at the boats with colorful sails passing by as if part of a parade. "Just let me think about it, okay?"

"Yeah. Of course."

He nodded at her, but heat began to climb up his neck.

Who was he kidding? Kaiah was an accomplished journalist. She lived in New York and flew all over the country, chasing her work. Why would she ever consider moving to a small town in the middle of nowhere?

He finished his drink, then tossed the cup and empty plate into a trash can. "We'd better get back to our posts." He pointed toward the lighthouse. "The line for the tours is getting pretty long." He started toward the lighthouse.

"Reid!" She hurried after him and grabbed his arm, stopping him in his tracks. Her blue eyes searched his. "Look, I don't mean to hurt you. I really care about you and Piper. I do. But I . . . I just need time." She paused, staring down at the ground for a beat before tilting her chin back up. "I got an offer from a bigger magazine. It was completely unexpected."

"Really?" He tried to keep his voice from betraying the shock currently rocking him at the core. He gave her a weak smile.

"Yeah. I was going to tell you, but I was waiting for the right time."

"That's . . . that's so exciting, Ky. Which magazine?"

"It's called *US Road Trip*. It's pretty well-known in my circle."

"I've heard of it." He nodded as disappointment and dread doused any shred of hope that she'd stay with him.

He was going to lose Kaiah. He had no idea how his heart—or Piper's—would ever recover.

"That's a big deal," he managed to croak out.

"Yeah, it is."

They stared at each other, and he tilted his head. "How long have you known?"

"Since this morning." She shifted her weight on her feet. "I checked my email when I went upstairs to get ready, and I found a message from a managing editor there." Frowning, she folded her arms over her middle.

"You knew this morning," he repeated.

She nodded, and another pang of disappointment and hurt radiated through him.

"Why didn't you tell me?" he asked.

"I-I didn't know how." She looked out toward the lighthouse and then back at him. "I guess I didn't want to hurt you." She cleared her throat. "My Coral Cove articles have been going viral, and an editor was impressed with my work, so she reached out and said she wanted to talk to me, and she included her phone number, but I . . ." Her voice trailed off, and she continued to avoid his gaze. He waited for her to continue, but she remained silent.

"Did you call her?"

"Not yet. I need time to think about it. I would have to move to Washington, DC." She rubbed a spot on her cheek. "I'm sorry, Reid. I've been waiting for an opportunity like this for years. It's just a lot to think about. I haven't fully processed it."

He rested his hands on her forearms. "Ky, stop apologizing. I'm so proud of you. You've worked hard, and you've earned this."

She gave him a small smile. "Thanks."

He tried to return the gesture, but his attempt at a grin felt like a grimace. "Listen, I get it." He kissed her forehead. "Congratulations."

"Thanks," she whispered again.

But as they walked toward the lighthouse, he was certain he'd felt a crack start to fracture his heart.

The last thing he wanted to do was hold Kaiah back. No matter how much it hurt him to let her go.

That evening, Reid handed Kaiah the keys to the Suburban so she could drive them home.

"I had a blast working at arts and crafts today," Kaiah said, making a turn toward Reid's neighborhood. "Piper and Astrid were great helpers when your mom brought them by." She peered in the back seat where Piper softly snored, and she smiled. "Piper is all tuckered out."

When Reid didn't answer, she studied him. He was staring straight out the windshield, seeming to be lost in thought.

"Reid?" She touched his arm, and his eyes snapped to hers. "You look like you're a million miles away."

"Sorry." His smile didn't quite reach his eyes.

She thought back to earlier in the day, how his demeanor changed when she told him about the job offer right on the heels of him asking her to say. Guilt burrowed deep in her gut. The job offer haunted her thoughts while she weighed whether to stay in Coral Cove or move to DC. The magazine would be a huge step forward in her career, but she was falling for Reid and loved his family. She felt stuck at a crossroads.

When she stopped at a red light, she spotted a cute pink bungalow with a *For Rent* sign in the front yard. A sign reading *Flamingo's Nest* graced the front of the house, along with a pink flamingo, of course. She took in the little front yard, small porch, and one-car garage.

This is perfect for me.

The thought startled her. But she decided to play along for a moment. If she were to take up Reid on his offer, she could rent a little house like that one and make Coral Cove her home. She could continue the hustle of her freelance career and maybe have the loving family she'd always dreamed of. But if she took the job with *US Road Trip*, she'd have the job she'd always longed for, with the resources and freedom to write about what she wanted. But she'd have to move to Washington, DC.

Was she ready to give up her career dreams and settle down? And what if it didn't work out with Reid? Or what if her freelance jobs dried up? How would she support herself?

Was there a way that she could have both—the fulfilling life of a journalist along with a family that included Reid and Piper?

Reid continued to sit quietly in the passenger seat, and the chasm expanding between them was breaking her heart. When she parked in the driveway, she took his hand in hers. He stared down at their entwined hands. His eyes finally met hers, and the pain she found there nearly sliced her in two.

"Reid, I'm sorry. I never meant to hurt you," she said softy, careful not to wake Piper and worry her. She sniffed as her eyes stung. "I haven't decided what I'm going to do yet. But no matter what, I need you to know that I care about you and Piper."

He gave her a melancholy smile. "I understand, Ky. It's a big decision, and I support whatever you decide."

She cocked her head to the side. "Do you?"

"Of course." He cupped his hand to her cheek, and she sucked in a breath, waiting for him to kiss her. Instead, he dropped his hand and pushed open his door.

They climbed out of the SUV, and he picked up his sleeping daughter. Piper rested her head on his shoulder and continued to snore softly.

"I'll see you in the morning," she told him. "Bright and early, right?"

"Yeah." He hesitated, and she held her breath, hoping he'd touch her. But he adjusted his daughter in his arms. "Good night, Kaiah," he said before heading toward the house.

She watched him go before hurrying up the stairs and retreating into the apartment. She sat on the sofa, powered up her laptop, and stared at Anita's message. The longer she looked at it, the more confusion swirled in her mind.

She opened a new document to start another article on the festival, but her thoughts kept returning to Reid's offer to stay and build a life in Coral Cove. The pain in his eyes when she'd rejected him sent another ribbon of sadness twisting her chest.

Clicking onto her internet browser, she typed the address for the little pink house into the search bar, and the home appeared on her screen. She scrolled through the photos—a small kitchen, a bedroom, a bathroom, a small den, and a little screened-in porch.

It really is perfect for me.

She studied the monthly rent and tried to imagine a life there—spending time with Reid, Piper, and their family. A family, *a real family*, something she'd craved since she'd lost her mother.

But what would she do about her career? And was she ready to trust another man with her heart?

And what if things didn't work out with Reid? What then?

Well, once again she'd simply have to find the strength to pick up the pieces and move on. But somehow she knew that if she lost Reid, rebuilding her world would be even more painful this time. Reid was so different from Hayes. He added so much love and joy and peace to her life, the opposite of Hayes, who seemed to take much more than he gave. At the same time, having a relationship with Reid meant she also had Piper to think about. If she made a commitment to Reid, then she'd have to make a commitment to Piper. And the last thing she ever wanted to do was break that little girl's heart.

Her head started to spin, and she collapsed against the back of the sofa. This was all too much to think about.

Her phone dinged with a text, and she found Kam's name on the screen.

Kam: Hey, sis! I haven't heard from you.
Everything okay?

Kaiah studied the screen and took a cleansing breath. She could call her sister and spend hours weighing the pros and cons of staying in Coral Cove as opposed to taking the job with *US Road Trip*, but she was too exhausted to rehash her hospital stay or her confusing feelings for Reid.

Instead, she just wanted to pour herself into another article, into sharing the fantasy of Coral Cove. After all, it was Monday, and the festival ended Thursday. She wanted to lose herself in her last few days of Coral Cove before she faced saying goodbye.

With her thumbs hovering over the phone, Kaiah texted back: Hey, Kam! How you feeling? I'm so sorry I haven't texted. I've been so busy with the festival and writing. Everything's fine. I'm heading to bed, but I promise I'll call later this week.

The dancing dots appeared almost immediately.

Kam: I'm fine. No problem. Talk to you later. Tell Mr. TDH I said hi, and have a fun week.

Releasing a long sigh, Kaiah opened a blank document on her computer and tried to concentrate on writing her next article instead of rehashing her confusing feelings for Reid, for Piper, and the life-changing decision she'd have to make way too soon.

Chapter 24

THE SWEET AROMA OF fresh funnel cakes mingled with popcorn and cotton candy as Kaiah walked past food vendors with Reid, Piper, Becca, Cash, and Astrid on Thursday night. It was the last day of the festival, and a carnival was set up in the elementary school's parking lot. Happy music played from the carousel while bells and whistles rang out from nearby games and voices of all ages shrieked as the roller coaster roared down the track.

The past few days had flown by while Kaiah had enjoyed the myriad activities she, Becca, and Reid had planned and the town had come together to create: a craft show, a town parade, a museum day filled with tours and historical booths, a fishing tournament, a talent show, and more live performances at the stage. They'd also hosted the mini-marathon with more than a hundred participants. Piper distributed the ribbons and trophies after the race, and Kaiah took photos of the winners. Over the past few days, Kaiah had done her best to soak up every happy moment with Reid and Piper. In between the flurry of activity, she'd also published another story about Coral Cove, though this one didn't go *quite* as viral—not that she was complaining. She still hadn't responded to Anita Williams's message, even though she'd spent each night staring at the ceiling, making a mental pros and cons list for staying or for taking the job.

Reid had returned to being his warm self. Neither of them had mentioned their brief conversation when he'd asked her to stay.

But the last day of the festival had officially arrived, and a bubble of sadness had been expanding in her chest all day long. How could it all be coming to an end?

Reid's voice from Monday night echoed in her mind.

Stay, Kaiah. . . . You can work anywhere, right? Why not make this your home base? You could travel all you want, write any story you want, and then come home to me and Piper.

"Can you keep a secret?" Becca asked, interrupting her thoughts.

"Sure," Kaiah said as Cash and Reid led the girls to a nearby vendor selling cotton candy.

"This hasn't been made public yet, but we've already raised so much money that we can not only renovate the school—we can upgrade the lighting in the lighthouse and refurbish the whole thing. Can you believe it, Ky? We're going to make the lighthouse beautiful again." Becca's dark eyes misted over. "The festival has been such a success, and it's all because of your help. If you hadn't gotten the word out about our sleepy little town, we never could have done this. I can't even begin to thank you enough."

Becca pulled her in for a hug, knocking Kaiah off-balance. She held on to her friend, and tears pressed against her eyes.

Keep it together, Ky! If you lose it now, you're going to be a snotty waterfall for the next twelve hours.

"Everything okay?" Reid asked.

Kaiah wiped her eyes and smiled at Reid. His handsome face flashed with concern, and the warmth in his expression made her want to sob like an idiot. Why did this man have so much power over her emotions?

She laughed it off. "Just sharing a girl's moment."

He held out pink cotton candy to her. "Want some?"

"No, thanks."

His eyebrows careened toward his hairline. "You don't like cotton candy?"

"I'm more of a big pretzel fan."

"Coming right up." He sauntered toward a vendor selling pretzels and popcorn.

Kaiah started after him. "Wait, Reid. You don't have to—" She stopped short when her phone rang in her pocket.

When she spotted *Coral Cove Car Care* on the screen, her hands trembled. She found a quieter corner near the far end of the parking lot. "Hello," she answered.

"Ms. Ross, this is Bill at Coral Cove Car Care. I was just wrapping up for the day, but I wanted to tell you that your car is ready."

"Oh. Already?" she asked, and then she covered her face with her free hand. What a stupid thing to say when she was expecting his call.

Bill chuckled. "I appreciate how patient you've been with us. We got the parts in yesterday, and we were able to fix it today. The mechanic just got back from a test drive, and it's running great."

Her eyes pinged to Reid and Piper standing by a row of dunk tanks where teachers, Principal Roberts, and Superintendent Edwards took turns sitting on the dunking platforms. The students were having a ball, literally—the line to dunk their superiors was too much for dozens of them to resist.

Reid's eyes met hers, and he waved.

Kaiah waved back, but her throat felt tight as the reality hit her: Her car was ready to drive, and the festival was coming to a close. She only had one last article to write about Coral Cove. Then it would be time for her to move on.

"Are you still there, Ms. Ross?" Bill asked over the line.

"Yes, I'm sorry," she said as sadness rolled in like a heavy fog. "Thank you for letting me know. I'll pick it up tomorrow."

"Perfect. We'll see you then."

Kaiah dropped her phone into the back pocket of her jean shorts and made her way over to Reid. Piper stood with Astrid, Becca, and Cash while they watched a boy take a turn pitching a ball toward a dunk tank where Superintendent Edwards sat looking nervous.

Reid handed Kaiah a large pretzel, and she thanked him. His dark eyes studied her. "Your phone call seemed kinda intense. Everything all right?"

"Yeah." She found her smile again and ate a piece of the pretzel before handing him one. "It was just my sister checking in."

He didn't look convinced. "Is she okay?"

"She's fine." She pointed to the dunk tank. "Look! That kid actually dunked the superintendent." She forced a laugh while the boy traded high fives with a group of kids.

Reid's warm hand was on her shoulder. "Kaiah. Do you want to talk?"

"I'm fine, Reid." She craned her neck, and her eyes met his. "Why?"

"You seem . . . distracted."

Her eyes slid across the parking lot. "Let's ride the roller coaster."

"What? Why?"

"Are you a chicken?" she asked, challenging him.

"Are you seriously calling a firefighter a chicken?" A captivating smile spread on his face.

She handed the remaining pieces of her pretzel to a befuddled-looking Becca before grinning at Reid. "Then prove you're not a chicken, Lieutenant Turner," she ordered before taking off.

"I'll show you!" Reid called after her.

She dashed toward the ride, but just as she reached the line, strong arms grabbed her around the waist and lifted her up in the air. She shrieked and giggled as Reid held her close.

"I'm not a chicken," he whispered in her ear, and his deep voice sent a riot of shivers cascading over her skin. "I accept your challenge." He set her back on her feet, tilted her chin up toward his mouth, and then lowered his lips to hers.

She held on to his shoulders and lost herself in the moment, not caring there were crowds of people around them. When he released her, she trailed her finger over his chiseled jaw and enjoyed the feel of his five o'clock shadow. She wanted to memorize every detail of Reid's handsome face, every muscle of his body, even the sound of his voice.

"There you go again," he said with a chuckle. "You keep zoning out on me, Ky. What's up?"

"Nothing." She pulled him toward the ride. "Come on, Lieutenant Turner. I'm still not convinced you're not a chicken."

He laughed and shook his head while they took their place in line. Kaiah scanned the large crowd moving around the carnival.

When they reached the front of the line, Kaiah hopped into the seat and fastened her safety harness while Reid climbed in beside her.

A teenage girl made her way down the line, checking all the harnesses and then giving a thumbs-up to a young man sitting in a booth.

"All right," the guy's voice called over the intercom. "Who's ready to scream?"

The roller coaster jerked to life and then started its journey forward, going up, up, up, up on the bright red track. Kaiah's stomach dipped before tying itself into a knot. She grinned over at Reid.

"Hold my hand," he said.

Gladly. Kaiah reached out and wove her fingers with his, imprinting the warmth of his skin and the feel of his calloused hand against hers.

The roller coaster came to the top of the hill, hesitated for a second, and then started its plummet. Kaiah sucked in a breath, opened her mouth, and screamed.

The roller coaster kept going down, down, down, twisting and turning and zooming away. She screamed again as the roller coaster took them upside down—still twisting and turning as it accelerated through more turns.

The roller coaster made another dip, and Kaiah gripped Reid's hand as she screamed with delight. After a few more dips, twists, and turns, the roller coaster slowed down and came back to the station. When the train came to stop, Kaiah released his hand.

"What'd you think?" she asked as they climbed down the stairs toward the souvenir stand.

Reid grinned. "Now *that* was fun."

"Should we go again?" she asked. "Or are you afraid?"

"I suppose I can do it once more."

"Yay!" She dragged him back to the line. "I guess you're not a chicken after all."

Piper sang softly to herself in the back seat of the Suburban, her hands moving the teddy bear Reid had won for her up and down to the beat of the song. Kaiah smiled at the little girl, and her heart felt heavy at the thought of saying goodbye.

The line of homes that had become familiar to her whizzed past the window. After riding the roller coaster two more times, she and Reid had met up with Becca, Cash, and the girls, and they rode the carousel, bumper cars, Tilt-A-Whirl, and other rides before playing games until the carnival finally closed.

Kaiah had enjoyed each moment with Reid and his family, but as the evening wore on, guilt nagged the edges of her conscience. She'd lied to him about the phone call. Reid had been nothing but kind, supportive, and generous ever since he'd picked her up at the mechanic's shop the day her car broke down, and he deserved better.

When he stopped the SUV at a red light, Kaiah took a quivering breath and then faced him. "Reid, I have to tell you something."

"Okay . . ." He rested his arm on the steering wheel.

"I lied to you."

His face pinched with confusion.

"My sister didn't call earlier," she said. "It was Bill at Coral Cove Car Care. He said my car is fixed."

"Oh."

Whatever the picture was in the dictionary for the word *crestfallen*, that's what Reid's face looked like.

"I'm sorry, Reid." She folded her hands in her lap. "I-I didn't know how to tell you."

He nodded slowly while something unreadable slid over his face.

A horn beeped behind them, and Reid's eyes flicked to the green traffic light. As he motored through the intersection, his posture became rigid, and the muscles in his shoulders tightened.

"That's—that's great," he said, but his words were barely audible, and his eyes were laser focused on the traffic ahead.

A tense silence filled the vehicle, and Kaiah kept her gaze trained on the passenger window. When they moved past the little pink house, the Flamingo's Nest, she studied the *For Rent* sign and wondered if she should sublet her apartment.

Kaiah glanced over at Reid as he steered the SUV onto the street leading to his house. His jaw was set, and his brow was rumpled. She searched for something to say to break the painful silence between them.

"Daddy, whose car is that?"

"I don't know, pumpkin," Reid responded to his daughter.

A silver Porsche Cayenne sat in front of the detached garage.

"Is that a friend of yours?" Kaiah asked Reid.

Reid shook his head. "I don't recognize that car."

Reid parked next to the Porsche, and Kaiah climbed out of the Suburban. When she found Hayes sitting on the top step while holding George's leash, her insides turned and dropped.

"What—how?" she began, confusion stifling her words.

Hayes's curly, light brown hair needed a trim, and his blue eyes sparkled in the evening light. Without a word, he released the leash, and her sweet golden retriever bounded toward her with his tongue lolling from his mouth.

George.

George is here.

Kaiah fell to her knees and wrapped her arms around her best buddy, holding him close while he licked her face. Tears overtook her eyes as she kissed the top of her sweet puppy's head over and over again.

"A doggie!" Piper appeared behind her. "Is this George? Can I pet him?"

Kaiah smiled through tears at the little girl. "Yes," she croaked.

"Hi, George. I'm Piper." She rubbed his ear, and when George began licking her, she squealed and giggled. "You're a nice doggie."

As she absentmindedly stroked George's soft fur, Kaiah shifted her focus to her ex-boyfriend, who had descended the steps and watched them all with curiosity. With the two men in close proximity, Kaiah couldn't help but compare Hayes with Reid. Hayes stood a few inches shorter than Reid. And Reid had definitely spent more time in the gym than Hayes. His bulging biceps and legs roped with muscle could attest to that.

When George returned to licking Kaiah, Piper eyed the strange man. "I'm Piper. You must be the friend who stole Miss Kaiah's dog." She glared at him. "Why did you take her dog and make her cry? That was soooo mean."

You go, girl! Kaiah bit back a snort.

Hayes seemed . . . embarrassed. Interesting. He hadn't seemed to care when he'd taken her dog and broken up with her *via text*. He hadn't even had the guts to tell her to her face.

Hayes touched his chest. "I'm Hayes, and you're right. I was mean when I took Kaiah's dog. I'm here to apologize."

Anger boiled in Kaiah's chest. "How dare you," she said, seething through gritted teeth.

Reid stood beside her, stone-faced, while he stared at her ex.

Hayes closed the distance between her and Reid, then sized up his competition. "Hayes Walker." He held out his hand to Reid, but Reid only scrutinized it with his stony eyes.

"Reid Turner," he grumbled before addressing his daughter. "Piper, we need to go inside."

Kaiah could feel tension coming off him in waves.

Piper giggled while George showered her with more affection.

"But Daddy, he's so sweet." She managed to move away from the kisses. "Come meet him."

"*Now*, Piper." Reid's voice held an edge of warning, but it seemed to be aimed at Hayes, which was where he kept his eyes focused. "You need to get your bath."

"Oooookay." Piper's grim expression was dramatic as she patted the dog's head. "I'll see you later, George."

Kaiah's heart began to break while Reid took Piper's hand and steered her toward the front door.

Once they were gone, Kaiah fixed Hayes with a look. "Care to tell me why on earth you're here?"

Chapter 25

"YOU WOULDN'T RESPOND TO my texts." Hayes slipped his hands into his jean pockets. "What else was I supposed to do?"

"Oh, I don't know. How about *take a hint*, Hayes?" Kaiah nearly spat the words at him. "I told you that unless you had something to tell me about George or you had a lead on a story for me, we have *nothing* to talk about."

George sat back on his haunches and patted Kaiah's thighs with his front paws. She rubbed his head, and a burst of love surged through her. She'd missed her little buddy so much!

"We have *plenty* to talk about, Ky." He jammed his thumb toward the front door. "For starters, who are those two?"

"None of your business."

"New boyfriend?"

She wasn't going to take his bait. He had no right to know anything about her life. He'd lost that privilege when he chose his career over their relationship. "How'd you find me?"

"It wasn't difficult. I read your latest articles—which are good, by the way—so I flew out to Wilmington, rented a car, and came here. Then I started asking around and figured out where you're staying."

She massaged George's head. "Asking around?"

"I'm a journalist too, remember? I'm kind of used to posing questions to strangers to find things out. I stopped at a few stores and talked to people at the festival." He rocked back on his heels. "Everyone's seen the pretty blonde reporter, and the rumor is that she's staying with a firefighter. I kept asking until someone told me where to find *your* firefighter." He eyed her up and down. "So you went from a journalist to a firefighter, huh?"

Fury swept a fire through her veins. "You need to leave. *Now.*" She pointed to his SUV.

"Hold on, Ky." He held his hands up in surrender. "Just talk to me. Please."

She huffed in frustration, and George whined, pushing his head under her hands. She hadn't even realized she'd stopped petting him. She rubbed his ears, and his big smile returned.

Hayes continued to watch her, and the months of anger and hurt that had accumulated in her gut merged together in a white-hot fury.

"Fine. If you won't leave, then I will." She began to back away from them, and George followed her. She started toward the stairs leading to the apartment while trying to fish her keys from the depths of her backpack purse. Where were they? Why did she always carry so much stuff in her bag? Wait—she didn't even need keys! The doorknob opened with a passcode. Hayes had her all discombobulated. She *had* to stop giving him so much power over her.

George whined, and she stopped moving. He rested against her leg, and her chest squeezed with love. She needed Hayes to go and her dog to stay.

"Ky, please," Hayes pleaded with her. "Just listen to what I have to say."

She glared at him. "If I listen, will you leave?"

"Yes, I promise."

"Fine." She sat on the landscape timber at the edge of the driveway and continued moving her fingers through her dog's satin fur. "You have five minutes."

Reid moved a slat in one of the shades facing the front of the house. "Piper, get ready for your bath, okay?" he called toward the hallway.

He winced at the vibration in his voice, but he couldn't help it. A storm of emotions raged in his chest—fury, anxiety, and grief. It was bad enough that her car was ready, but having her ex-boyfriend waiting for them when they got home nearly sent Reid over the edge. He should've known that clown would show up when Kaiah said she hadn't responded to his text messages. What man in his right mind wouldn't fight for Kaiah?

"Are you watching Miss Kaiah and her friend?" Piper, wearing her *Little Mermaid* robe, stood in the den doorway.

Shame bloomed in Reid's cheeks. What kind of example was he setting for his daughter by spying out the window? But he couldn't lie either. "Yep."

Her little nose scrunched. "Why is he here?"

"I don't know." But it couldn't be good. Most likely Hayes was begging for her to forgive him and go to wherever he was living, and he was using her adorable dog as a bargaining chip.

Seriously, what a jerk!

Reid hoped Kaiah didn't fall back under the spell of the guy standing in his driveway, who drove a Porsche and wore designer clothes. It was obvious the guy was successful, but he didn't think Kaiah would be fooled by that. At least he hoped not.

"Let's get your bath, Piper."

While his daughter talked nonstop about the carnival and Kaiah's dog, Reid wallowed in his anger and hurt over Kaiah. He longed to know what she and Hayes were discussing, but he feared he knew the outcome—Kaiah was going to leave, and he and Piper would face another loss and heartbreak.

A strange emotion crept through Reid, something ugly and almost painful that squeezed the air from his lungs.

"Are you okay, Daddy?" Piper asked while Reid helped her into her pajamas.

"Yup." He brushed her hair.

"Can you and Kaiah read me a story?"

Reid shook his head. "She's with her friend and George."

"I want to see George." Piper made a beeline toward the hallway.

"Piper, *no*."

Reid rushed after her, but she was already out the front door.

"I'm sorry," Hayes dropped down onto the landscape timber on the other side of George.

Kaiah eyed him with suspicion. "You mentioned that in your texts."

"I mean it. I shouldn't have run out on you. And I shouldn't have taken George with me."

Although he appeared contrite, she'd learned not to take this man at his word. Instead of responding, she continued to scratch George's chin.

"I love you, Kaiah, and I want you back."

A bark of laughter exploded from her throat. "Could've fooled me."

"I mean it, Ky. And I'm here with a proposal."

"A proposal?" A year ago, that's all she would've wanted. But now? Yeah, not so much.

"Come to California with me," he said. "Let's try again."

"*No.*" She stood and swiped her hands over her shorts, sending tufts of George's golden hair floating through the air around her.

"I have a proposition for you."

"I thought it was a proposal," she quipped.

"I got promoted. Now I'm a managing editor at *Global Media*. I was instructed to hire an editor for the travel section, and I thought of you. You're the most talented and qualified journalist I know. That's why I've been trying to get in touch with you."

Her head started to spin. *Another* job offer? How was it raining jobs all of a sudden?

She tried to focus and comprehend his words. "What are you talking about?"

"You heard me." Hayes angled his body toward hers. "You'll write stories for the travel magazine, which is in print and online. The salary is at least twice what you make now, probably more than that." He swept his hand through the air. "It's full-time and includes benefits—medical, dental, vision, all that, plus a 401(k). You'll have an office and everything."

Her eyes widened, and she froze. Now she had a *second* offer that would be another step toward her goal of working for *Travel and Culture*. This was what she'd been working for since college. She'd finally travel and write about exotic places and people. It was everything . . .

"It's your dream job." Hayes echoed her thought.

Her hands began to sweat. "I-I thought you went there as a staff writer. How did you get the managing editor job so fast?" she whispered. But then she got control of her wits, and she sat up straighter. "Wait, forget I asked. I don't even care. Just go home, Hayes. Oh, and I'm taking George. I'm not negotiating on that." She grabbed George's leash and started toward the stairs leading to the apartment.

"Wait." Hayes ran after her, grabbed her arm, and spun her to face him. "Kaiah, how do you even know this guy? Is he married?"

Kaiah tried to yank her arm away, but his hand only clamped down tighter around her bicep. "Hayes, don't you dare touch—"

"Hi again!" Piper bounced toward them. "I wanted to say good night to George and Kaiah."

Kaiah ignored Piper, keeping her glare on her ex. "Hayes, let go of me or I'll scream," Kaiah warned through clenched teeth, and he released her. She pulled Piper against her midsection and reveled in the smell of her clean hair. "Sweet dreams, honey." The bubble of grief that had been expanding inside her all day long burst, and she swallowed a sob.

Piper pulled away. "Miss Kaiah? Why are you crying?"

"I just love you so much," she whispered, holding back more tears.

Piper kissed her cheek. "I love you too, Miss Kaiah."

When Kaiah stood, her gaze landed on a large figure leaning against the frame of the front door.

I love you too, Reid.

The thought nearly stole her breath away.

Reid's expression remained frigid while he walked to the edge of the driveway and crossed his arms over his wide chest.

Kaiah faced Hayes. "I need you to know that things are over

between us." She sent him a steely glare. "But since I'm interested in furthering my career, I'll let you tell me more about this job. Let's meet for breakfast in the morning at Pancake Palace. Nine o'clock."

Hayes seemed relieved. "Great."

"Now *go*," she hissed.

Hayes turned to walk to the Porsche, then looked back over his shoulder at Kaiah. "See you tomorrow." Then he climbed into the SUV and backed out of the driveway.

Piper hugged George and began telling him how much she loved him.

Kaiah tried to decode Reid's icy stare as he watched Hayes's Porsche rumble into the night.

"Reid," she began, but he continued to focus in the direction of where Hayes's SUV had gone. "Reid, please look at me." She could hear the tremble in her voice. He finally met her plea with a guarded expression. "I had no idea he was going to show up today. I hadn't responded to him, and I never told him where I was staying."

"No big deal." He took three steps away from her. "Piper, it's getting late." He pointed to the sky where the sun had begun to set.

Kaiah followed him. "Reid, wait. Talk to me."

He swallowed. "You and Hayes have a history. Of course he came after you." He shrugged, but his expression was anything but casual. "I'm happy for you two."

"I'm *over* him, Reid." Her voice sounded strained. "I didn't tell him I'd go with him."

Reid watched her. "I wouldn't blame you if you did."

"Do you mean that?" Her voice hitched, and her body felt heavy with grief.

"Come on, Piper," Reid said. "Let's go."

Piper kissed George again. "Night night, doggie." Then she hugged Kaiah's waist. "Good night, Miss Kaiah."

After Kaiah kissed Piper's head, the little girl flounced toward the front door.

Kaiah studied Reid. "Let's talk about this, okay?" she asked. "Maybe after she's in bed?"

He rubbed a spot on his sternum with the heel of his hand and shook his head. "There's nothing more to say, Kaiah. I never really expected you to stay, and I could tell that you really never intended to." His cold expression sent a chill through her. "It's been fun. But it's over now."

Her eyes brimmed with tears, and she brushed them away. His words had cut her to the bone.

"You don't mean that." Her voice was a strained whisper.

"Come on, Daddy!" Piper hollered from the front door.

"Good night, Kaiah." His deep voice sounded rough. "Thanks again for everything. Have a safe trip home, or wherever you wind up next." Then he turned on his heel and stalked into his house.

As she watched him go, an ache started in her belly and worked its way up to her chest as her heart began to shatter.

Reid kept his eyes locked on the ceiling in his bedroom later that night. He'd been tossing and turning for hours while his last conversation with Kaiah replayed in his mind.

It had torn him in two to tell her to go with Hayes, but he knew it was the best solution. He could tell as soon as he set his eyes on Hayes that he had plenty to give to Kaiah. Plenty of money. Plenty of stories to write. An opportunity to explore the world and achieve the dreams she'd had since she was a kid. All Reid had to offer was his heart.

Reid pressed his hand to his forehead while a headache throbbed. He felt like an idiot for falling for this woman when he knew as soon as he'd met her that she was going places—far, far away from the little town of Coral Cove. But he'd been attracted to her the moment he'd seen her walk into the Roast Shack. He wasn't just drawn to her beauty; he'd fallen for her sense of humor, her generous spirit, her intelligence, her work ethic. She had not only written the articles that had drawn the crowd to their festival, but she had also rolled up her sleeves and helped make it all happen. Aside from that, Kaiah was the first woman who had not only captured his heart but also captured Piper's.

Groaning, he rolled to his side. How on earth was he going help Piper heal when he had no idea how he'd ever get over losing Kaiah himself?

Reid nestled deeper under the covers. He had to find a way to get through this. He'd already endured one loss. How would he recover from a second one?

But he knew one thing for certain—he'd never be the same after Kaiah left Coral Cove.

Chapter 26

KAIAH YAWNED AND RUBBED her eyes while she sat in a booth at Pancake Palace the next morning. After only managing to sleep for a couple of hours, she finally got up around eight and took George out for a walk, then gave him breakfast from the food she'd had delivered. After George was settled, she called an Uber to take her to Coral Cove Car Care to pick up Daisy. She'd considered asking Reid, but after the way last night ended, she couldn't bring herself to face him again.

His words had echoed through her mind nearly all night long.

You and Hayes have a history. Of course he came after you. . . . I'm happy for you two.

She'd tried to make sense of it. Why would Reid ask her to stay and make Coral Cove her home but then reject her?

She'd managed to make a mess of everything, and now she was more confused than ever. She had two killer job offers and Reid had pushed her away. Was that a sign to take one of the jobs? But would a job take away her longing to be with Reid and Piper?

Kaiah cupped her hand to her mouth to shield another yawn just as Hayes walked into the restaurant. She tried to bury any thoughts of Reid as Hayes took a seat in the booth across from her.

Hayes beamed at her. His smile had once set her heart aflame, but no longer.

"How'd George do last night?" he asked.

"Fine." She tried to sound more neutral than she felt. "He slept at my feet like he always did."

"He missed you." Contrition filled Hayes's face, and he took her hand in his. "We both did, Ky. I'm so sorry for hurting you like I did. I'll do anything to make it up to you."

She pulled her hand away and shifted on the bench seat, trying to put some space between them. "Cut it out, Hayes," she hissed. "I want to hear more about this job offer."

Hayes studied her for a moment and then sat up straighter. "Fine. I messed up, and it's over between us, yada, yada, yada. But hear me out: I want you to consider this job." He tapped the tabletop. "You're a great writer, and I need you on my staff," he continued without missing a beat. "I think you'll like the salary." He told her the amount, and she tried to mask her shock. It was more money than she could ever dream of making as a freelancer. "I can ask for more if that'll help with your decision."

A middle-aged woman with frizzy gray hair and a pencil balanced behind her ear appeared at the end of the table. "What can I get y'all?"

"I'll have the pancake special and a coffee," Hayes said.

The woman wrote on her notepad and then turned her attention to Kaiah. "And you, sweetie?"

"Uh." Kaiah's head was spinning, and food was the furthest thing from her mind. "The same."

"Great." The woman scribbled the order, took their menus, and left.

Hayes leaned toward her. "Kaiah, think about it. This is everything you've wanted," he said. "You'll have the freedom to write all kinds of stories, anything you want. And the sky's the limit. If you want to go to Alaska and write a story about the Indigenous people there, you can. Or if you want to go to the Amazon and write about how people are protecting the rainforest, you can. We have a tremendous budget, and all you have to do is pitch the articles that mean something to you, anything you want to sink your teeth into."

She narrowed her eyes at him. "So what's the catch?"

"No catch." He held up his hands. "I'm just offering you a job."

She studied him with suspicion. "Really? Just a job, huh?"

"Yes. I know it's over between us. You've made that clear, and I respect it. But just consider becoming a staff writer for me. Please. You're the best person I know for this position. I mean that."

She moved her fingers over the cracked vinyl bench while she mulled over everything Hayes was offering her—a career with a salary that would give her a decent life and the freedom to write stories that mattered.

This was it. This was her dream coming true right in front of her eyes.

But if it was the best choice for her, then why was she hesitating to say yes?

The server set two mugs of coffee on the table along with a small container of creamers and then walked away again.

Hayes stirred creamer into his mug and took a sip. "So what do you say, Ky?"

She glanced out the window, then back at him. "I need time to think about it."

"How much time?"

She paused, considering. "I don't know."

Silence settled in the booth, and she stirred creamer and sweetener into her coffee but couldn't bring herself to drink it. Nothing was appetizing right now.

"And who's that Reid guy?"

Kaiah studied her coffee and considered how much to tell Hayes. Even though Reid had rejected her, she still felt compelled to protect him and Piper. "A friend."

"How'd you find this place?"

"I was on my way to South Carolina and my car broke down." She slumped back against the booth. "Reid rents out his apartment, so I stayed there. I got Daisy back this morning."

"What took so long? Did the engine blow up or something?"

She shook her head. "The parts were on order from the UK."

"So you started writing about the place since you were stuck here. That's why you wrote about the festival and the lighthouse, right?"

"Something like that," she muttered before sipping her coffee.

The server brought their food, and she picked at hers while Hayes wolfed down his pancakes and talked on and on about how wonderful his life and job were in California.

She only half listened. The other half of her brain was pondering if Reid had really meant what he said. That it was over, and that it had been "fun." Those words had gutted her.

Surely Reid was as heartbroken as she was.

"Kaiah? Did you hear what I said?"

Her eyes cut over to Hayes's, and she found him watching her. "I'm sorry, what?"

"I said that you really need to consider the offer," he said. "I told my boss about you, and he's impressed with your work. If you want it, then I'll get you a plane ticket. We can find a service to bring your car for you." He paused. "This is a great career move, Kaiah, and you deserve it. You've paid your dues. Don't let this opportunity pass you by."

She moved her fingers over her mug.

He took a drink and then nodded. "How much time do you need to think about this? I have to be back in California on Monday."

"Give me until the end of the day."

He smiled. "That'll work. I hope you'll say yes."

"I almost called you in the middle of the night," Becca told Reid while they sat on her deck and drank sweet tea. "I woke up and had this awful feeling. It almost reminded me of when . . ." Her voice trailed off, and she focused her eyes toward the backyard.

Reid sipped his drink. After his restless night, he had dropped Piper off at school and then gone straight to his sister's house. He was grateful Cash was working so that he could talk to her in private. He'd craved relief from his foul mood and broken heart, and just being with his twin gave him comfort.

"I'm so stupid, Becks," he admitted. "I actually believed she might stay. And when I saw her ex in the driveway, I realized how naive I've been."

"You're not naive, Reid. I thought she'd stay too." She shook her head. "I saw how you two look at each other. Even Cash noticed it, and he doesn't notice *anything*." She tapped his arm. "Don't give up hope, Reid. She's not gone yet."

"But why would she stay here? This is a small town. She's used to the city and exciting adventures. What can I possibly offer her?" He set the glass down on the table and covered his face with his hands. "I've known her a grand total of three weeks. What am I thinking?"

"Love knows no timeline, bro."

"Love?" He gave her a humorless laugh. "Please."

She gave him a look of disbelief. "You can't lie to me. I can feel it." She touched her chest. "You care about her—*a lot*."

"Yes, but love her? No."

Yes, I do. I'm crazy about her, and I thought she was crazy about me.

He rubbed his eyes. "Let's talk about something else. Have you gotten a final number for how much money we raised?"

"No, but Misty Rodriguez is supposed to call me with the total later today. I know we already exceeded our goal, but I can't wait to hear by how much." She gave him a sad smile. "Thanks to Kaiah."

His nostrils flared. Even the sound of her name was a stab to his soul.

She tapped his shoulder. "Chin up, Reid. She'll decide to stay."

"I doubt it."

"Don't be such a pessimist."

"I'm not. I'm a realist. And it's best if things go back to normal and it's just Piper and me again."

Becca shook her head. "You two have already been alone for too long. It's time to open your heart and home to someone who can make you happy. Both you and Piper."

If only it was as easy as his twin made it sound.

~

Kaiah left the restaurant and drove aimlessly around Coral Cove. She parked in front of the Roast Shack and let her head fall back against the headrest.

She stared at the front window of the coffee shop and thought back to the first time she saw Reid. She'd immediately been drawn to him, and when he'd handed her the vanilla latte, there was something about him—something so authentic and mesmerizing. When she'd gotten to know him, she realized her first impression of him was accurate. He was kind and loving, funny and smart, and super generous. He was an incredible father, and for the short time she'd known him, he'd been a wonderful boyfriend.

But when the going got a little tough, Reid had pushed her away.

Since there was no place for her in Coral Cove, maybe she should take the job in California. But then she'd have to work for Hayes. She couldn't think of a more awkward working relationship. She'd have to talk to him about her projects, get his approval, allow him to edit her stories. He'd be up in her business all day every day.

Unlocking her phone, Kaiah opened the email from Anita Williams. She still hadn't responded to her and wondered if the job was still available. She could move to Washington, DC, and start a new life there.

Kaiah's eyes stung, and she squeezed them shut. How could the idea of leaving this place, somewhere she'd only been for three weeks, hurt her so deeply?

Opening her eyes, she turned toward the lighthouse and felt it beckoning her. She drove the two blocks over, parked, walked out on the boardwalk, and dropped down onto the sand. She breathed in the familiar scent of salt water as the calming cadence of the waves crashing into the shore washed over her.

Memories rained down on her—seeing the striped tower when she first limped Daisy into town and then walking to it after running into Reid at the coffee shop. She remembered touring it with Reid the day she came up with the idea for the festival, holding on to Reid and kissing him for the first time after he surprised her with the white lights, and watching the fireworks with him and Piper the night the festival began. The lighthouse had become important to her—just like this town and its wonderful people. It had felt like a beacon that was calling her home, filling her with hope.

Right then she felt her mother's presence as she stared at the light that had led people safely to shore for more than two hundred years.

"I could use your advice right now, Mom," she whispered. "I wish you were here to tell me which path to choose." She sniffed as her throat thickened. "I miss you, Mom. I miss you so, so much."

Her tears spilled from her eyes and flowed hot down her cheeks while she weighed each option—taking the job in California, taking the job in DC, staying in Coral Cove with Reid and Piper and their wonderful family.

And then, a knowing clicked into place.

She needed to stay in Coral Cove.

She didn't need a fancy job to be happy. She could write stories that mattered as a freelancer and make Coral Cove her home base. And she could do it while coming home to two people who meant the world to her.

She belonged there. With Piper. With Reid.

She just had to convince him that she wanted to be part of his world.

Excitement pulsed within her chest as she stood, brushed the sand off her jeans, and faced the lighthouse. "Thank you," she whispered. Then she dialed Hayes's number.

"Yeah?" Hayes said when he answered.

"I can't go to California with you," she told him while walking to her car.

"What do you mean?"

She climbed into the driver's seat. "I said, I'm not going with you."

"What? Why not?"

"I don't want your job," she said. "Go back to California and forget about me."

"Kaiah, I've told you I'm sorry multiple times." Irritation vibrated in his voice. "Just *take the job*. Don't let your stubbornness cloud your judgment. This offer is better than any other job you're ever going to find."

"That's your opinion, Hayes," she said. "Thanks for the offer, but no thanks. So goodbye forever. Don't contact me again. And by the way, I'm blocking your number."

Kaiah hung up as she started the car, turned off her phone, and slapped on her blinker to exit the highway. As she merged over into the right lane, the opening chords of Shenandoah's "Next to You, Next to Me" started to play, and her heart swelled.

She glanced down at the bracelet Reid had given her with the beads that spelled out *Coral Cove*. She knew it to the bottom of her heart—she belonged in Coral Cove. Now she just had to tell Reid.

A plan came together in her mind, and she couldn't wait to put it into action.

Chapter 27

NEARLY THIRTY MINUTES LATER, Kaiah parked in Reid's driveway next to his Suburban. She picked at her fingernail while she mulled over what to say. Then she pushed open her door, slipped the package she'd purchased into her backpack purse, and hurried up to the apartment to retrieve her dog.

"Hey, sweetie." She hugged George and then led him down the stairs. "Let's do this."

George gave her a happy bark and wagged his tail before following her to the front porch.

Her pulse skittered as she knocked on the door. Then she jammed her hands into her pockets.

The door swung open, and Piper threw her arms around Kaiah.

"Miss Kaiah!" Then she dropped to her knees and hugged George. "Daddy! Miss Kaiah and George are here," she called over her shoulder before returning her attention to Kaiah and petting George. "I missed you. I was sad when I got home from school and you weren't here."

"I missed you too," Kaiah admitted.

Reid walked slowly to the doorway and leaned against it, and when his bottomless brown eyes met hers, her stomach dipped.

They stared at each other for a moment, and the speech she'd mentally prepared dissolved in her mind.

"Can we talk?" she finally asked.

Reid touched Piper's head. "How about you take George out to the backyard to play so I can talk to Miss Kaiah alone?"

"Okay!" She took George's leash. "Come on. Want to meet my cat?"

"No, no, no," Reid said. "Take him *outside*. Don't introduce him to the cat."

Piper did as she was told and led George toward the back door.

Reid opened the door wide. "Come on in."

She followed him into the den.

He scrubbed his hand over the stubble on his chin and sat on the arm of the sofa. "I didn't expect to see you again. I thought you left with Hayes." His expression looked as if he'd eaten something sour.

"I have something for you." She pulled the package out of her purse and handed it to him.

He studied the bag and then looked up at her. "What's this?"

"Open it, Reid. Please."

He pulled out the lighthouse suncatcher Kaiah had seen when she first came into town, and confusion clouded his features. "Why are you giving me this?"

She stood across from him. "When I drove into Coral Cove, the first thing I noticed was the lighthouse. And when I walked into town, I saw this hanging in the window at a gift shop, and it reminded me of my mother." She paused and pulled in a deep, trembling breath. "She loved lighthouses. And the summer before she died, she bought a suncatcher in New England that looked just like this one."

He swallowed, and his Adam's apple bobbed. "You told me that." He moved his fingers over the suncatcher and then held it out to her. "You should keep this as a memento from your time here."

"I don't need a memento, because I don't want to leave."

His eyebrows shot up. "What do you mean?"

"I came here to tell you that I don't want to go."

"But you got that job offer in DC. Your dream job."

She shook her head. "That's not my dream anymore."

He opened his mouth and then closed it. The only sound they could hear were Piper's giggles and George's happy barks from beyond the sliding glass door.

His expression clouded with a frown. "What happened when you had breakfast with Hayes?" His question held a thread of caution.

She sighed. "He tried sweet-talking me, and I told him to cut it out. Then he offered me a job." She explained how he had been promoted to managing editor, and he offered her a high-paying job that would allow her to travel and write. "I asked him to give me time to think about it. When I left there, I drove around, and I wound up at the lighthouse. That was when I figured it all out."

He leaned toward her. "Figured out what, Ky?"

"That I don't need some fancy job or to travel the world to be happy." Her hands trembled. "What I need is right here"—she pointed to the floor—"in Coral Cove."

"What are you saying?" His words were measured.

"What I'm saying is that I believe that the lighthouse was calling me home." Tears pooled in her eyes. "My mom passed away when I was eleven. Ever since then, I've been searching for a place where I felt like I belonged and also for a family of my own. I think

I finally found it here, Reid. This is my home." Her voice broke, and she sniffed.

Reid set the suncatcher on the sofa and stood, his eyes softening. "Ky . . ."

She held up her hands. "Wait. Please let me finish." She pulled in a shuddering breath and then pointed to the suncatcher on the sofa. "I gave you that suncatcher because it reminds me of my mom and my dream of having a family."

Kaiah watched his mouth form a small round *O* as his deep chocolate eyes misted over.

She pulled in a deep breath through her nose. "I felt a connection with you the first time I met you. And the more I got to know you, the more you and Piper and Coral Cove felt like home." Her words shook, and she pointed toward his deck. "The night we sat on your deck under the lights, you told me that I needed to figure out where my heart is." She paused again and cleared her throat. "Well, my heart is right here, Reid, because I fell in love with this place." Tears slipped down her cheeks. "And I fell in love with you and Piper."

He closed the distance between them and wiped away her tears with the tips of his fingers. "And we fell in love with you too." His voice was husky.

"Then why did you tell me to leave?"

He cupped his hand to her cheek, and she leaned into his touch. "I thought you deserved better than me. I thought you needed a guy like Hayes, a guy who could give you adventure and a future."

"I don't want him, Reid. I want *you.*"

He gave her a weak smile. "I'm relieved to hear that. But I can't offer you much."

"All I want is your heart."

"You've had that ever since you stole my coffee cup, Cayenne."

She laughed, and he dipped his chin and brushed his lips over hers. She closed her eyes and let all of her worries dissolve. All that existed was her and Reid, along with this perfect moment.

When he released her, she held on to him for balance. "I love you, Reid," she whispered.

"I love you too," he said. "I didn't think I could love again, but you've shown me how." His fingers traced her lips and her chin, making every cell in her body leap to life. His lips met hers again, and she tunneled her hands through his hair. When he pulled away, they both worked to catch their breath.

He grinned at her. "I'm so relieved you're staying. I guess that means we're officially dating."

"I thought you were *already* my boyfriend. I told the doctor you were."

He threw back his head and laughed.

"I've already found a house I want to rent," she said. "I can still freelance and maybe even get a job at the newspaper."

"And we'll be a family." He took her hands in his. "Thank you for bringing me out of the dark and into the light again."

"Thank you for doing the same. Now kiss me again, Mr. TDH."

His grin was wolfish, sending a sizzle of electricity through her veins. "Gladly."

Then he lowered his lips to hers.

Epilogue

One year later

KAIAH HELD HER BREATH while she stood with Reid, Piper, and George on the pier by the lighthouse and listened to Mayor Whittington give the opening remarks for the Second Annual Light the Dark Festival.

"I'm excited to share the new seal for Coral Cove," Mayor Whittington announced. "We've added our beloved lighthouse to it." She held up an updated Welcome to Coral Cove sign featuring the lighthouse and a seascape. The massive crowd cheered.

"And now, everyone, join me as we Light the Dark for Coral Cove!" she said before white lights lit up the outline of the lighthouse and the lamp shone brightly into the dark night.

Just then a *whoosh* was followed by a *boom* as colorful fireworks lit up the sky.

Piper sat on the ground beside George and rubbed his back

while holding his leash. "You don't need to be afraid, George. The fireworks won't hurt you."

Kaiah and Reid shared a smile.

The past year had flown by at lightning speed. After Kaiah and Reid reconciled, she signed a lease to rent the Flamingo's Nest. She went back to New York to pack up her things and to formally end her apartment lease. Then she moved into the pink house and continued writing travel stories as a freelancer in between her part-time stint writing for the local paper. She was grateful Reid and Piper traveled with her on assignments, and she enjoyed their time together on the road—on an airboat tour gliding over a Florida swamp, flying over crop circles in Kansas, and riding an Amtrak train across the Rockies. Kaiah couldn't wait to take them on more trips soon.

Kaiah was also excited to learn that the first festival had raised enough money not only to renovate the school but also to refurbish the lighthouse. The Coral Cove Historical Society took the lead on the project. The wiring in the entire building was replaced, and the inside and outside of the lighthouse were repainted. It looked brand-new, and Reid was thrilled that the historical society had also opened the lighthouse to the public, reinstating tours. The mayor and school officials were so pleased with the festival that they decided to make it an annual event.

During the past year, Kaiah had also worked to reconnect with her father, and she, Reid, and Piper had traveled to Arizona to spend a week with him and her stepmother. She was also delighted to meet her new niece, Kendall Rose, who had been born to Kamryn and Devon. She still made fun of her sister for giving her daughter a *K* name, but Kam was determined to keep the tradition alive.

"Ky."

When Kaiah turned, she found Reid was down on one knee, and her insides fluttered. "Reid?" she asked. "Are you okay?"

He grinned. "Yeah, I'm fine, but I have a question for you."

Another firework exploded, and she jumped with a start. "Reid, what are you doing?"

Reid smiled at Piper. "Are you ready?"

Kaiah's confused look bounced between them. "What's going on?" she asked.

Reid pulled something out of his pocket and then nodded at Piper. "Let's do it." He cleared his throat, "One, two, three . . ."

"Will you marry us?" Reid and Piper yelled in unison.

Kaiah gasped, pressing her hand to her chest while her eyes focused on a jewelry box holding a large, round diamond surrounded by smaller stones in a gold setting. "Reid . . ." Her eyes brimmed with tears.

"Do you like the ring, Miss Kaiah?" Piper asked. "I helped pick it out."

"I love it, sweetie." Kaiah sniffed.

"Daddy told me that I had to keep the ring and the plan a secret, and I did it." Piper glimpsed up at Reid. "Right, Daddy?"

"You sure did, pumpkin, and I'm so grateful." Reid swallowed, and worry flickered over his face. "So, Ky? What's your answer? Don't leave me hangin' here . . ." He stood and gave a nervous chuckle. "Will you marry me? And adopt Piper?"

His daughter touched Kaiah's hand. "Will you be my mom, Miss Kaiah?"

"Say yes," Becca said as she, Astrid, and Cash moved through the crowd and came to stand by them.

Kaiah nodded as tears streamed down her face. "Yes. I'd be honored to be your wife, Reid. And I'd love to be your mom, Piper."

Reid slipped the ring on her finger, and it was the perfect fit.

"Yay!" Piper exclaimed while a chorus of claps sounded around them. "We're gonna have a wedding! And *I'm* going to be the flower girl!"

Kaiah laughed as Reid pulled her against him.

"Welcome to the family," Cash said as Becca, Astrid, and the crowd around them cheered.

Reid touched her face, his expression radiant. "Thank you for being my lighthouse, Ky."

Kaiah moved her hand over his cheek. "Thank you for giving me the family I've always dreamed of, Reid."

"I love you," he whispered.

"I love you too," she told him. "And I can't wait to be your wife and Piper's mom."

She brushed her lips over his, and as he deepened the kiss, their future as a family filled her mind as the fireworks continued to explode in the sky.

Acknowledgments

AS ALWAYS, I'M THANKFUL for my loving family, including my mother, Lola Goebelbecker; my husband, Joe; my sons, Zac and Matt; and our five spoiled indoor cats and our one outdoor cat. I'm blessed to have such an awesome, amazing, supportive, and purring family. Special thanks to Zac, who is always ready to recommend a cool country song and/or answer my endless car questions.

Thank you to my awesome firefighter and supercool brother-in-law, Jason Clipston, who generously (and patiently) answered my questions. I'm beyond grateful to you, Jason! You're a blessing to our family and your community.

I'm so grateful to my wonderful church family at Morning Star Lutheran in Matthews, North Carolina, for your encouragement, prayers, love, and friendship. You all mean so much to my family and me.

Thank you, Zac Weikal, for your help with my social media plans, my website, my online bookstore, and all of the other amazing things you do to help with marketing. I would be lost without you!

To my agent Natasha Kern—I can't thank you enough for your guidance, advice, and friendship. You are a tremendous blessing in my life. I hope you enjoy your retirement with your family—especially your precious grandsons.

I would also like to thank my new literary agent, Nalini Akolekar, for her guidance and advice. Nalini, I look forward to working with you on future projects.

Thank you to my wonderful editor, Lizzie Poteet, for your friendship and guidance. I appreciate how you've pushed me and inspired me to dig deeper to improve both my writing and this book. I'm a better writer because of you, and I'm excited to keep learning from you.

I'm grateful to every person at HarperCollins Christian Publishing who helped make this book a reality.

I'm grateful to editor Amy Kerr, who helped me polish and refine the story. Amy K., you are a master at connecting the dots and filling in the gaps. I'm so thankful that you worked your magic on this book, and I hope we can work together again soon!

To my readers—thank you for choosing my novels. My books are a blessing in my life for many reasons, including the special friendships I've formed with you. Thank you for your email messages, Facebook notes, and letters.

Thank You most of all to God—for giving me the inspiration and the words to glorify You. I'm grateful and humbled that You've chosen this path for me.

Discussion Questions

1. At the beginning of the novel, Reid is focused on being the best dad possible for Piper and isn't interested in dating. What do you think causes Reid to change his mind about opening his heart to love again?

2. Kaiah is heartbroken that Hayes not only broke up with her but also took their dog, George, whom they had adopted together. Have you ever been hurt by someone close to you? If so, how did you cope?

3. Becca, Reid, and Kaiah pour themselves into planning a festival to raise money for much-needed school renovations and to help bring more visitors to Coral Cove. Do you have a special charity or ministry? If so, what is it, and how does it inspire you and those around you?

4. Although Hayes broke Kaiah's heart, he shows up in Coral Cove uninvited after she ignores his text messages. And he expects Kaiah

not only to forgive him but also to accept a job offer and move to California with him. Do you think Hayes has a right to be forgiven by Kaiah? And what would you do if you were in Kaiah's shoes?

5. Reid lost his wife in a car accident and still struggles with grief and guilt after four years. Have you ever lost a beloved family member? If so, how did you cope?

6. Kaiah is close to her sister Kamryn. They talk or text nearly every day. Do you have a special relative with whom you're close? If so, who is that relative, and how has he or she influenced you and your life?

7. Piper lost her mother when she was a toddler and so has no memory of her. As a result, she dreams of having a mother figure in her life. Were you close to your biological mother? If not, did you have another mother figure in your life? What difference did your mother or mother figure make?

8. What has Reid learned about himself by the end of the novel? How does that influence his thoughts about a future with Kaiah?

9. By the end of the story, Kaiah decides to stay in Coral Cove and build a life there with Reid and Piper. Have you ever experienced an overwhelming change in your life? If so, how did you adapt to that change?

10. Have you ever visited a small coastal town like Coral Cove? If you could go anywhere for vacation this weekend, where would you choose to go?

About the Author

Dan Davis Photography

AMY CLIPSTON is an award-winning bestselling author and has been writing for as long as she can remember. She's sold more than one million books, and her fiction writing "career" began in elementary school when she and a close friend wrote and shared silly stories. She has a degree in communications from Virginia Wesleyan University and is a member of the Authors Guild, American Christian Fiction Writers, and Romance Writers of America. Amy works full-time for the City of Charlotte, North Carolina, and lives in North Carolina with her husband, two sons, mother, and five spoiled rotten cats.

Visit her online at AmyClipston.com
Facebook: @AmyClipstonBooks
Instagram: @amy_clipston
BookBub: @AmyClipston